In *Return to Taylor's Crossing*, Jani
Civil Rights era through the experier
African American who came of age i
turbulent time. It is a story of sadness, and revenge, and hatred, and ignorance. It is a story of growth, and change, and hope, and renewal. It is a story of forgiveness. And it is a story we must never forget.

—Raymond L. Atkins, author of *Sweetwater Blues*

Janie Dempsey Watts is a fine storyteller, weaving her tale of love and loss with scenes from a landscape she knows well. *Return to Taylor's Crossing* is a bold and brave story, whose characters you will love.

—Cassie Dandridge Selleck, author of *The Pecan Man*

Return to Taylor's Crossing is a 1950's story about a time that continues to haunt African Americans in the South. It is a compelling story of hate, love and victory. The author, Janie Dempsey Watts, tells this must-read story from different points of view, engaging the reader into history and the secret lives of the people of Taylor's Crossing.

—Ruth P. Watson, author of *Blackberry Days of Summer* and *An Elderberry Fall*

RETURN TO TAYLOR'S CROSSING

~ Janie Dempsey Watts ~

Return to Taylor's Crossing
Janie Dempsey Watts

Library of Congress Control Number: 2015916543
CreateSpace Independent Publishing Platform, North Charleston, SC

1. Southern—Fiction. 2. African-American Historical—Fiction. 3. Romance—Fiction.

ISBN-13: 978-1517372194
ISBN-10: 1517372194

DEDICATION

For my grandchildren, so they will know the shadow history of the South, and understand the struggle.

"A farewell is necessary before we can meet again, and meeting again after moments or a lifetime is certain for those who are friends."

~ Richard Bach ~

INTRODUCTION

Although the place in this book is not real, the area where I have imagined it to be is in Northwest Georgia not too far from Taylor's Ridge. Like much of the South during the 1950's and 1960's, the people who lived in this area were caught up in the conflict stirred up by the Civil Rights movement. The history around many of the events that took place is mostly oral, handed down by those who witnessed attacks or had friends or family caught up in the violence. In the 1950's and 60's, African-American homes were often the target of cross-burnings, arson and bombings. One African-American farm worker was targeted to be driven away from the area near where I grew up. This man was someone I knew and admired when I was a very young girl. After he was run off, I never saw him again.

For many years I wondered what became of this man, and thought about how being terrorized had affected him. I only know how it affected me. The attack on him opened up my eyes to a world full of senseless hate and racial inequality, and left me angry for years. On some days, I am still angry.

This story is not his but was inspired by what happened to him. No one really knows exactly what went on the night of the attack except him and those who hurt him. Nothing will make up for the violence he experienced that night at the hands of his attackers.

In this fictional story I explore how a racially motivated violent event might have affected the lives of those involved. In telling what might have happened to Abednego and Lola, and to some of the other characters I have created, I hope to inspire others to work diligently for racial harmony and peace.

—Janie Dempsey Watts

Chapter 1

ABEDNEGO HARRIS
May, 1959, Taylor's Crossing, Georgia

On a still cool early May morning, the arrival of a new bull in Taylor's Crossing was the biggest news since the Tuckers' dairy bull had been killed by a copperhead a week earlier. A group of men gathered around the working pen awaiting delivery of the new Holstein scheduled to arrive at the Tucker Dairy at any moment. The only dark man in the group, Abednego Harris, a wiry nineteen, held a rope and a bucket of feed in his right hand. In the back pocket of his worn blue jeans, the top curve of a copper bull nose ring peeked out. Abednego's boss, Barton Tucker, and his grown son, Henry, both red headed and wearing overalls and feed store caps, stood alongside the pen chatting with their neighbor, Sewell Buttrill, a slim man whose blond head seemed to be just a notch higher than any of the others. Although he was already dressed in his suit for his job at the bank, Sewell, like most country folk in Taylor's Crossing, could not resist a chance for some excitement.

"Where'd you say the snake bit your other bull?" asked Sewell.

"Right in the face," said Barton. "His nostrils swelled up and he suffocated."

"Like me, can't breathe. This cold is killing me," said Sewell. He pulled a monogrammed handkerchief from his pocket and blew his pink nose for emphasis. "Where'd he get him? In the barn?"

"Naw, snake got old Captain out in the breeding yard," said Henry.

Sewell snickered. "Going after the gals can be risky, even for a smart old bull," he said. Barton and Henry laughed along with him. Abednego did not. His eyes focused on the main road, watching for the delivery truck.

"How much this one weigh?" asked Sewell.

"About twelve hundred," answered Henry.

"Think so, Sir?" said Abednego. Henry was near his own age, but was his boss and white. "Awful big for a yearling." He was careful how he spoke so he wouldn't look smarter than Henry.

"What you think he weighs, boy?" Sewell's voice rose in a challenge. He blew his nose again.

"Don't reckon I know," answered Abednego, although he did. He had been with Henry down in Calhoun to pick out the bull, and he was certain the animal wasn't a pound over 900. "Look like we gonna see here directly." He nodded his head in the direction of the wood-paneled truck heading up the dirt lane.

"Get that gate, boy," old man Tucker ordered Abednego, who had his hand on the gate and was in the process of pulling it open. He propped the gate against the fence and loosely wrapped the chain so he could quickly shut it once the bull came down the truck ramp into the pen. The men would line up on either side of the ramp to guide the bull into the enclosure.

The truck backed in and came to a halt. The driver and his helpers, Amos and Luke, two farm hands in their twenties, climbed out and came to the rear of the truck.

"How do, Sir," said Luke. "You want him in this

here pen?"

"That's right," Henry answered. "You lead him down. He halter broke?"

"Yes, Sir," he answered. "Hand fed from a bottle since he was born. Luke, get up there and get that rope on." Luke opened the back gate of the truck and wedged himself through, approached the bull, talking to the large hot animal in a low voice.

"Easy boy, gonna bring you out in a minute," he said, tying the rope into the halter. "You just follow me, alright? Okay, Amos, I think he's ready to come out." Amos moved slowly and quietly as he opened the truck's rear gate. Luke kept talking to the bull in a reassuring voice. They started down the ramp slowly.

A loud sneeze ripped out of Sewell Buttrill. Bellowing in fright, the bull jerked away from the handler and charged down the ramp, lowering its head as it ran right at Henry and Barton Tucker. In an automatic defensive gesture, Henry threw up his arms to shield his father, and the bull suddenly whirled around towards Sewell, who appeared frozen. Abednego stepped over quickly to shove Sewell out of the way so the bull could pass. The bull charged past and loped towards the cow pen. Seeing Sewell on the ground, Abednego offered his hand to pull him up from where he'd fallen in the dirt. He waved Abednego away and stood up on his own, brushing the dust off the back of his navy blue striped pants with his monogrammed handkerchief.

"Sorry, Sir," said Abednego. "Don't want them horn getting you." Sewell's intense green eyes glared at the black man.

"I know my way around cattle, boy," he said. "I tell you one thing, no *bull* never knocked me to the ground."

He twisted to the side and kept brushing his pants although no more dirt was visible.

"Real sorry, Sir," Abednego said.

"Get the ring on the bull, boy," said Barton.

"Yes, Sir. Just give him time to settle down, Sir." Abednego pulled the copper ring out of his back pocket. "Something done spook him," he added, although he and everyone else knew it was Sewell's ear-splitting sneeze. Abednego moved away from the men and walked slowly and quietly towards the cow pen where the bull stood staring at the cows. He put his hand into the feed bucket, let the feed run through his hand to ping against the side of the metal bucket. The bull flicked his ear at the sound. Abednego talked softly, moved like a hunter in the forest. Coming up on the other side was Henry. He carried the bull staff, a pole that would be snapped to the ring once it was in the bull's nose.

Looking at the feed bucket, the bull licked its pink tongue. Abednego kept his eyes on the beast but acted as though he were going to walk past the bull to the cow pen. He kept shaking the feed. The pinging grew louder. When he was about five feet from the bull's head, he set down the feed bucket and backed away. The bull took a few steps towards the bucket, sniffed at the feed, and lowered his head to eat. Abednego sneaked up the bull's side, reached his hand toward the bull's head, and grabbed the halter. The beast yanked up its head. Abednego held on tight to the halter. His body rose into the air as he clung to the animal's neck with his left arm and reached for its head with his right hand where he grasped the open copper ring. He deftly inserted the ring through the bull's septum, pushing hard to get it through the cartilage. The bull groaned, blew out air and blood in a futile effort to make the pain go away. Henry leapt forward with the staff and clipped it into the copper ring. Abednego nodded, took the staff from Henry and held on while the bull tried to fight it.

Luke shook his head and spat on the ground. "Dang!"

"Pa ain't gonna believe this," said Amos. "He just clipped that bull all by hisself." Why I never saw a man put in the ring by hisself."

"Nigger's showing off if you ask me," said Sewell. "Don't know his place."

Absorbed in working the bull, his hands covered with splatters of blood, Abednego was too busy to hear any of the talk.

"You gonna be alright, big boy," Abednego told the bull. "Settle down, there." He talked softly until the bull quit fighting against the stick. Henry attached a rope to its halter. With Henry on one side and Abednego on the other, they moved the new bull towards the barn that would be its home.

Chapter 2

ADELAIDE BUTTRILL

With her husband Sewell gone for the day, and the children miraculously still asleep, Adelaide lay in her poster bed trying to steal a few more minutes rest. Staring down at her swollen belly, she could not believe her fourth child would be arriving in two more months. Her stomach was at the bursting point and she did not think she could make it another week, much less eight. Of course, as long as the baby was inside her she had one less to care for. Ever since her colored lady, Susie, had left three weeks before on account of her arthritis, the running of the home, the cooking, the care of her three children, had all fallen on Adelaide. Being pregnant and watching her two boys, three and four, what her sister called "Irish twins," and her toddler girl was proving too much. Old Susie had promised her teenaged niece would come up from Rome as soon as school was out. Adelaide was counting the days till her arrival. The $20 a week her husband had to pay for help was worth it. With Sewell's salary as a bank vice president, they could well afford it.

She rolled over on her side and looked at Sewell's pillow. She saw a blond hair, one of his, and plucked it up with her puffy fingers. She let it drop behind the headboard where it could be lost in the dust balls that had surely gathered since Susie's departure. For the past week, Adelaide had been too exhausted to change the sheets, usually Susie's chore. She wondered if she could get away with just changing the pillow cases. Perhaps Sewell wouldn't notice the rest of the sheets, although she would.

She ran her hand along the stiff spot in the center of the bottom sheet. He had insisted again last night even though she had been asleep when he had sneaked up under her nightgown. At least she could not get pregnant again till after this baby came. Perhaps in a few minutes she would get up, peel off the sheets and drag them downstairs to the utility porch. Sewell had purchased her a front loading machine when little Emily was born so washing wasn't a problem. Her huge belly seemed to always get in the way. She would have to squat to get the sheets in the machine. She heard the slam of the screen door from downstairs. Could Crandell and Coke have slipped out of bed already and sneaked out?

Heavy footsteps thudded on the wooden stairs. Sewell. He came through the bedroom doorway unbuckling his belt. Goodness gracious, did he expect to do it again this morning?

"The nigger shoved me in the dirt," Sewell said. "My pants are filthy." He let them drop to the floor.

"What nigra?" she asked.

"What nigger? Like the valley is filled with them. There's only one lives down here. Tucker's boy, works at the dairy."

Adelaide climbed out of the bed, held on to the side of the mattress and squatted down to pick up her husband's pants.

"Why would he push you?" she asked. She saw a tiny bit of dust on the seat of the pants. Maybe she could get it off with a wet washcloth?

Sewell was searching the closet for a new pair of

trousers.

"First, stupid moss head sasses me. Thinks he's a big shot with cattle. The new bull gets loose, and the boy acts like it was going to charge me. I wasn't nowhere near that bull when the nigger knocked me down."

"Surely he wouldn't do that on purpose?" she said.

"Surely he wouldn't," he mocked her in a high falsetto. "My hind end he wouldn't! Their kind will get away with what they can."

"What did Barton Tucker do?" she asked, hoping to deflect her husband's anger onto someone other than herself.

"Fool didn't do a damned thing," he said. He held up a pair of wrinkled trousers. "Is this the only clean pair of navy pants?"

"I haven't done the ironing this week," she said, when in fact it had been three weeks. He stepped into the pants, pulled them up his hairy blond legs.

"If anyone asks I'll just tell them my nigger maid quit and my wife is knocked up and big as a house." He walked by and pinched her on the butt. "If I wasn't running late, we could have ourselves a little party. Maybe this evening." He turned to the mirror and adjusted his tie.

"If I had some help around here I might have more energy for you," she said.

"I'll drive over to Crow Town this evening and talk with Susie about her replacement."

"That's a good idea," Adelaide answered, and added, "Honey." He smiled at her, turned and left. The low wail of the baby came from the nursery. She waddled over to the closet, worked her puffy feet into bedroom slippers. She glanced in the full-length mirror as she passed by. She hardly recognized the round-faced, large woman staring back at her. What Sewell said was true. She did look as big as a house, the result of four pregnancies in five years. She arranged her chestnut curls around her face, not that baby Emily would care. But Adelaide did. Her long curls, her aquamarine eyes, they hadn't changed, and she knew it was important to make the best of your assets. At least Sewell still doted on her, although she didn't really enjoy lovemaking in her current condition. As long as he wanted it, she would go along. With three children, and one on the way, she couldn't afford to lose her husband like her sister had. After he ran away with a girl he met at the carpet mill, her sister and children had moved back in with her parents. Their daddy was so mean to the children that her sister had said she would soon as marry the Purple People Eater as long as he had a place of his own and didn't beat her. The baby's cries intensified. Adelaide toddled out of her bedroom and headed in to check on little Emily.

Chapter 3

ABEDNEGO

A few days after the arrival of the new bull in Taylor's Crossing, Abednego saw a shapely young woman in the Buttrills' field near the road picking flowers. Surrounded by hundreds of yellow daffodils, Lola towered above all like a tall chocolate rose. He watched as she bunched the flowers in her hands and placed them on her apron, pinned it to form a sling. For a moment, she straightened up from her picking to rest. With delicate hands she dabbed sweat off her neck and face. The angles of her damp face shone in the sun. She stared into the distance, towards the Buttrills' two-story home, at the columned, covered front porch. Was she daydreaming about the future, to a day when she had a man? She'd make someone a good wife if she wasn't already taken. Who wouldn't fall for such a fine looking gal? Silhouetted against the field of opened blooms, she shifted ever so slightly. He sensed she was about to turn and catch him looking at her. That wouldn't do. He clutched his paper bag in his right hand, resumed walking down the dusty red road, and whistled "Sleepy Time Down South" just loud enough so she could hear. He imagined her turning towards the melody and seeing his white tee shirt straining against his wide back. She would wonder who he was. Thinking this, he flexed his biceps as he walked. As he moved his head in rhythm to the tune, he looked like he hadn't a care in the world instead of who he was--a farmhand running late to the evening milking.

At the dirt lane leading to the Tucker Dairy he turned and headed to the one-story dairy barn, a cool building that smelled like milk and Clorox. Henry was already pouring feed into the troughs. With a ready grin and a shock of red hair falling into his blue eyes, Henry seemed more like a teenager than a man of twenty-one. He handed Abednego an empty bucket. The herd of cows waiting at the door to be let inside began to stir.

"Old Bessie was wondering when you'd be here," said Henry. "What you bring us?" he asked, looking at the brown bag. Abednego set his paper bag down in the corner.

"Orange Crush. You find a cup we can split it," he said.

Henry laughed. "You dog, you. You know I like Coca Cola."

"Yes, Sir," Abednego said, smiling. He walked over to the sink where some rags soaked in a mixture of Clorox and water. He pulled out a rag and squeezed out the excess liquid.

"You're a smart one, ain't you Bing?" Henry teased, calling Abednego by his nickname. "Makin' sure you bring the drink I don't like."

"If you say so, Sir." He waited by the milking station while Henry opened the gate to let in Bessie and three other cows. They headed towards their usual spots and began eating the feed while Abednego wiped off their udders with the damp cloth. He hooked their teats to the teat cups, and the milking began. He stood by the cows while Henry lined up the cans that would store the milk.

"Sir, what you know about that gal up to the Buttrills?" he asked. Henry laughed again.

"I was wondering when you'd notice her, you two being the only coloreds working in this neck of the woods," he said. Many Negroes lived in Crystal Springs just over the bridge, but Abednego was Taylor's Crossing's sole Negro resident. His mother and sister had moved away two years earlier to Chattanooga to be closer to his mother's job at the Read House Hotel. "Old Susie's arthritis was flaring up again so she brought up her niece from Rome to help Mrs. Buttrill. You know Mrs. Buttrill's in the family way again?"

"No, sir," said Abednego, although he had heard. Mrs. Buttrill seemed to always be expecting, he had overheard some of the ladies at the store saying, adding that Mr. Buttrill should be ashamed of himself. Mrs. Buttrill was looking awful worn out with all those babies.

"The new colored gal, they say she's a hard worker and right quick, which is a good thing since that house is bigger than the Memorial Auditorium and she's chasin' them kids all over. She's right pretty, ain't she?" Henry said.

"Yes, Sir," Abednego answered.

"Built like a brick shit house," Henry said.

"Her face and hands is nice," Abednego said. To which Henry burst out laughing.

"Bing, most men would've noticed something else first," he said. Abednego wished he'd never spoken. Suddenly he felt flushed and hot. He walked away from Henry, went over to the feed storage area, clanged open one of the metal lids and dipped the metal scoop into the coarse pellets of feed. Why did Henry twist everything around and make it sound nasty?

Chapter 4

SEWELL BUTTRILL

The meeting at the bank with the board of directors had not gone well. Sewell took his anger out on the gas pedal, pushing hard as he headed down the Old Alabama Highway towards Taylor's Crossing. He couldn't wait to get home and get out of his suit. And maybe Adelaide would be rested now that the new girl had started working. Perhaps she would be ready for a party tonight. He reached down and let his palm run down across his thigh. He sure hoped she'd be in the mood.

He pulled up the long gravel drive and into the car shed. Walking up to the back entrance of his house, he was greeted with the smells of dinner. Although he hadn't met the colored girl yet, the strong scent of collards and a baking ham was a good sign she was as talented as old Susie. Probably another plump one. Good cooks usually were. It had been weeks since he'd had a decent meal. Adelaide was good in bed, but lousy in the kitchen. He quietly opened the screen door and entered the utility porch area next to the kitchen and peeked in.

Standing in front of the stove, Lola's back was turned to him, giving him time to assess the girl from the rear. He noted her full hips and narrow waist, letting his eyes linger over her bare and glistening neck. She had pinned up her black hair to keep herself cool he imagined. The tawny skin looked naked, almost vulgar, yet he was attracted to the bareness of her neck. He quickly felt angry with himself for thinking this way, especially about a nigger girl.

At the bank, just last year, when he found himself attracted to one of the new tellers, a saucy brunette, he had figured out a way to handle it. He picked on her constantly, kept pointing out her mistakes, told her to dress more like a professional, less like a floozy. Before too long she came into line. Now she kept her head down and did her job. He found himself not attracted to her at all. He knew how to handle women who acted like Jezebels.

He moved back across the porch, opened the screen door, let it slam shut behind him. Startled, the girl whirled around.

"Good evening, Sir," she said. "I'm Susie's niece, Lola."

"Evening. You making cornbread to go with those greens?" he asked. Lola gestured towards the oven.

"Should be ready in a few more minutes," she said. Sewell glanced at the table, already set.

"Where's my onion?"

"Sir?"

"You might as well learn now, gal. I have a quarter of fresh Vidalia with my supper every night. Didn't Mrs. Buttrill tell you?" Lola wiped her hands on the apron and started across the room towards the cellar door.

"She told me, Sir. I forgot."

"You need me to show you where they are?"

"No, Sir. I already saw the root cellar when them boys play hide and seek."

"Go ahead then. I'll be expecting to eat promptly at six." Lola opened the door and pulled the string to turn on the dim overhead bulb before heading down the stairs into the damp cellar. Sewell loosened his tie and headed towards the parlor.

Surrounded by the children, Adelaide sat on the arm chair reading a golden book aloud.

"And when they got to the top of the hill, they counted themselves. One, two, three, four. One little puppy wasn't there."

"Booger man ate him!" Coke yelled.

"You ate boogers!" Crandell shouted back. Little Emily joined in.

"Boog, boog," she said.

"Boys go get washed up," said Sewell. "Time for supper." The children ran to hug their Daddy around the legs. He ruffled their hair and herded them towards the hall and the restroom.

"Soap and water," he called after them. They raced each other to the bathroom. He walked over to the chair where his wife sat.

"How's my pokey little wife?" he asked. Before she could answer, he leaned in to kiss her mouth and run his hands up under her chestnut curls, let his fingers linger on her ivory neck, so warm and dry, not sweaty like the nigger gal's.

Chapter 5

ABEDNEGO

The next afternoon, a Saturday, Abednego saw the flower girl again. Between milking times, he had been relaxing at home in his cabin the Tuckers provided as part of their arrangement. Situated in a low place near the stream, the cabin was partly hidden by trees and bushes, sheltered from the harsher weather and the prying eyes of white neighbors who didn't like folks who looked different. He sat out back of the cabin with his younger sister, nine-year-old Marvelous, visiting for the weekend. Seated on two old milking stools, they tried to spot turtles in the slow-running branch that ran behind his back porch. A slight girl with voluminous sable hair reined in by a narrow red cloth hair band, Marvelous was a restless child at her home in the city. At the farm visiting her big brother, she was not. There, she was content to spend hours looking at birds, squirrels, possums and turtles in the branch.

"I bet I see them cooters come up before you can," said Marvelous. She liked to make a game of spotting turtle heads surfacing in the creek. "Look," Marvelous yelled. She pointed at the reptilian head that rose slowly to the surface. The turtle gasped for air, then dove back again.

"You sure that ain't no water moccasin?" Abednego teased.

"Ain't no snake," she said and slapped him on his arm.

"You sure?" he asked.

"That's a gator," she giggled,

"You a trip, gal. I be going inside and get us some peanuts and Crush." He walked around the side of the cabin towards the dirt road that ran in front of his place. The flower picking girl was coming his way, walking steady and straight towards the Buttrills' place where she worked. He ran over to stand beneath the hickory nut tree and watched her come closer.

"Hello flower gal," he said. "How you doing this fine afternoon?" He saw the beginnings of a smile on her lips. She stared straight ahead and kept walking. He was close enough to hear the swish of her skirt as she moved past, close enough to smell soap—an almond scent?—that had touched her bare skin that morning. He felt a flush of heat pass through his body. His belly felt like fish were swimming round inside. He reached out and held onto the solid trunk of the old hickory, watched her walk out of sight. He had to find out her name.

"Bing? You gonna get us that drink, or what? I'm thirsty," Marvelous called out to him. He had almost forgotten what he was doing. He turned to go back inside his cabin.

A few days later, a summer storm swept into the valley. Late in the afternoon after the thunder and lightning passed and a gentle rain fell, Abednego walked over to Elmwood's Store to get some things for supper. When he entered the store, he spotted Lola concentrating on the shoes displayed underneath a table of overalls. She picked up a pair of gray galoshes and went to the counter to pay for them and a bottle of lotion of some sort. He nodded at her, yet didn't speak. He didn't want to give nosey Mr. Elmwood gossip fodder. Even though folks said women were busybodies, he had found that men were just as bad. He grabbed a loaf of bread, some corn meal and a can of Vienna sausages, paid, and rushed out the door to catch up.

The rain had picked up and she was ahead of him walking briskly with a paper sack held over her head to keep dry. She wore her new galoshes but had no umbrella. He ran up beside her and began to walk in step with her.

"Them galoshes ain't enough," he said, and raised his umbrella over her head. "You don't want to get wet."

"Thank you, I'm fine." She kept her gaze on the Buttrills' house. The wind blew a curtain of rain into them.

"Please, you getting drenched," he said. Her blouse was soaked, and the paper had grown soggy and limp.

"Don't think I know you," she said.

"Abednego Harris," he said. "Work at the Tucker farm just down the road from the Buttrill place. And you Miss Susie niece. What they call you?"

"Lola, Lola James," she said. Her voice was low and smooth as honey dripping off a spoon.

"Well, get under here, Miss Lola James, before you melt," he said.

"Melt?" she asked.

"Like sugar getting wet," he said. She smiled and let him hold the umbrella over them both. They continued walking side-by-side.

"I work at the dairy, with cows," he said, feeling dumb as he said it. What else would he be working with at the dairy? Pigs?

"You good with horses, Mrs. Buttrill say. You broke they colt last summer. She say you not afraid of horses, or bulls either. Is it true what folks say about you putting the ring through that bull's nose by yourself?"

"Yes, Ma'am." Thinking of mastering the bull, he

lifted his chest a little and stood taller. He glanced at her soft cheek so near to his under the shelter of the umbrella. He inhaled the scent of her, almond and something else he couldn't figure out. Sweet cherry? Too soon they arrived at the end of the Buttrills' long driveway lined with oaks, elms, and hickory nut trees.

"I can walk by myself from here," she said. She stepped out from under the umbrella. He moved quickly to cover her head again to keep the rain from falling in those big eyes.

"Wait. You be going to the fish dinner over to Crystal Springs Saturday?" he asked, referring to the picnic organized as a fundraiser for the new African church a few miles away.

"I'm gonna work the food line with the church ladies. Maybe I see you there?" She ducked out from under the umbrella, grabbed the hem of her wet skirt, and sprinted away for cover beneath the large branches of the trees. He called after her.

"Want me walk you to the front porch?" His words were lost in the patter of the rain. Lola continued alone, sheltered by the long branches above the tree-lined driveway. He watched her retreat safely into the distance toward the big white house on the hill. With her wet skirt clinging to her hips, he could see her curves, a pleasing shape. Lola, that was her name. He couldn't wait to see her again.

Early Saturday morning, his older brother Shadrach pulled up in the old Plymouth to drop off his sister Marvelous for the weekend. While Abednego worked in the dairy, Marvelous rode horses with Barton Tucker's daughter, Iris, who was about the same age. At noon he caught the Tucker's draft horse, Sassy, bridled and saddled her, and led her over to his cabin where he tied her up under the hickory tree. After washing up, he put on his best blue cotton shirt and ran a dab of Brill cream through his short hair. Going out front, he untied Sassy, climbed on, and pulled Marvelous up behind. They set off on the dirt road leading to Crystal Springs and the picnic.

Only three miles away, Crystal Springs was a different world altogether, not at all like Taylor's Crossing. The residents were all Negroes. Their houses were older, smaller, closer together, and most days someone sat on the front porch. Abednego always relaxed when he passed over the bridge that marked the Eastern edge of Crystal Springs. Here he could be himself; here he felt safe.

Arriving at the cool hollow where the dinner was held, he was greeted with the aroma of grilling fish and chicken and the laughter of the three dozen or so picnickers gathered on blankets all around. Marvelous jumped off the horse and ran to find the other children. Abednego looked around the crowd and spotted Lola, taller than most of the women, and prettier, too. She stood at the serving table helping the other ladies. He got in line and waited patiently while she dished out potato salad, coleslaw, and beans. When it was his turn, he spoke.

"Miss James, you be surprising me." She looked up at him and smiled, served him a huge plate with a generous scoop of coleslaw and a mound of green beans.

"Why that, Mr. Harris?" she asked in a whisper since all the ladies seemed to be watching.

"You ain't melt after all," he said, and whispered, "Sugar." She slapped a final spoonful of potato salad on his plate and handed it over.

"Fish and chicken at the next table," she said.

"I'm gonna save a place for you in the shade," he

said, and followed Marvelous to sit on a blanket under a towering pine. When one of the children came to take Marvelous off to the sack races, Abednego walked over to the dessert table and picked up two pieces of pecan pie. He approached Lola, who was just finishing putting away some of the food.

"Care for some pie?" he said.

"I'm putting away this slaw," she said. Old Miss Lizzie, who wore red lipstick that matched her New Testament she carried in her pocket, piped up.

"Go ahead, Lola, I take care of it."

"Are you sure?"

"Go on, now. You ain't had no break all day," she said. Lola took off her yellow apron and followed Abednego over to a spot under a fragrant magnolia. He held the pie while she took a place on the soft blanket. Under the cool shade of the tree, sitting next to her, he felt proud and lucky to be sitting next to the best looking girl at the picnic.

He learned that although she was from Rome, she was staying at her Aunt Susie's place in Crystal Springs and working over the summer.

"In the fall I'm gonna move back home and finish high school," she said.

"You ain't finish high school? How old you, gal?" he asked.

"Seventeen," she answered.

"You seem so grown up," he said.

"Some days I feel like thirty. Chasing them Buttrill babies plenty a work," she said. He reached across the blanket, touched the back of her hand lightly with his fingers.

"Don't be saying you look old or nothing. You act

like a much older lady, like you figure everything out, like a queen or something."

"Queen?"

"A queen of flowers," he said. She smiled. He continued. "A queen who need to get out once and a while and do something fun. Don't you be getting awful lonesome sometime?"

"I stay busy with my house chores, and them kids, when I'm not busy being a queen," she said. He laughed.

"What time you done with work?" he asked.

"After I clean up from supper, I head back to Auntie's."

"Sounds exciting," he said. Lola laughed.

"You want to leave early some evening, go to the picture show?" he asked. She sat her pie plate down, tilted her head, and stared at the ground.

"That ain't likely to happen," she said. "Auntie won't allow it. You think wrestling that bull was hard?" She glanced over at Aunt Susie, who sat across the field hidden under a wide-brimmed, feathery purple hat. She had been staring at them the entire time.

"Ain't she a widow woman?" he asked.

"Uh huh, Uncle Leroy been dead for a long time, ever since I can remember." Abednego rose from the blanket.

"Excuse me, Miss Lola, I got me some wrestling to do." He headed over to where the aunt sat in a group of chattering ladies. Besides Susie, two of them wore elaborate hats. One was a royal blue, covered with beads and the other was light pink with chocolate feathers. He stood by them with his hands behind his back.

"Ladies, I been asked to choose the lady wearing the best looking hat today," he said. "And I say it wouldn't be no fair contest, what with that purple one clearly the winner." Aunt Susie looked away as though she didn't hear him. "And that a shame. The prize a dollar more for the church building fund and free lawn mowing for a month to the winner."

"Miss Susie, her hat the nicest," said one of the ladies. The others nodded and murmured in agreement." "Un huh," another agreed. "You take that prize, Susie."

"I can't do it," she said. "Not for myself." The others leaned forward to urge her on. "The Lord, he need his church built," said Sara. Susie reached up and touched the brim of her hat.

"I gonna do it for Jesus," she said.

"Amen," Sara said. A round of "Amens" followed.

Abednego reached into his back pocket, pulled out his wallet, and fished out a crisp dollar bill, handed it to Aunt Susie.

"Ma'am, when would you like me mow your lawn?" he asked.

Chapter 6

LOLA JAMES

By the time Lola returned home from work Monday morning, she was ready to sit down and eat supper, then fall into bed. The boys, Crandell and Coke, wild as a couple of Billy goats, had a food fight and flung creamed corn all over the floor before she could stop them. After being told to clean up the mess by Mr. Buttrill (she already had the wash rag in her hand and was wiping up the floor when she heard his booming voice ordering her to do so), she had to bring the clothes in from the line, fold and put them away, and wash dishes. She had not expected maid work to be so hard. No wonder Auntie's legs had just about worn out.

As she approached Auntie's house, she heard someone whistling and hammering. From the back, with his wide shoulders and big-muscled arms, she knew it was that Abednego from the fish fry. Why was he here?

"Evening," she said as she tried to slip past so she could wash up. It was a hot and humid day, and dust stuck to her sweaty face after the three mile walk from Taylor's Crossing. He turned and flashed a smile her way.

"Good evening, Miss Lola," he said, smiling as he spoke. "I be joining ya'll soon as I finish fixing these old rocking chair. Let me hear when the supper ready."

"Uh huh," she said, passing him to go inside. She stood at the wash basin in the front room, dipped a cloth in the water and splashed water on her face. How did he talk his way to their supper table? She had enjoyed his attentions at the picnic but she wasn't so sure she wanted to be socializing with a farm hand. Her mother had warned her to be careful of country boys she might meet. They could be fresh, Mama had said. This fellow was moving along too fast. She had thought about him some since the picnic and although she was flattered by his attentions, she really wasn't interested. After she finished high school, she planned to go work with Dr. Doushaun, the Negro doctor in her hometown. The good doctor wore a suit, tie, and Old Spice to work, drove a Cadillac and, more importantly, as her mama had pointed out, was not yet married. Lola's mother was good friends with his mother. She had implied Dr. Doushaun might have more than a job in mind for Lola.

Mama had told her before she left, "You meet anyone up there, you don't be giving them the time of day, you hear? You don't need be getting mixed up with no sharecroppers, no farm hands." Lola's father was a sharecropper and her mother had just turned seventeen when she gave birth to Lola. Her father had run off the minute he found out his young wife was expecting. Lola had never met him. When her mother gave her the speech on sharecroppers and farm hands, Lola listened, and nodded in agreement. That, of course, was before Abednego Harris had pushed his way into her life.

Lola applied a generous dab of Jergens lotion on her hands and patted a little along her throat. She liked keeping her hands soft, but what she loved was the cherry-almond smell. She heard Auntie call from the kitchen.

"Time to be setting the table, three places," said Auntie. "My knee killing me." Lola went into the kitchen, opened the silverware drawer and took out some forks.

"Three?" Lola answered, trying to see how Auntie

would explain herself. Usually Susie wasn't one for having company over.

"That boy a worker. He mow the lawn, clip them weeds, sweep the porch, and now he be fixing them broken chair. About time we had someone help keep this place up. You don't have no time to do it and I ain't able," Auntie said.

"Yes, Ma'am," was all Lola could answer.

A few minutes later Abednego came in and sat at the table with Auntie and Lola. Auntie said her usual blessing, "This is the day the Lord has made, let us rejoice and be glad in it."

"Amen," said Abednego and Lola. Over steaming collards with ham hocks and buttery cornbread, the two women listened to him talk about the lawn mower needing tuned up and how he would put in some oil and such. How he would paint the stairs real soon, and chop fire wood to bring over when they cleared off the back pasture. Auntie seemed so nice around Abednego that Lola wondered if she was sweet on him, except she was a good thirty years older.

Lola didn't speak much but listened as Abednego carried on about the chores, how he was saving to buy his own farm, about how gentle the Tuckers' horses were. Instead of talking, Lola studied Abednego's face, his broad nose, the serious set of his mouth while he worked his magic, all so that one day Auntie would allow him to take Lola to the picture show. She wasn't planning to go out with him, but Lola admired him for trying so hard. As he talked to Auntie, Lola thought about the first time she had seen him.

She was out picking daffodils for Miss Buttrill and stood up for a minute to look at the colors of the sunset behind the tree tops on the horizon. She was thinking how the pinks and blues were so pale but only for a few moments. In ten more minutes the sky would be a different color. Sunsets changed quickly, so she always made a point of stopping to look. She heard someone whistling and saw an energetic looking man wearing a straw hat walking down the road. With those big muscles in his arms and his dusty jeans, she could see he was a farm hand. She was happy to see another colored person. In her short time in Taylor's Crossing she already felt lonely being the only dark person among all the whites. She liked the way Abednego walked, jaunty like he was happy or something.

The next time she saw him was when she went down to the store to pick up some milk for the Buttrills. That time, she didn't like the way he smelled like cows and Clorox, or the way he acted so friendly. When he asked her name, she didn't want to answer. Her mother had told her not to talk to strangers, and she was sure that included a farm worker. Caught in the storm, and offered a spot under his umbrella, she decided it was better to talk to a stranger than to catch a cold from getting wet. Mama wouldn't have minded. And even serious Dr. Doushaun would have said, "Miss James, you stand under that umbrella and take care of your health."

By the time of the fish fry, she had planned to tell him she didn't have time to see him. She just wanted to do her work every day and go back to Auntie's, sit on the porch after dinner, and watch the glowing lightning bugs in the dusk. At the picnic Abednego had saved a place for her. She didn't want to be rude, so she sat down with him. When he told her how sweet she was, how she looked older, and started talking about queens and such, she finally understood what Mama had meant about farm boys being fresh and all. What her Mama hadn't told her is how good it felt to be talked to this way. Could there be anything wrong with letting a farm boy talk? Auntie nudged her arm, brought her back to the present.

"Lola be wanting to climb on a horse since she was three," Auntie said. "Ain't you, gal?"

"Never been around no horse," answered Lola, getting up from the table to bring over some dessert.

"One day between milking I set you up on one," said Abednego. "Right after I saddle up the horse for the Tucker gal. She ain't mind, long as you don't, Miss Susie." Auntie looked at Lola, now dishing the cobbler into small bowls.

"You like to set up on that horse?" Auntie asked. Lola shrugged as she handed Abednego a bowl of peach cobbler.

"Couldn't hurt nothing to try," she answered. After all, it wasn't a date or anything, and she had always wanted to see how the world looked from up so high, a different perspective than hers. And if Auntie approved, what could be the harm?

Chapter 7

MARVELOUS HARRIS AND IRIS TUCKER

The next Friday afternoon was warm with a light breeze, perfect weather for riding if you were someone named Lola, Marvelous whispered to her friend Iris, a red-headed girl with freckles who also loved horses. Marvelous stood by the fence in the pasture with her hands on her hips and wearing a sour expression. The two girls watched as Abednego led his new friend around on Gypsy, the white mare the girls usually rode. Iris whispered, "She's pretty."

"So what? She don't know how to ride no horse," Marvelous answered. "I wish she fall off so we could have our turn." Iris giggled.

"I'll bet your brother would catch her in his arms before she hit the ground," she said. Marvelous reached down and grabbed a fistful of pine cones.

"Not if I spook that horse and make her fall off," she said. Just as she was about to launch the cones, Abednego helped Lola off the horse and motioned for the girls to come over. Marvelous threw down the pinecones. She and Iris ran to Bing so he could boost them up on Gypsy's broad back. They liked to ride double.

"Thank you girls for letting me ride your horse," said Lola.

"You're welcome," said Iris.

"Let's go, Iris," said Marvelous. She kicked Gypsy, spurring her into a trot. They headed for the swimming hole by the lazy running Little Chickamauga Creek.

"I don't see why Bing spend time with no gal," said Marvelous. Iris kicked the mare into a gallop.

"He's old enough to have a girlfriend," said Iris. "I wish Lawson had one."

"Your brother too ugly to get one," said Marvelous. Iris laughed.

"Ugly and mean," Iris said. The girls rode up to the edge of the muddy creek, and Marvelous slipped off the horse, tied the reins to a sycamore branch. Iris followed, pulling a curry comb out of her pocket.

"You think Bing and Lola gonna fall in love?" Iris asked, brushing the horse's forelock.

"Nah, Bing too smart for that. I'm never gonna have me no boyfriend," said Marvelous as she stroked the mare's neck.

"Me either," said Iris. "I'd rather have me a horse."

"You already got one," said Marvelous.

"Gypsy is yours, too." Marvelous reached out to Iris and looped pinkies, their secret handshake.

"Best friends," Iris said.

"Forever," said Marvelous.

A few days later, a heat wave made daytime riding miserable for the horse and the girls. They had already waded in the swimming hole and spent hours designing fairy nests of grass and stones. They hid the nests in Iris' backyard where the fairies, but not Iris' snoopy brother, Lawson, would find them.

The girls missed their riding time and thought about riding after supper, but Iris' mother called her inside after dinner for a bath and bedtime, even though it was light outside. Iris sat on the bed and let her mother brush out her long, fine hair.

"Mama, since it's so hot, can Gypsy stay in our yard tomorrow so I can spray her off with the hose?"

"I'll ask your daddy, but I don't see why not. Gypsy could eat down the grass, and then your daddy won't have to mow," Mrs. Tucker said. "You'll have to clean up after her."

"Sure," said Iris, slipping under her lavender chenille bedspread.

The next day, Iris learned her father had agreed with her plan. At dusk, she brought Gypsy inside the fenced yard and latched the gate. She patted her goodnight and went in for supper, bath, and bed.

Iris fell asleep re-reading "Black Beauty" but woke to a soft blowing noise outside her bedroom window. She rose and walked over to the open window where her mare beckoned, her white fluffy body outlined by the moon's silvery light. Hearing no noise in the house, Iris knew her parents were asleep. She quietly pushed against the window screen and eased out onto the mare's wide back, passed under the rustling leaves of the crabapple tree and headed for the gate that enclosed the yard.

Although it had been a hot day, the evening had given way to a nighttime freshness or coolness. Iris wore a thin nightgown, and the warmth of her horse felt good against her bare legs. At the edge of the yard, she leaned down low over Gypsy's neck and unlatched the gate. They trotted down the lane into the night.

Moonlight washed against the windows of the cabin where Marvelous stayed with her brother, Abednego. Hearing a tapping noise at the window, Marvelous woke up and treaded lightly over to the window and pulled back the old flour sack curtains. She saw Iris' pale, grinning face. Carefully timing her steps to her brother's inward snores,

Marvelous tiptoed over the creaking floorboards. Once outside, she took Iris' hand and let herself be pulled up behind her friend onto Gypsy's wide back.

"Ain't we gonna get in trouble?" Marvelous whispered.

"Who will know?" asked Iris. Marvelous wrapped her slim arms around her friend's waist and hung on as they headed across the road and moved through a grassy field. The horse cut a wake as it moved through the tall, silver green grass. Iris kicked the horse into a gallop, and the girls laughed as the wind blew on their faces. Afterwards, the girls sneaked back into their beds.

The clandestine rides continued whenever Iris could talk her father into letting the horse stay in the yard by the house. Lawson protested saying the manure smelled and was furious with Iris after their father one day asked him to shovel it up into a wheelbarrow and roll it over to fertilize the tomatoes. He barricaded himself in his room with his CB radio, and Iris was glad for the distraction. He was so busy talking to people all over the place, he never seemed to hear what was going on right under his own nose. That was fine with Iris. The nighttime rides remained the girls' secret, brought them closer.

On days when it was cool enough they tried tricks on the horses in front of Abednego's cabin. Marvelous liked to stand on Gypsy while Iris led her around. Then Iris would get on and ride backwards while Marvelous led her. One Saturday afternoon after a rain had cooled off the air, they were trying stunt moves on the horse in Abednego's front yard. They asked him to snap some pictures with Iris' Brownie camera. They posed for the picture, Marvelous behind Iris but turned the opposite way, so they were back to back. Marvelous' hands were on her hips, and she was trying her best to look puzzled. Iris had her hands turned up to the air as if to say, "I don't know what's happening."

"You cooking now," Abednego said as he snapped the photos. In another shot, Marvelous was on the horse but lying forward with her head against its neck, her dark curls mingled with the mare's flaxen mane. Iris sat behind her, leaning forward into Marvelous' back. Her long, straight red hair hung over Marvelous white blouse. Abednego was shooting their picture when a car slowed down as it passed by.

"Eeny, Meeny, Minny, Moe, catch a nigger by the toe," a man yelled out before the car sped up and pulled away. Abednego put down the camera and tried to see who it was, but couldn't.

"D.D.T.," yelled Iris after the car. Abednego hushed her.

"Ain't no sense stirring up trouble," he said. "What do D.D.T. mean anyway?"

"Drop dead twice," said Marvelous. Abednego laughed.

"That man an ignorant fool," he said. "Nothing to worry about." But as he said it, he led the horse around to the back of his house by the creek, away from the road, out of sight.

Chapter 8

ABEDNEGO

Abednego kept showing up at Auntie's to perform chores. When he finished painting, sweeping, chopping, trimming, or hammering, Auntie would invite him in for some cold iced tea or supper. Later when it cooled off, they would go sit on the front porch in the rocking chairs and talk. As the sun set over the ridges, Auntie would proclaim, "This is the day the Lord has made, let us rejoice and be glad."

"My mama say the same thing every sunrise," said Abednego.

"Auntie say it at sunrise, sunset, and in-between," said Lola. Auntie nodded.

"Nothing wrong with telling God he's appreciated," said Auntie.

"Amen," said Abednego. "Sure is pretty tonight. Like one of them Hawaii sunsets I seen in the picture show."

"I'd like to see me a picture show with a beach and palm trees and an ocean," said Auntie.

"I think *South Pacific* playing. We can go see it," he said. "You, me, and Miss Lola." He explained that his married friend, John, and his wife Rose, were going Saturday night. Miss Susie nodded.

"We can pay our own way," she said. When Saturday evening arrived, John, Rose, and Abednego pulled up out front of Auntie's. Wearing one of her elaborate hats—a green feathered number that tilted down low over her face, Auntie strutted down the stairs like she was headed to Paris, France, not Ringgold. Dressed in a simple lavender cotton dress that couldn't hide her curves, Lola followed. Abednego ushered the ladies into the back seat on one side, then went around to the other side of the car so he could sit next to Lola.

At the Ringo Theatre up in town, with Abednego holding Auntie's elbow, the group followed the sign "Colored" to the balcony section. Abednego sat between Lola and Auntie, who had to take off her hat and hold it in her lap so it wouldn't obstruct the other patrons' view. As they watched Mitzi Gaynor wash that man right out of her hair in *South Pacific,* Abednego eased his arm around the top of the seat where Lola sat, but nothing more. Auntie was so absorbed in the movie she did not notice. He was content to inhale Lola's cherry-almond scent and be near to her in the dark theatre.

They all had such a good time, the next weekend Abednego organized another outing to see the latest John Wayne movie. At the last minute, Auntie had a flare up of her arthritis and could not go. Lola could, she said, as long as John and Rose chaperoned. When they pulled up to Auntie's to pick up Lola, Auntie limped out to the car spouting marching orders.

"That gal better be back here by eleven or I be madder than a wet hen," Auntie said.

"Yes, Ma'am," came a chorus of answers from the young people. Everyone knew that in her younger days, Auntie had once pulled a pistol on her daughter's boyfriend over some perceived slight.

The couples were seated in the balcony once more

and watching a fight scene during "Rio Bravo" when a frightened Lola shivered and edged her shoulder into Abednego's chest. He put his arm around her, squeezed her shoulder, and left his hand resting there until the movie was over. In the darkened theater, at that moment, he felt as though his world was perfect.

Within less than an hour, it all turned around when three white teenaged boys harassed them in the parking lot. John and Rose had already gotten into the black Chevy. Abednego and Lola were climbing into the back seat when one of the white boys spat brown tobacco juice all over their front bumper. Abednego watched the ugly slime snake its way down the silver chrome. The spitter, a skinny fellow with a beak of a nose, laughed with his friends and smirked at Abednego.

"What you gone do about it, nigger?" he asked Abednego, who hesitated before getting in the car.

"Let's go, Abednego," urged John.

"Did ya'll hear that? What kind of name is that?" said the tobacco juice spitter. "A dumb nigger name." With Lola safely in the car, Abednego turned to face the teenager.

"Bible name," he said. "Book of Daniel." He climbed into the car as another stream of spit hit the bumper. John cranked it up and pulled away.

"A bunch of rednecks up from Alabama," John said. "Don't usually have no trouble up here in Ringgold."

"Best to pay them no mind," said Rose. Lola murmured in agreement, but Abednego spoke.

"I'd like to catch him alone one night and rip that chaw right out of his cheek."

"You be better off putting your hand in a cow pie, Bing," said John. They all laughed, except Abednego, who put his arm around Lola protectively. Later, when the two men were alone, John told Abednego about the two couples, sharecroppers, who had been killed down at Moore's Ford Bridge about sixty miles south of Atlanta.

"I remember hearing bout that. Long time ago, weren't it?" asked Abednego.

"In the forties," said John. "What difference do it make? In case you hadn't noticed, not much changed around here." Abednego nodded.

For the next few weeks they did not travel up to Ringgold, or to the movies. Abednego had learned the best way to stay out of trouble was to avoid it. He continued to stop by Auntie's and do her chores. One night on the porch when Auntie was out of earshot, he whispered for Lola to stop after work to see him at the Tuckers' barn where he tended to their horses. The next afternoon he took his time cleaning and trimming the horses' hooves, looking up at the wide doorway from time to time, hoping she would appear.

Gypsy flicked her ears toward the barn opening and Abednego looked to see Lola standing there with the sunlight framing her tall form. Lord, if the gal didn't look like an angel with all that light around her.

"Come on in, cooler in here," he said. She came and stood next to him, watched as he focused on filing the edge of the horse's hoof. "I'll be done soon as I get them cockleburs out of Gypsy's mane."

"Can I do it?" Lola said. He handed her a comb. She worked the comb in above the burrs, then tugged down to free them from the tangled mane.

"I been thinking about your name," Lola said. "How you end up with a name like Abednego?"

"My mama name me and my brothers after her favorite Bible story. These three brothers, Abednego,

Meschack and Shadrach, don't do what the king say. He tell them to bow down to a gold idol. The king get real mad and toss them into a hot furnace. You know what? An angel come along and made that furnace feel like a cool breeze. Them three brothers don't burn up."

"I remember that story," Lola said. "I like your name."

"Yeah, but me and my brothers get tease plenty when we was in school. Now Lola, that a good, easy name. You got yourself a story?" Lola shook her head.

"Mama say she just like the name."

"So do I," said Abednego. He stood up and took the curry comb from her hand, let his hand linger on hers. She smiled and pulled away.

"Auntie gonna be wondering where I am," she said. "She knows what time they let me off work." Abednego took off his apron, put down his tools and walked her outside.

"Why don't you stop by tomorrow? I want to show you something," he said.

"Maybe," she said. "What you going to show me?" she asked. He smiled.

"A surprise," he said. He watched her as she walked away towards the road. "See you tomorrow."

"Maybe," she said. He saw her shrug her shoulders but knew she would come. She would be curious to see the surprise.

The next afternoon, Abednego was sitting astride a hay bale wiping down a saddle with saddle soap when he heard the chain clinging against the gate. It was Lola, who even in her light blue uniform covered with some sort of green stains, looked good.

"Come for your surprise?" Abednego said, laying

the saddle across a wooden saddle horse. He wiped off his hands on a clean rag.

"Maybe," she said. He laughed and took her hand, led her outside through the pasture, down towards the creek.

"We has to be quiet and wait. You gonna see your surprise soon." He took her to a spot near the creek, a small mowed meadow. They both stood behind the wide trunk of a large elm so they were hidden yet had a clear view of the meadow, the trees that lined the creek, and the lowering sun.

"What we looking for?" she whispered. "The sunset?"

"My friends," he said. "They come by every evening about this time. Just be quiet, and they be here in a minute." He took her hand and squeezed it while they waited, listening to the birds in the trees and inhaling the light fragrance of blackberry blooms. Within half an hour three rabbits hopped into view, a larger white-tail and two smaller ones.

"How'd you do that?" she asked.

"I told you, they my friends," he said. She grinned, and they watched the rabbits chase each other around a thicket of white blackberry blooms bordering the fence.

"Mama and babies?" she asked.

"I think so," he said. "Looky there." He pointed to a round bale of hay where a black and white cat lurked. "That cat thinking about supper." One of the baby rabbits twitched back its ear, and sensing the cat, sped away into the thicket. The others followed.

"She must of warned the others about that cat," said Lola. "How'd you know the rabbits were going to be here?"

"I didn't," said Abednego. "Just knew we'd see something. Sometime it a turtle, larger than a dinner plate. Another time, a heron or wild turkey, or duck. Tonight it was rabbit. All kind of life down here in this pasture." A loud rustling noise came from the thicket, which trembled from the movement of something inside. Lola and Abednego looked up to see two of the rabbits rush out of the thicket and cross the open the meadow.

"Where's the other baby?" asked Lola. Abednego pointed to the thicket.

"Probably in there, with the cat," he said. "Cat got hisself some supper."

"Cat can't eat no rabbit," said Lola. "Can he?"

"Afraid so," he said. "Or maybe he'll just bat it around a little, mess with it, for fun." Lola picked up a fallen branch,and headed for the thicket.

"I'll show that cat some fun," she said.

"Won't do no good," he said. "That's what cats do. Don't go too close to them bushes."

"Why not?"

"Saw a rat snake in there the other day," he said. Lola threw the branch down.

"I hope the snake will bite the cat," said Lola. Abednego laughed and took her hand. They walked down to put their feet in the cool stream.

On another sultry summer evening when Lola stopped by, Abednego had a paper sack of snacks for the horses. He pulled out a handful of carrots, broke them in half, and gave her some. She put most of the carrot pieces in her dress pocket but left one in her hand.

"Lay the carrot flat on your palm," he said. Lola was still a little shy around horses but did as he said. The sorrel gelding, Jupiter, always the friendliest when a treat was at stake, came over and brushed his lips against Lola's palm. Lola started laughing and tried to pull away but Abednego encouraged her. "He ain't going to hurt you, gal." The horse took the carrots, and Lola turned to Abednego giggling.

"It tickles," she said.

"Tickle? I show you tickle," he said, and reached his arms out towards Lola. She bolted away, and he chased her around the field while the curious horses watched. When he finally caught up to her, she held out her arms and breathing hard, commanded, "Don't you dare tickle me, Mr. Abednego Harris!" He bowed at the waist and backed away.

"Yes, your majesty," he said. "Anything for the queen of flowers." Then she motioned him to come closer. She reached in her pocket, pulled out another carrot piece, and put it on her extended hand. He leaned down and gently kissed the damp palm of her hand before taking the carrot in his mouth.

"You one friendly horse," she laughed, and ran away again. He made neighing noises and galloped after her, finally caught up to her as she stood by the honey suckle covered fence. They stood side-by-side, breathing hard.

"You one fast filly," he said. She tilted her head towards him, opened her eyes wide.

"Think so?" she asked. He stepped closer and put his hand out to touch her forearm.

"You a thoroughbred, gal," he said. "Like one of them race horses." He broke off some honeysuckle blossoms and brushed the hair away from her face.

"Hold still," he said, tucking a sprig of honeysuckle behind her ear. His fingers touched her soft skin. He took in the perfumed fragrance of the blossoms, of her. He couldn't help himself. He leaned in and kissed her lips. She didn't move away, let his lips touch hers. The kiss was short, sweet. She tasted like he knew she would, a nutty flavor that made him want more. When he pulled away, he saw a startled look in her eyes.

"First time?" he said. She nodded and glanced up at the sky for a moment, then stepped closer to him and tilted up her face. As their lips came together again, he felt the sensation of her kiss wash over him. He felt his body heat up, wanted to press her against a round bale of hay, and make love to her. He knew he would not. She was young. Although he had been with a woman once before, this felt different. He did not want to take advantage of her. Lola pulled away and looked up at the sky again. Following her gaze, he saw a sickle of a moon in the twilight sky. An omen, he thought, that they were meant to be together. He pulled her to his chest, hugged her tight. Lola's narrower body fit perfectly there against his broad chest. With her in his arms, all was right in the universe.

Chapter 9

LOLA

What Lola remembered most about the evening Abednego first kissed her was the overpowering smell of the honeysuckle, the way his eyes softened when he reached out to tuck the blossom behind her ear. She had never been close to a man before, and she found herself staring into his ebony pupils wondering if she looked long enough would she see his soul? And if she did what would it look like? This was what she was thinking when all of a sudden he kissed her.

She liked the way it felt having his warm lips press against hers, yet she was scared. Auntie had told her if she let a man have his way with her she would be struck dead by a lightning bolt. She quickly looked up in the sky and saw not a storm cloud in sight. The sky was clear with a sliver of a moon. Auntie was wrong—she would not be killed if she kissed him again. She moved her face close to his. As their lips touched, a tingle began in her stomach, shot through her like an electric current. The lightening! She pulled away to see where it had come from but saw nothing but sky deepening into indigo, punctuated with a pearly crescent. Auntie had not told her the truth, and now she knew why. She had never felt anything like this except for one time at church when she was singing "Amazing Grace" and felt a yearning, a surrender, to the melody that vibrated through her body.

From that night on Lola didn't think anymore of staid old Dr. Doushaun or her plan to go back to Rome in the fall. She let herself forget that there was a time beyond each warm summer evening she spent with her farm boy. Instead she let herself be consumed with thoughts of Abednego and how he enjoyed seeing her laugh, how she melted when they kissed. While she fried the okra in the iron skillet at the Buttrills, she found herself staring at the clock above the stove counting the hours till she could leave and stop by to see him on the way home. As she scrubbed the skillet and pots after supper, she sang one of his tunes in her head. "Sleepy Time Down South." The work was drudgery. Hopes of seeing him carried her through changing little Emily's diaper, cleaning the toddler's spit up, and even scrubbing out the toilet.

On most afternoons on the way home she stopped at his cabin and took a seat beside him on his front porch. Together they watched the lowering sun wash golden light over the grass fields across the dirt road.

"How your day, gal?" he would ask, taking her hand.

"Better now," she said. She loved the way he smiled at her and sometimes brushed her hair away from her eyes.

"Yeah? My queen be feeling good?" he'd say. She smiled and nodded.

"How them cooters?" she said, knowing full well he would lead her around to the back porch not to see the turtles but to give her a kiss or two when they were away from the road. They had to be careful not to let anyone see them because she was afraid Auntie would find out and forbid her to see Abednego. To avoid making Auntie suspicious, Lola told Auntie that Mrs. Buttrill was getting so big with that baby in her belly, she had to work late to wash up the supper dishes and put the children to bed. When Auntie asked if she ever saw Abednego in Taylor's Crossing, Lola told her she waved at him when she walked by the dairy. She felt she could not tell the truth, that Auntie would not want to hear she was falling for a farmer. So she lied to Auntie, told her Abednego was like a brother, if anything at all.

There was nothing familial about the way he pressed his body against hers when they kissed, the way his hand cupped the small of her back. When she felt herself getting carried away, she always pulled back. Her cousin Mary had warned her that kissing could lead to "the snake in the grass" that could make her belly swell like Mrs. Buttrill's. After working with the three children all day, she knew she was not ready for a baby of her own although she was curious about "the snake." One day she would allow herself to find out, but not until she was married. She told Abednego this, and he answered, "The best thing in life be worth waiting for."

While standing in the shade of the mature beech tree one sultry afternoon, after Lola and Abednego had kissed till their lips were pink and swollen, Abednego said he was going to show Lola how much he loved her. He pulled out a knife from his back pocket and began carving their initials into the smooth, gray bark.

"Will it hurt the tree?" she asked.

"Don't think so. The A.H. and L.H. gonna be here a long time."

"You mean L.J."

"I know what I'm carving, gal. And your name gonna be Harris one a these day." Hearing him say that made Lola smile inside and out. When he surrounded their carved initials with a huge heart, she thought she might melt. She could not believe someone loved her this much, and was not afraid to show it.

Every time they had to part, Lola hated to go, but when dusk approached, Abednego would offer to walk her home to Crystal Springs. She always refused his offer and set out on her own. She was afraid someone would pass by and report back to Auntie that she had a boyfriend. Taylor's Crossing was a fish bowl of a community where folks seemed to mind everyone else's business more than their own, and especially colored folks' business.

One evening after she walked the two miles from Abednego's, Lola arrived at Auntie's to find her in the kitchen crying. She was afraid Auntie had heard about her and Abednego. How would she explain about him? She approached her aunt cautiously.

"What's wrong, Auntie?" Her aunt stood up and started yelling.

"They done burn Miss Lizzie and Mr. Sam's house down! There ain't nothing left."

"Were they hurt?"

"They all shook up. Everything gone. She didn't have no time to collect nothing. She left her red New Testament Bible on the bedside table when she rush to get away from them flames."

"Who would do that to two old folk?" Lola asked. She remembered how kindly Miss Lizzie had treated her at the fish fry.

"Who you think be torching houses round here?" said Auntie as she wrapped a ham in tin foil before placing it in the oven, her usual response to disasters great or small.

"The Klan?" she asked.

"Not before this, I don't say so. I'm afraid, yeah, it them white hoods bring they hate up our way," said Auntie.

She shook her head in disgust. "John and Rose be by after a while to take her some food and clothes the church ladies gather up. Lizzie and her husband staying with her brother up in Chattanooga tonight." She handed Lola a bowl of green beans to string. Lola took the bowl, and suddenly feeling tired, sat down at the kitchen table. She methodically tore the strings away from the beans and broke them into pieces. She thought about Miss Lizzie's house and could see the flames licking up the side of the cheery yellow clapboard, consuming Miss Lizzie's red-covered New Testament. Poor Miss Lizzie. Who would have thought the Klan was anywhere that close? She thought of the ugly tan spittle coursing down John's bumper that night outside the movie theater up in Ringgold. Were the teenagers who had bothered them outside the picture show that night really from Alabama as John had said, or were they part of some new, local Klan?

Chapter 10

ABEDNEGO

Just after dawn the next morning, Abednego finished his morning milking and returned home to his cabin to get some breakfast. He sat on the front porch steps pulling off his work boots and was surprised to look up and see Lola walking down the lane towards his cabin. She had never stopped by on the way to her work before, but he was happy to see her. When she came onto his porch, he grabbed her hand to pull her around back and give her a kiss. He stopped when he saw the tears in her eyes.

"What's wrong?" he asked.

"The Klan burn down my friend's house last night," she said. He held her in his arms, cradling her as she cried. "In the night she take a heart attack and die. The Klan scare her to death."

"Don't make no sense," said Abednego.

"Like that cat and them rabbits you show me," said Lola.

"Except that cat hungry," said Abednego. "The Klan be pure hate."

"I'm scared," she said. "They might come down here and burn up Auntie's house. Or yours." Abednego tried to reassure her that Taylor's Crossing was safe.

"No Klan round here, gal," he said.

"Maybe not right down here in the valley, but they getting close."

"They won't come here," he said, stroking her hair. But he really wasn't sure. All he knew was he wanted to hold her and keep her safe from the ugliness of the world.

"Stop by after work and we do ourselves some turtle watching," he said. She pulled away as she heard the sound of a car engine coming down the road. She squeezed his hand and promised she'd come see him on the way home. As he watched her walk down the lane, he wished he could skip the milking and his farm chores and be with her all day. He also wished he could kill the ignorant fools who had burned down a house, killed an old woman, and hurt his Lola.

All day Abednego could not get her off his mind. As he and Henry weeded the garden and picked some early tomatoes, he thought about Lola going through her chores weighed down by a heavy heart. He wondered why this had to be?

He had heard stories about the Klan and how they ran folks off since the trouble down in Alabama. Rosa Parks had started it on the bus, followed by the bus boycotts. The Klan had gotten meaner after the federal court ordered the desegregation of the buses down in Montgomery. Some folks said the Klan was growing since the new law came into effect. That was down in Alabama. Not here in his county.

Lola lived a good three miles from him, too far for him to help if someone tried to burn down her house. If only she lived closer to him, if only they lived together.

"Bing, you awful quiet today," said Henry. "Cat got your tongue?" Abednego looked up from picking tomatoes in the garden.

"That old tomcat pawing up the garden again?" asked Abednego. Henry tossed an over ripe tomato at

Abednego, who caught it mid-air.

"You in another world, boy," he said. "Thinking about that gal again, ain't you?"

"Yes, Sir," Bing lied. "Been thinking about taking her fishing up to the river." He did not want to talk about the burned down house, which he was not sure Henry had heard about yet. And if he did, he would probably think it was an accident caused by "some dumb nigra."

"That gal fish?" asked Henry.

"If I put the worm on," he said. Henry laughed.

"Hadn't ever met a girl who wanted to put on the bait," he said. "Well, you watch yourself, and don't get that gal in trouble."

"No, Sir," said Abednego. He plucked off an aphid and squeezed it to death between his fingers. Henry had no right to talk about his love life. Did he think Abednego stupid?

"I'd hate Sewell Buttrill to come after you with a shotgun," he said.

"He wouldn't have no chance," Abednego said. Henry stopped picking, stared at Abednego like he was crazy. Seeing his boss tense up, Abednego continued, "Anything happen to Lola, her Auntie Susie done shoot me with her pistol before Mr. Buttrill have his turn." Henry chuckled.

"You right about that, boy," he said. "They say old Susie shot a robber once. In the back. I can finish up the picking here. Why don't you go on and fix that fence down by the creek?" He referred to the repairs needed in the barbed wire and cedar post fence that surrounded the acreage.

"Yes, Sir," said Abednego, glad to have a chance to get some time by himself, time to sort out his own thoughts. He went back to the barn, gathered up the wire, staples, pliers, and a hammer, and tucked them into his tool belt. Pulling his straw hat on tight, he headed out into the heat.

Chapter 11

LOLA

With her heart heavy with the news of Miss Lizzie's dying, Lola's morning did not go well. She heated the milk bottle too long and had to hold the screaming toddler in her arms while waiting for it to cool. Just leaving for town, Mr. Buttrill overheard and came in to see "what the Sam Hill was she doing to little Emily." Although she tried to explain, he snatched the girl from her arms and took her upstairs to Miss Adelaide, who was still lying in bed resting. Lola returned to mopping the kitchen floor while wrangling the boys who were not coloring as they were supposed to, but were instead breaking the crayons in half and throwing them.

"Crandell, Coke, stop it," said Lola. She grabbed a handful of the crayons off the table and shoved them back in the box. "If y'all don't color the right way I'm fixing to put up them crayons." The boys began wailing, just as Mr. Buttrill returned down the stairs. He shook his head in disapproval.

"You need to keep them quiet, gal. My wife needs her rest. Why don't you take them outside? Mop that floor some other time."

"Yes, Sir," Lola answered. Mr. Buttrill watched her as she untied her apron strings. Probably waiting around to tell her how she was doing it wrong. She hated his nosing around in her business and especially when Miss Adelaide had already told her what chores to do today. She propped the mop back up in the bucket and set it in the kitchen corner. She wondered how she would get the floor done, the vegetables chopped for dinner, and fix the meatloaf Miss Adelaide had requested, all by noon and while keeping an eye on the children. She sighed, took the boys' hands, and headed outside.

Standing under the grand magnolia tree at the side of the house, she watched the boys toss a ball back and forth, aiming for but often missing each other. She thought about Miss Lizzie and shivered. How could the Klan come after an old woman? She looked at the boys' pale, chubby faces and wondered would they, too, grow up to join the Klan? She did not think Mr. Buttrill was a member but who knew? He was always going off to town for meetings. Although he did some kind of work at the bank, he seemed to come and go as he pleased. Coke, the younger one, threw the ball into Lola's skirt and laughed as Lola startled.

"Watch where you aiming, Mr. Coke," she said. She tossed the ball back to him. He then threw it at Crandell's face, hitting him in the eye. Crandell touched the right side of his face and screamed in pain, then ran towards Coke and pushed him down to the ground, and jumped on top of him. They tussled with one another, rolling around over the dropped magnolia blossoms. As Lola reached down and separated them, she wondered why did boys always want to fight, to hurt each other. Were the Klan nothing more than big boys who wanted to fight and hurt just because it was their nature? Was there nothing she could do to prevent it or change nature's course?

"Y'all going to use your words from now on," she said. "Animals fight like this, like y'all. Big boys, they use they words and talk things out." She didn't really believe what she was saying, not for a minute. Still if she worked on them a little, day by day, maybe they wouldn't grow up to burn down an old Negro woman's house one day, maybe even hers. She heard a voice coming from the upstairs window.

"Lola?" called Miss Adelaide. "Could you come up and get Emily? She needs to be changed." Lola grabbed the boys' hands and headed back in. Had Miss Adelaide, the mother of three and one on the way, suddenly and inexplicably forgotten how to change a diaper?

Up in the large and usually airy bedroom now filled with little Emily's massive stink, Lola found Miss Adelaide lying under the covers still dressed in her pink print nightgown. Little Emily lay giggling and playing with her mama's long auburn curls. The boys jumped up on the bed to torment their little sister.

"Doo doo butt, doo doo butt," taunted Coke. Crandell poked at the baby's soft stomach which made her laugh.

"After you change her, bring her back. The boys can stay in here with me," said Miss Adelaide.

As Lola wiped off the baby's bottom with a damp cloth, the baby looked up at her with trusting blue eyes. Lola felt sorry for her. How much attention would the girl get once the new baby was born? Would she run with her rowdy big brothers and turn into a little demon, too? Lola felt helpless to do anything about the baby's future. All she could do was give Emily as much attention as she could between her other chores.

Five minutes later, Lola brought the baby back in, freshly powdered and looking like a golden-haired angel. Miss Adelaide had made it out of bed and moved to her blue-upholstered divan. She watched the boys play hide and seek under the sheets, although their clothes were covered in dirt from their earlier rolling around under the tree.

"After they're done playing, you'll have to change the sheets," said Adelaide. "Mr. Buttrill hates finding any kind of dirt in our bed." The baby kicked and waved her arms at her mother. Lola carried her to Miss Adelaide and handed her over. Getting some fresh sheets out of the closet, Lola added the bed changing to her list of chores. She had hoped to leave early so she could meet Abednego.

"I have some sad news," said Miss Adelaide as she brushed little Emily's downy hair. "An old nigra couple up in Ringgold had their house burn down last night. I believe your aunt may know them?" Lola nodded.

"Yes 'em, Miss Lizzie come down to our fish fry and sometime to Sunday evening meeting."

"Mr. Buttrill said it was probably caused by a cigarette."

"Ma'am? Miss Lizzie and her husband don't smoke."

"Well, maybe they had them some visitors who smoked. Maybe someone from out of town. One of those Atlanta nigra preachers up there in their house trying to stir up trouble. You heard of any preachers from out of town coming up around here?"

"No Ma'am," Lola said. She knew Miss Adelaide was referring to the movement to change the Jim Crow laws, but down here, colored folks didn't get involved in such. They knew better, Auntie had said.

"Well, you can tell Miss Susie I am sorry to hear it was her friend who died," said Miss Adelaide. "You get that meatloaf made up yet?"

"No, Ma'am," answered Lola. She felt bothered by

Miss Adelaide's offering her condolences in the same breath as the meatloaf, and sounding much more concerned about the meatloaf than the death.

"Well you run on down and get it put together. Be sure to use quarter onion, not a whole. I don't need gas on top of everything else. I'll keep the boys up here for a while. Mr. Buttrill will be back promptly at noon, and he'll expect a hot dinner on the table."

"Yes, Ma'am," said Lola. "I need to take off early to set with Mr. Moses."

"Can't some of the other nigras do that? I need you here."

"I'm sorry. Auntie told me I had to, Ma'am."

"How long? You'll have to make it up," Miss Adelaide said.

"A couple of days, Ma'am. I be glad to make it up."

"Make up some extra when you cook our supper," she said. "Put it in the Frigidaire for tomorrow so we'll have something to eat."

"Yes, Ma'am," Lola answered. She turned and headed out of the room, mumbling to herself. Didn't she think Mr. Moses who had just lost his wife could use her help, needed Lola more? And where had Miss Adelaide come up with such nonsense about the Atlanta preachers? Miss Lizzie's grandson was a pastor from down in Alabama. She couldn't wait to tell Abednego what Miss Adelaide had said.

Chapter 12

ABEDNEGO

When Abednego finished the evening milking, he returned home and sat on his front porch shucking and eating peanuts. He took an occasional swig from his Orange Crush and stared at the road as though trying to make Lola materialize in the shimmering August heat that rippled up from the gravel road. He went back inside his cabin to look in the mirror and rehearse what he was going to say to her. He looked at his face, adjusted his frown to an almost smile, not too serious but not grinning too big, either. He didn't want her to think he was kidding.

"Love come on all of a sudden sometime. And when that happen, a man got to do something about it. I don't know you very long, just long enough to know I fall in love. With you, everything about you. Your soft hands, your shining face, your kiss that taste like walnut. I want to care for you, hold you in my arms at night. Queen of Flowers, will you be my wife?"

That didn't sound quite right. Maybe he should start out calling her Queen of Flowers and present her with a bunch of flowers, tiger lilies? Yes, that was a good idea. He would walk her back near the creek and sit her down on the hay bale, then make her close her eyes. He could give her the flowers, then kiss her, then ask her to marry him. Or should he kiss her, then give her the flowers, then ask her? Maybe the order did not matter. Maybe she would say no whatever he said. He had no idea how she would respond, and he surprised even himself when he set his mind to asking her. It was the right thing to do. He wanted to keep her close. With the Klan's attacking just eight miles up the road, he felt he had to. The only right way to keep her safe was to be with her at night when the white hoods, those cowards, slinked around in the dark like a pack of wolves on the prowl. He would get John to drive him to Ninth Street up in Chattanooga one night, and he would buy a pistol. If the Klan came, he would be ready.

Just after half past she arrived. He heard her before he saw her, her light step on the crunchy gravel of the lane. He stood up and saw her face, contorted in grief and damp with the day's toil. He held out his hand and led her past the sweet shrub bush to the coolness of the stream bank. He took her in his arms, squeezed her tight against his body. When he felt her shaking, he pulled away, saw her tears mixed with sweat.

"So sorry your friend die, Lola," he said. She shook her head.

"No, it's Mrs. Buttrill. What she say cause the fire. She try to blame it on Miss Lizzie having some preachers up from Atlanta smoking cigarettes and stirring up trouble. Miss Lizzie, she don't have no people like that in her house, she don't know nothing about no Silver Rights." Abednego felt the anger rise up in his throat as she spoke.

"She wrong, just plain wrong," he said. "The heat and all them babies be making her one crazy white lady."

"No, it was Mr. Buttrill told her a cigarette caused that fire, she say. Old Moses can't barely breathe he so old. He never smoke. Miss Lizzie don't allow no smoking around him. Mr. Buttrill, he lying." Abednego pulled her close again, lowered his voice to a soothing, confidential timbre, and stroked her head.

"You and I know who done it. Every colored in the county know who. The Buttrills can't be changing the truth." And they sure know how to ruin me asking my gal to marry me, Abednego thought. "Why don't you set down and let me get you something to drink, gal? A Crush or something? You hungry?" Lola shook her head.

"I feel so mad I don't want nothing. Besides, Auntie expect me home shortly. John and Rose gonna drive us up to town to set with Mr. Moses. I'm off tomorrow, and Auntie want us to stay up in town with Mr. Moses till after the funeral."

"Let me walk you home, Lola," he said.

"What about Auntie?" asked Lola. "Or someone seeing us?"

"I turn around before we get all the way there," he said. "Hold up a minute. Let me get something." He stepped back inside. A minute later he returned with the tiger lilies hidden in a brown paper bag. He pulled them out of the bag and handed them to Lola.

"Thank you. Mr. Moses will like these," she said.

"They for you, gal," he said. Clutching the flowers in her left hand, she threw her arms around his neck and hugged him.

"You make me feel better," she said. "I love you, Bing." That's all he needed to hear. He grabbed her hand and led her towards the road.

"I'm gonna show you a short cut," he said. "If we cut through the back pasture, it'll take off about half a mile to your house. Come on." He took her hand, and they walked across the hot road into the cool grass of the Tucker's pasture.

Under the elm tree, at the place where he had shown

her his rabbit friends, he stopped and pulled her to his chest, kissed her long and hard. Then he whispered in her ear.

"Shut your eyes, my Queen of Flowers," he said. "I have a surprise for you." He watched her eyes close, her head tilt up slightly in anticipation.

"What you up to, Bing? You gonna put a frog on my head or something?"

"Nah, hold your hands out, palms down," he said. He picked a field daisy and quickly fashioned it into a circle, tied the stem into a knot. "You sure you not peeking?" She shook her head no. "Good," he said, taking her left hand in his hands. He slipped the daisy ring around her third finger.

"Miss Lola James, would you marry me?" he asked. Her almond eyes opened wide and she looked at the flower ring, then at Abednego. She laughed. She put her hands on her hips.

"You real funny, Bing," she said. "I like this ring." He grabbed her hand.

"I ain't teasing, Lola. Will you be my wife?"

"Marry you?" she asked. "Really?" Bing ran his finger over the daisy ring, stroked her finger.

"I don't have no time to get a gold ring, but yes. Marry me, live with me, let me keep you safe." Lola jumped in the air. She threw her head back, held her slender arms out, and twirled around in a circle.

"Yes, yes, yes!" she sang.

Abednego ran over and grabbed her waist, took her in his arms, and covered her mouth with kisses, combed his fingers through her dark curls, his future wife's curls. He felt like the luckiest man in the world—until he heard something rustle in the brush. He stopped kissing her, shifted his head to look over Lola's shoulder to see a patch of blue cloth retreating into the thicket down by the creek. He couldn't tell who it was, but someone had been spying on them. Was it Henry? He was supposed to be in town picking up barbed wire, not walking the pasture. Or that creepy Lawson Tucker? Or a neighbor?

"What is it?" Lola asked. No use upsetting her, scaring her. She had been through enough for one day.

"Nothing, baby, nothing. Thought I saw one them mean old cats."

Chapter 13

LOLA

At the side of the road by the bridge, Lola gave Abednego a final kiss and headed towards Auntie's, her step light and quick. She did not want to think about how she would tell Auntie, or her mother. All she wanted to do was feel the joy she had felt when Abednego proposed to her. She had no clue how or when they would marry. That did not matter. They would do it somehow. Maybe she would finish high school before they married, or perhaps they could marry and she could finish high school somewhere up here. She had promised her mama she would get her diploma. And that she would work at Dr. Doushaun's. Her mama would be disappointed, but not after she met Abednego. She would tell her mother she would go to school in the mornings and work at the Buttrills after, work into the night if she had to. To be with Abednego who made her so happy, she would do anything to make it happen.

She arrived at Auntie's to see John and Rose's car pulled up out front. Rose, who was standing by the side of the car, held up her hand to stop her.

"Your Auntie madder than a wet hen," she said. Rose looked down at the flower ring on Lola's finger, at the orange tiger lilies, and arched an eyebrow. "Where you been?"

"Them boys got into them flowers, making things.

Don't want me to leave. Are you early?"

"We're not, Lola. It's seven thirty." Lola dashed up the stairs and into her room to change out of her uniform. She gently took the daisy engagement ring off her finger and hid it in the top drawer of her dresser under some lingerie. She felt a warm rush tickle her stomach as she thought of Abednego touching the daisy ring, now lying against the cool white cotton of her underthings. She had to force herself to focus on her flour sack nightgown she packed in a grocery bag and all the other clothes she would need for the next several days. Carrying the bag and the tiger lilies, she returned to the car and climbed in the back seat next to a pouting Auntie.

"I'm sorry I had to work late, Auntie," she said. "These flowers are for Mr. Moses. Think he'll like them?"

"If he be awake when we get there," Auntie snapped. "Couldn't you get Mrs. Buttrill to let you off early, gal? Don't you tell her where you was going?"

"I tried, Auntie. She say the fire was Miss Lizzie's fault. Say Miss Lizzie had them Atlanta preachers up here smoking and stirring up trouble."

"Say what?"

"That's right. Miss Adelaide think Miss Lizzie had her some Silver Rights preachers in her house talking about them Jim Crow laws."

Auntie began to work her lips around, as if she were tasting an old and bitter pecan.

"Miss Lizzie grandson, James, he gonna be here tonight. He usually too busy preaching God's word to come up here, ever since he took over his church down in Alabama. Where in the world Mrs. Buttrill come up with that idea?" asked Auntie.

"Mr. Buttrill say it. And she say to tell you she

sorry about your friend," said Lola.

"She ain't sorry," said Auntie. "Next thing you know she be asking you to mend them white robes for her." Lola thought her aunt was joking but tried to remember what she had seen inside the Buttrills' closets, never any white robes or hoods or anything suspicious. Of course she hadn't been in the tool shed Mr. Buttrill kept locked. She did not think they would hire a colored person if they were in the Klan. Or would they? White people confused her.

"Miss Susie, could she be talking about your grandson preacher friend who stopped by on his way to the revival last month?" said John from the front seat. "You suppose they figure him to be part of the SCLC?"

"Even if he is, Miss Lizzie no fool," said Auntie. "She wouldn't bother with that. Miss Lizzie too busy talking about Jesus, and nothing else."

"Amen," said Rose.

"I think they burned down the wrong house," said John. "That's what happened." Lola shivered as he said it. She thought how easy it would be for the Klan to make a mistake. She wished she and Abednego were married now, not later. She crossed her hands, let her fingertips run over her naked finger where the daisy ring had been, where just an hour ago Abednego had touched her. She remembered the way she felt when his arms were wrapped around her, the safe feeling he gave her. As Auntie and John continued to talk about all the violence, about the Klan and the fools who joined it, she allowed herself to dwell in another place, the world she and Abednego created when they were together, a place without violence, a place where only love existed.

Chapter 14

MARVELOUS

That evening, after Lola left to sit with Mr. Moses, Abednego's sister Marvelous arrived for a week-long visit. With lightning bugs winking at them, brother and sister sat on the back porch of Abednego's cabin dangling their bare feet above the tall alfalfa while they fished. They talked and watched their bobbers float on the surface of the lazy creek.

"You like that gal, Bing?" asked Marvelous.

"Sure do, Miss Marvelous," answered Abednego. "She sure think you pretty." He tugged at her wild mane of hair, fastened into a plump ponytail.

"You just sayin' that, Bing."

"Nah, she mean it."

"Am I pretty as her?" asked Marvelous.

"Shoot, gal, no one as pretty as you," said Abednego. Marvelous freed her hair from the rubber band that held it and tossed her curls around.

"My hair is longer," she said.

"That right," said Abednego. "You ever wish you had a big sister help style that hair for you?"

"Nah," said Marvelous. "I can do it." She ran her fingers through her hair. "Iris is like my sister."

"Yeah, if you had a big sister, she could be helping you style that hair."

"Bing, you know that ain't gone happen."

"Don't be so sure of it, baby," said Abednego. Marvelous jumped up, handed her brother the pole.

"You sure talking funny, Bing. You sick in the head or something?" Marvelous crossed her arms as she spoke.

"Set down and don't scare them fish," said Abednego. Marvelous complied, sat back down but not before spinning her index finger around near her temple to indicate her brother was nuts. "If I be marrying Lola, you be getting yourself a big sister."

"Marry? You can't marry her!"

"Why not? I love her," said Abednego. Marvelous looked down and away from her brother, and toyed with an empty Orange Crush bottle.

"What about me?" she asked. Abednego threw his arm around her shoulder, pulled her in for a hug.

"I'm gonna love you just the same, and Lola gonna be like your big sister," he said.

"She gonna live here in this cabin?"

"Don't know yet. Wherever we live, you be visiting us all the time," he said.

"She gonna have a baby?"

"No, Ma'am," said Abednego. "Not for a long while, she ain't. When she do, you gonna be an aunt." Marvelous jumped up again, put her pole down on the porch.

"Me? An aunt? I got to tell Iris," she said and started off in the twilight.

"Wait," said Abednego, rising and following her. He grabbed her arm. "We wasn't planning on telling no one." Marvelous shrugged.

"Iris ain't gonna tell. I make her cross her heart, don't you worry about it. I'm gonna be an aunt!" She couldn't wait to share the news with her best friend. She dashed for the road and did not see the black sedan puttering their way.

The brakes screeched, and the car swerved to avoid hitting her, almost ran into the ditch. Abednego ran after her and watched her turn around to see the source of the screeching sound. She looked at the red-faced white man who leaned out of the window and shook his fist at Abednego. He didn't say a word—he didn't have to—his eyes narrowed into slits, his thin upper lip twitched. Marvelous could feel the hate; she had seen this look before. The man jerked the shifter into gear, turned the wheel slightly, and floored the gas pedal. Gravel flew out behind the wheels as he pulled away. As soon as he was out of sight, Marvelous ran back to her brother.

"That a mean man," she said. He threw his arm around her.

"Don't worry," he said. "He ain't from around here." Somewhat reassured, Marvelous looked up at him.

"Can I go tell Iris?" she said.

"About that mean man?" asked Abednego. "Don't you be telling her and get her upset. He just some dumb fool passing through."

"Nah, Bing, about me being an aunt."

"Yeah, alright. Wait. I told you not for a long time. You tell her when me and Lola marry, after a good long while, you gonna be an aunt. In a few year. Maybe."

"Okay," said Marvelous, already starting to pull away.

"Hold up," said Abednego. "You promise you look before you cross. I don't wanna be scraping your skinny butt up off this road." She laughed, took giant steps, and headed for the road, slowly turned her head left, then right, then bolted across.

Up at Iris' house, Marvelous found her friend in the living room with the fancy flowered wallpaper and new rug that smelled like hay. Iris was switching on the new TV the family had just gotten the week before.

"I got a secret, but you can't tell nobody," said Marvelous. "Bing gonna marry, and I get to be the aunt when they have their baby." Iris grabbed Marvelous' hand and pulled her down in front of the TV.

"I told you he was sweet on that Lola," she said. "They can't have babies till they marry. First he has to kiss her in front of the preacher."

"I know that," said Marvelous.

"Look, there's Bob Brandy." Iris pointed at the screen to a tall man dressed like a cowboy. "Do you think Rebel will be on today?"

"Probably," said Marvelous. "After Bob talks to them Brownie Scout," she said. "I wish I could get on Rebel and ride him right out of the TV into this room."

"Yeah, he'd probably dump manure all over the floor," said a male voice from behind them. The girls turned around to see Iris' brother Lawson had sneaked up and was standing behind the new brocade sofa. "I'm not cleaning horse poo. That show is stupid and so is Bob Brandy." He walked across the rug in front of the girls in order to turn the channel to another program. Iris jumped up and shoved his hand away. They glared at each other.

"You're gross, Lawson. It's my time to watch," said Iris. "Your turn starts after Bob Brandy. Mama said so."

"Would ya'll move over?" said Marvelous. "They about to give away the Moon Pie." Lawson stood to the side of the TV and watched his little sister sit back down in front of the TV next to Marvelous.

"Wouldn't you love to win one of those silver

dollars?" Iris asked. "I bet if we were on the show, we would."

"I know we would," said Marvelous, taking Iris' hand. They held hands and looked up at the screen as Bob handed a grinning boy a cellophane wrapped cookie.

"Fairies," said Lawson. He turned and walked out of the room.

"What he talking about?" asked Marvelous.

"I don't know," said Iris. "Probably just jealous because we're friends. He doesn't have any."

"Less you count all them cooties he have," Marvelous said.

"Shush," said Iris. "If he hears you he'll tell Mama. Hey, look, there's Rebel now!" The girls looked at the TV screen as the horse walked into view.

Back in the cabin later that night, after Abednego tucked her in bed, Marvelous lay staring at the walls—a collection of old newspapers pasted against the wood boards to keep out the wind, so different from the fancy wallpaper at Iris' house. She thought about the man who had almost run over her and wondered what he would have done if Iris had run out in front of him. Would he have jumped out to see if she was alright? Would he have said how sorry he was? She thought about Lawson and wondered what a fairy was? She liked fairies, so if he thought she and Iris were fairies, well, that was good. Wasn't it? Maybe he'd been spying on them when they made the fairy nests. Did fairies eat Moon Pies? Did fairies ride horses? She fell asleep thinking of pink and green fairies riding silver horses that took off flying when they galloped.

While she was deep in her dreams, Marvelous did

not hear the car that pulled into the driveway, or the man's voice that contrasted sharply with the cicadas' gentle chorus.

Chapter 15

ABEDNEGO

Abednego jumped up off the couch where he was sleeping when he heard the scrape of a car's oil pan against the rut in his dirt driveway. He pulled aside the curtains, looked out the window to see the dark outline of a car. He heard a deep voice. "Nigger, I'm warnin' you, we don't want your kind around here. If you know what's good for you, you'll pack up and leave Taylor's Crossing."

Abednego checked the lock on the door, secured the wooden crossbar he had installed to keep out intruders. Who was this person who had come to disturb his sleep? And why had someone suddenly decided he should not be here anymore? Probably had something to do with the Klan burning down that house. Or maybe it was the man who had almost run over Marvelous. He paced up and down near the front door, trying to calm himself from the fear he felt at the stranger who had appeared to shatter his sleep. He walked over to the thin cot and found Marvelous sleeping soundly. Returning to the couch, he lay back down but kept his eyes on the front door till dawn, and time for the first milking.

He woke up Marvelous before he left and told her he had heard something outside the night before, that she should keep the doors locked until he returned. When she asked what it was, he lied and told her he thought maybe a bobcat, or maybe just a raccoon. He didn't want to frighten her, but he didn't want her to be asleep if someone came back.

"Something break in, you crawl out that window and go out to the porch," he said. "Then follow the creek up to the Porters' house." Marvelous looked at him like he was crazy.

"I ain't scared of no animals. They can't get in here. If they do, I'll hit them in the head with your iron skillet." Marvelous sat up as she spoke. Her face looked tough and fierce for a girl of ten.

"You right, baby. Just want to make sure you know I'm leaving. If you put on that wood slide, nothing gonna mess with you. Besides, raccoons and bobcats, they mostly come out at night." Like those cowards in the Klan, he thought but did not say. He headed for the front door with Marvelous trailing along behind him in her lavender nightgown. "Now just slide the wood bar across."

"Okay," she said. "Unless he a giant, that bobcat ain't coming in here, no Sir." As he stepped off the porch, he heard the bolt slide into place. He realized then that anyone coming into the cabin would be slammed in the head with the back side of the skillet. Marvelous, was, after all, his baby sister and a Harris. She knew how to defend herself. He smiled at the thought, realized he did not have to worry during the two hours it would take to milk the cows.

In the milking barn after he hooked up the first cows to the milkers, he spoke to Henry about the threats made by the stranger who came in the middle of the night.

"I wouldn't worry about it," said Henry. "Probably just some high school boys out for a joy ride."

"Don't know, Sir," said Abednego. "With that house burn down up the road, it might be one a them Klan.

The man, he have a deep voice, sound older than high school."

"Abednego, you know there ain't any Klan down here," Henry said. "Down in Alabama, yes, but there's none of them boys down here in Taylor's Crossing. Besides, you work for us and mind your own business. They like to run off folks who drink or beat their women. You don't beat your gal, do you?"

"No, Sir," said Abednego.

"You just keep doing your work, keep to yourself. You ain't going nowhere. I couldn't keep all these cows milked without you."

Abednego knew it was true. The other fellow, Flint Lockerby, had broken his arm when he fell off a horse, leaving only Henry and Abednego to handle the entire dairy operation.

"He sure sound like he mean it, Sir," Abednego said. Henry was quiet through the first three rounds of cows before he told Abednego he would mention the incident to the sheriff the next time he went into town to buy feed.

"Appreciate that, Sir," said Abednego. "My little sister visiting, and I hate for her be scared."

The rest of the day, and the next, passed uneventfully, although he missed Lola and could not wait for her to come back from helping Mr. Moses. He wanted to tell her how much he loved her, and how he was excited they would soon be husband and wife. He wanted to talk about when they would get married and where they would live. Most of all he wanted to hold her and inhale the sweet smell of soap and sweat that emanated from her, and make love till they both fell asleep in each other's arms. After the first milking for the next few days, he returned to his cabin and made breakfast for Marvelous, then walked her up to the barn where he knew he would find Iris feeding and grooming the three horses. While he worked in the garden or helped Henry cut hay, he knew the girls would stay busy with the horses. With Iris, Marvelous would be safe.

Chapter 16

MARVELOUS

While it was hot outside, Iris and Marvelous stayed in the barn with Gypsy, Jupiter and Sassy, brushing their coats and pulling cockleburs out of their tails. They braided each horse's mane and tail and added red, blue and yellow ribbons at the ends. In the middle of the day, when the heat was almost unbearable, the girls "bathed" the horses, squirting water from a garden hose over the horses' backs, and each other. One afternoon, Abednego pulled out the clippers and file, showed them how he trimmed the horse's hooves. As the afternoon began to cool off, the girls would climb aboard Gypsy and ride double all around the house and nearby fields, pretending they were in a parade. In a mowed field near Iris' house, they constructed jumps from broken tree branches and taught Gypsy to go over them. In the evening after supper, Iris rode Gypsy over to Abednego's cabin, tied her up on the back porch rail, and sat on the bank by the branch with Abednego and Marvelous.

Abednego tried to fish, but he kept catching turtles which he threw back in. He finally set the pole down and along with the girls, watched the turtles rise out of the murky water, their heads looking like snakes. They would move slowly and surely to the surface and then dive back out of sight. Eventually the girls lost interest and started singing "Ain't Nothin' But a Hound Dog." They began howling like dogs at the full moon as it came up over Taylor's Ridge. Abednego picked up his fishing net, held it like a guitar, and strummed as he joined them as they segued into "Blueberry Hill." Just after dark, Henry showed up to collect Iris. The girls said goodbye, promising to see each other the next morning. Abednego announced it was time to turn in for the night. He had to get up early the next day to check on a cow about to birth a calf any minute.

Lying on the narrow cot, Marvelous saw Abednego had fallen asleep while she was wide awake with restless thoughts. Why couldn't the moon always be shining? Why did it have to disappear for a few days sometimes? She liked the way its light kept the earth from being in total darkness, the way its light made her feel protected from the dark.

When she heard a faint thud of hoof beats, Marvelous jumped up, went to the window, and pulled back the curtain. She waved at Iris who was standing in a pale wash of moonlight. She motioned with her finger that she would be there in a minute. She wiggled out of her nightgown, stuffed it and her pillow under the covers along with some other clothes, so it would look like she was still there asleep, and then tiptoed over to the chair by her bed and put on the shorts and blouse she had worn yesterday. Carrying her boots in her hand, she went to the window, opened it slowly and quietly, and climbed out. She put on her boots and went over to Gypsy and Iris, held out her hand so Iris could pull her up. Sitting behind Iris, Marvelous put her arms around Iris' thick waist.

"Hang on," Iris whispered, "and don't let go. We're going somewhere new." Iris dug her heels into Gypsy's side, and the horse set off running for a night adventure.

Chapter 17

IRIS

After the ride, Iris let Marvelous off in front of Abednego's cabin and returned home to her own bed. She fell asleep thinking of riding through the tall grass, high on her horse, safe from the world. In the middle of the night, she startled awake when she heard dogs barking. She remembered the German Shepherds that had chased them, and wondered if they were out roaming by themselves or had a neighbor, seeing her with Marvelous, unleashed them on purpose? Many times sitting around Grandma's supper table with her father, mother and uncle talking all at once, she had often heard about mean men who tried to hurt Negroes. She heard about cross burnings and bombings, always "up the road a ways" or "down yonder a piece." She worried about Marvelous. Her grandmother assured her no one would bother "our colored friends." The Tuckers were well respected and her granddaddy and his sons, William and Henry, were powerful men known for their strong tempers. They had once caught a horse thief trying to steal one of the foals. The man had begged for them to call the sheriff, but they had already pulled out the horsewhips. His screams echoed across the valley that night. Everyone knew not to cross the Tuckers. At least in the valley, she hoped.

Ringgold was different. One time Henry took Iris and Marvelous along to pick up feed. While they waited in the truck, the girls both felt thirsty and ventured out to find some water. The fountain marked "colored" was broken, so Iris encouraged Marvelous to drink out of the "whites" fountain. Marvelous hesitated.

"No one's around," Iris said. Marvelous quickly stepped forward, put her lips over the gurgling water, and gulped while Iris kept a look out. She hadn't seen anyone, but someone inside the feed store must have. When Henry came out, he scolded Iris.

"You ought to know better than to cause trouble," he said. The following day Lawson had lectured her on keeping her distance from Marvelous in town. Some boys in school had teased him and called the Tuckers "nigger lovers." A few days later when they were weeding in the garden, Lawson had grabbed her wrist and urged her to stop hanging out with Marvelous.

"You're getting too old to be her friend," he said.

"What do you mean?" Iris had asked.

"Liking coloreds when you're little is one thing, but you're almost in junior high," he'd said.

"What's changed?" she had asked.

"It's time to stop being a child and see the world the way it is," he'd said. "You need to grow up." At sixteen, he was five years older, and a head taller, so she listened, for a second.

"She's my friend, and nobody's going to change that," she yelled. Her brother shook his head and simply walked away leaving her alone with her thoughts and three rows that needed weeding.

Chapter 18

ABEDNEGO

After Abednego had tucked his sister in for the night, he went to his own room, and peeled down to his undershorts. Clutching his pillow, he fell asleep thinking of Lola, who would be back the next week.

Sometime in the night, he thought he heard something, but when he rose and pecked into the back room to check on Marvelous, she looked like she was tucked in tight under the covers. He checked on the door bolt and found it undisturbed. After a few moments, thinking of his hard day ahead, he let himself fall back to sleep.

He awoke to the cold butt of a pistol at his temple. His eyes startled open to see a group of white-hooded figures standing around the couch, the light from their flashlights making pale circles on the old wood floor. When he moved to get up, one of the hoods leaned down over him and Abednego looked up at the cut out circles where the eyes were supposed to be and saw the light of the flashlight reflecting against eyeglasses. The man shoved him hard, back onto the mattress.

"Roll over, boy," said the voice from underneath the hood. Abednego felt his hands being tied behind his back, felt a gag--an old rag that smelled like gasoline and stung his nostrils--be placed tightly between his lips. Several pairs of hands roughly rolled him back over and when he saw there were at least ten of them, he didn't even try to struggle. He hoped they had come in through the front and not seen Marvelous asleep in the back room.

"Boy, you were warned. We don't want niggers down here. You hear me?" a muffled voice came from under one of the hoods.

Abednego tried to answer but his "yes, Sir" was muffled by the gag. There was a brief period of silence. Then he heard someone fumbling through a bag of tools, the clink of metal to metal. He hoped they had not brought a hammer and nails. Sometimes the Klan nailed the victim's nuts to a bench. He felt like throwing up.

"Get up," instructed a muffled voice, this one sounding somewhat familiar, a gravelly smoker's voice. Abednego stood up from the sofa and tried to walk. Instead, the men in white robes shoved him along through the back room, past the cot that sat by the south wall. Amazingly, thankfully, they were so intent on pushing him out the back door they didn't seem to notice the cot or his sleeping sister. When they arrived outside, he realized why.

Standing just off the porch, the path he was being pushed into was lined with white hooded men holding bats. As he was shoved down the line, he felt the slam of bats against his shoulders, back, buttocks and legs. He stumbled and fell down but was pulled back up by rough hands—farmers' hands? Hands that jerked him up so he could receive another blow. It took only about thirty seconds to travel through the line of men, but it felt much longer. Each blow felt harder than the last, as though the men were trying to outdo each other. A final shove landed him on the soft, damp, welcoming moss of the stream bank. He heard one of the men giving orders.

"Pour some gas on the nigger's sofa," he said.

Abednego tried to yell to tell them about Marvelous, but the sound that emerged through the tight gag was that of a scared animal. He thought of Marvelous dying in a fire and kicked and struggled to free himself. He felt himself being lifted up off the ground.

"Like a wild boar, ain't he?" one of the men said of the writhing, kicking, fighting Abednego. He called out for the others to come help, and in the end, it took eight men to get Abednego to the car in the driveway. The last thing he felt was a sharp blow to his skull.

When he came to, he opened his eyes to darkness, breathed in the gas smell of the gag. He thought of Marvelous alone back at the cabin, perhaps now in flames. He felt like he was suffocating. He tried to focus on the bumping up and down happening underneath his body. When he kicked out his legs, his feet were stopped by something hard—the walls of a car trunk. They had thrown him into the trunk and were taking him somewhere. He felt the car shift gears, and his body rolled towards the rear. They were going up a hill, around some curves, he guessed, probably to the top of Taylor's Ridge where the locals dumped old washers, stoves and dryers. Unwanted things, things they wanted to get rid of. They would toss him out like so much trash, after they beat him to death, or if he was lucky, shot him instead.

The car slowed to a stop. The trunk lid lifted, letting in moonlight that filtered through trees. He felt himself being lifted out, felt himself being thrown to the ground. A boot slammed into his thighs. He glanced up and saw the outline of a tool of some sort. A hammer? They would nail him to a log. He kicked his legs and tried to get away but a dozen hands held on tight. Two of the hoods moved up close to his face. The last thing he saw before they blindfolded him was moonlight reflecting off eyeglasses worn under one of the hoods. He felt a sharp kick hit his back.

"We don't want no niggers down here in the valley," said one of the men in his deep, nasal voice.

"You move away from here and stay away if you don't want nothing to happen to your little nigger whore," said another. How did they know about Lola, he wondered. "She can disappear real easy. We don't want no niggers down here. That means you, boy. You don't go back down to the valley. And don't you tell no one what happened here tonight. You hear?" He tried to answer "yes" but his voice came out a muffled groan. A sharp blow landed on his shoulders—one of the bats.

"Clyde, he can't answer with the rag in his mouth," said another.

"Shut up you stupid cuss," said another voice. "Now we have to make sure he don't talk."

Then the arguing started.

"Get the nails and let's hammer him down real good to the log over yonder."

"Let's beat him to death first."

"Get the bats."

"Naw, let's cut him. Make it easy for them buzzards to pick over them leftovers."

Like he was some kind of leftover plate of ham at a covered dish supper. Abednego wasn't going to be anyone's supper. The voices grew louder but seemed to move away from him. A good time to make a move, he thought. He gently rocked his body from side to side.

"I think we should do what they done to that boy down in Alabama."

"That nigger shacked up with a white lady," said

another voice.

"He whistled at her."

"Would of raped her if they hadn't killed him first," said another.

"Let's find a stout tree. Bring a rope." He heard the scuffling of feet moving over the dead leaves. For the moment, he was forgotten as they searched for a sturdy tree in the woods.

He heard another sound, a straining engine, the shifting of gears. A car coming up the ridge road. Abednego rolled away from where the sound came and came to rest downhill from the voices. He dug his chin into the dirt and dampness of the ground, and trying to ignore great pain, used his knees to inch his injured body through the woods. The arguing men lowered their voices as the car came closer. It sounded like the car pulled over, and a door opened then slammed shut. He heard footsteps.

"Dumping's not allowed up here," said the voice.

"We ain't dumping nothing, Billy."

"What are y'all doing here this time of night?"

"Coon hunting."

"Boys, the GBI been snooping around after that house burnt up. I think it best you all went on back home tonight and let the coons be. Party's over." As he heard them talking, heard their footsteps thudding towards the sound of the man who seemed to be in charge, Abednego scooted his body further along using his chin and knees. He ignored the bits of soil and decaying leaves that pressed into his nose and mouth, the jolting pain in his knees. He rocked his body back and forth until he rolled away. His body began to spin on its own, headed down a slope, he realized. He let himself roll until his shoulder bumped up against something hard and cold. An old appliance. If he could get on the other side of it, away from their voices, he would be hidden from their sight. Once again, he drew up his knees, dug in his chin and scooted away from the voices. He hoped he was on the downward slope, hidden by the washer or dryer or stove. With his face in the damp musty leaves and earth, he lay as still as a possum and waited.

"Where'd that coon run off to?" someone said from far away.

"Go on, ya'll. I mean it." It was the man in charge. Abednego heard the sound of the car engines start up. After he heard the cars pull away, and let a half an hour so pass in silence, he reached up to touch the cold metal of an abandoned metal sink with sharp edges. He worked the rope back and forth against the sharp metal edge until he felt the rope give way. He loosened the rope that bound his hands. When his hands were finally free, he lifted the blindfold and looked all around to see the hulking shapes of old washers, dryers and a stove. Looking up through the tree branches, he saw the full moon partly covered in gray clouds. A tarnished moon.

He bent over to unbind his feet so he could make his way back down the mountain to the cabin. He had to get Marvelous, if she hadn't already burned to death. Thinking of his baby sister, he kicked his feet free, stood up on wobbly knees. His shoulders, back, thighs and buttocks smarted from the blows. One knee felt like it was broken. He tried to ignore the pain and limped down the dirt road that ran down the ridge, back towards Taylor's Crossing. The sky behind him was still dark. Soon dawn would rise up behind him bringing light.

Chapter 19

MARVELOUS

After Marvelous jumped off Iris' horse and tiptoed onto the back porch of her brother's cabin, she was surprised to see the back door flung open. Now she would be in big trouble. Perhaps Abednego had gone looking for her. As she moved towards the door, she thought she smelled something burning. She walked through the back room past her cot and moved into the front room where her brother slept.

In the scant light of moonlight, she could see smoke curling up from the sofa.

"Bing? Bing?" she yelled. No one answered.

The sofa was smoldering! She ran back out on the porch, grabbed a tin pail, turned on the spigot, and filled the bucket. She dumped water on the sofa until the smoke had nothing left to feed upon.

Although the couch was already tattered and ancient, it was now mostly ruined, all because of her. If she hadn't sneaked out to ride the horses, Bing wouldn't have come after her, and the couch wouldn't have burned. She grabbed a broom, swept the excess water towards the back door. She should never have gone riding with Iris. After she had finished sweeping the water out the door, she sat down on the porch and dangled her legs over the edge. It was hard to believe only a few hours earlier that she, Bing, and Iris sat in this same spot laughing and singing while Bing played on his fish net "guitar." She looked at the moon reflecting off the water and wondered just how mad Bing would be.

Chapter 20

ABEDNEGO

Walking the distance from the ridge top to the valley—less than two miles—would on a normal day have taken Abednego about twenty minutes, but with his knee swelling with every step, it took him a full hour to get home. As he approached the cabin, he was glad to see it was still in one piece and did not look damaged by fire. When he opened the front door, he saw the couch and yelled out.

"Marvelous?"

"Out here, Bing," she said. He found her on the porch looking frightened but otherwise unharmed.

"You okay, Marvelous?" he asked. He held out his arms, and she ran into them.

"I'm sorry, Bing. I'm sorry."

"The Klan hurt you?" asked Abednego.

"No," she answered, truthfully.

"Good," he said. "They coming back. We got to leave. Let's get all our things together." He let go of her and limped over to grab some paper bags from the closet.

"Where we going?" she asked.

"To Crystal Springs, then up to Chattanooga, to Mama's," he said. "I be taking you home, baby girl."

"How?" asked Marvelous. "We gonna walk?"

Abednego didn't know how to answer. Sitting down on the cot in the back room to collect his thoughts for a moment, he suddenly felt broken, overcome with tiredness. Chattanooga was too far away. He didn't know how they could get there. He touched his hot and swollen knee, and knew it would not be on foot. He did not want to ask Henry for help because Henry would be more concerned with the morning milking. He wouldn't understand why Abednego had to leave the valley at once. As a white man, Henry could not imagine how it felt to be gagged, beaten, and almost lynched. Abednego's only hope was to get to Crystal Springs where he knew he could find help among his people, three miles away. He would never make it with his knee hurting like it was. His head thrummed as waves of pain overcame him. He groaned. His sister stood by the cot looking at him with concern.

"Marvelous, my leg hurt. Now here's what you gonna have to do." As Marvelous listened to his plan, what he expected her to do, she shook her head.

"I can't do that, Bing. It's wrong."

"You want the Klan get us?" he asked. She shook her head no. "I know it seem wrong, Marvelous, but you gonna write a note and leave it. You not stealing nothing — you borrowing. Now go get a scrap of paper and pencil, and write what I tell you. Quick now. We ain't got much time till it's light."

Chapter 21

MARVELOUS

The paddock was dark. She felt like a thief as she crawled through the rail fence and walked over to the horses. They neighed softly when they saw her.

"Shush," she whispered. She walked up to Sassy, the big draft horse, offering a carrot. The mare arched her huge neck and pushed her nose down towards the carrot in Marvelous' hand. She eased on the bridle, led the horse to the gate, took her through, closing it softly as she left. She rolled up the note and tucked it into the latch where Iris would certainly see it. She pulled the rubber band from her ponytail to secure the note even tighter to the latch, so it wouldn't blow away. As she led Sassy towards the cabin, she hoped no one saw her or heard her. She felt badly betraying her friend, taking the big draft horse without asking first. She felt like a thief. She knew Iris would understand when she saw the note.

Chapter 22

IRIS

The Tuckers were eating breakfast around their big circular table when her father announced that Sassy was missing and that he thought Abednego had taken her. A neighbor up early gathering eggs from his hens had heard something and walked over to look through the fence row to see what it was. He saw what looked like a grown colored man with a little girl riding behind him on a huge horse. He said it looked like "your nigger boy but couldn't really see nothing on account it weren't yet dawn."

"He wouldn't have stolen the horse," said Henry. "He's not like that."

"Never trust a nigger is what I say," said Lawson, tearing a piece of bacon in half.

"He didn't steal her," said Iris.

"He didn't show up to work, and the horse is gone," said her father.

"He must have had a good reason to borrow her," said Iris. "Maybe Marvelous got sick in the middle of the night, and he went for help."

"Maybe they decided to take the horse for a joy ride, like some other folks do around here," said Lawson, turning to look at Iris.

"You'd know, wouldn't you?" replied Iris. "I heard you sneaking out the door this morning. What were you doing, anyway? Maybe you took the horse."

"Stop it, you two," said their mother. "Lawson, since you've got on your boots already, why don't you go with your father to look for Sassy?"

"I need someone to help milk the cows," said Henry.

"I'll go with Daddy," said Iris. She pushed away her half-eaten toast and ran to the back porch to put on her boots. "Daddy, you'll need someone to ride Sassy back when we find her." She made a face at Lawson and followed her father out the door and into the truck. They headed down the road leading to Crystal Springs, barely cruising along at five miles an hour, searching fields alongside the road.

Less than a mile down the road, Iris spotted Sassy's huge dark form first, standing near an intersection, tied to a fence post. Sassy arched her thick neck and turned to see the truck. When Iris jumped out and approached, the mare nickered softly.

"Good girl," said Iris. She untied the reins and petted the mare.

"Well, I'll be," said Iris' father. "They didn't take her too far from home, did they?"

"I told you, Daddy. Abednego wouldn't steal her. Boost me up."

"Bring her to the truck bed," said her father. "She's too high for a boost." Iris led the horse to the tailgate, which her father had opened. She scrambled up onto the mare's wide back.

"You go ahead and get her back to the barn," said her daddy. "I've got to ride into town to see the sheriff."

"Why, Daddy?" she asked.

"Can't have Abednego thinking he can do this again."

"Don't tell the sheriff. They'll put him in jail."

"No, honey," said Tucker. "The sheriff will just come down here and scare him some."

"Please, Daddy," Iris begged. Her father sighed.

"This is a grown up matter," he said. "And Abednego should have known better. You go on home now. You need to help Lawson and Henry with the milking since Abednego didn't show up. What in the Sam Hill was he thinking?"

Iris turned Sassy and headed back down the lane, kicked her into a trot. She wished she had a way to warn Abednego about the sheriff, but she didn't know where to find him. Her daddy said the cabin looked abandoned. She would talk to Marvelous later—she knew there would be an explanation. As she bounced up and down to the movements of the horse, she couldn't help wondering if her friendship with Marvelous hadn't somehow started the whole mess.

Chapter 23

LOLA

When Lola and Auntie came home from the funeral, the first thing Lola heard as she climbed out of the car was a low whirring noise that seemed to come from the woods. When she almost stepped on a cicada, she leaned down to take a look at its orange pop-out eyes.

"Why you care about that bug?" asked Auntie. "There be a thousand more where he come from."

"See that orange trim on the wings?" Lola asked. She squatted down to look. "It's a pretty thing, ain't it?" Auntie did not have a chance to answer before a neighbor lady, Pearl Hawkins, ran up to tell them what had happened.

The Klan had kidnapped Abednego, had tried and failed to burn his cabin, she said. After escaping, he and Marvelous had ridden over to Crystal Springs on a stolen horse. Everyone had seen the horse, but no one wanted to return it for fear of getting into trouble. Finally Samuel Mills had agreed to take the horse to the end of the road not far from the Tucker farm. Samuel had just gotten back, as a matter of fact.

"What about Abednego?" asked Lola. "And Marvelous? Was they hurt?"

"Abednego, he pay the Jones boy to run him up to Chattanooga," said Miss Pearl, who had a way of telling a story in her own roundabout fashion. "That car of his almost die up on the highway, it so raggedy. Can't get it started most mornings. Say it might be the battery."

"Was Abednego hurt?" asked Lola.

"What you think, sister? Say the Klan beat him up with bats and aimed to string him up. They say he leaving for up North. Not coming back here no more. And I don't blame him. Them white hoods like to have killed him."

"Where is the Jones boy now?" Lola asked.

"I don't know," said Pearl. "Maybe at his house." Lola rushed down the road to find him, which wasn't too hard. Approaching Jamie Jones' house, she saw his big feet sticking out from underneath his ancient Cadillac.

"Jamie?" she called. "Come out from under there and tell me about Abednego." He scooted out and stood up brushing his pants off.

"I drive him up to the hospital," he said. "He tore up real good."

"Can you take me in to see him?" asked Lola. Jamie looked down at his big feet before answering.

"My car broke," he said. "And he ain't there at the hospital anyway."

"Where is he?"

"At his Mama's, if he ain't left for up North," said Jamie. "Say to tell you don't try to come see him. It ain't safe, he say. He gonna mail you a letter when he get up North."

"He's not coming back?"

"No, Ma'am," said Jamie. "He can't do that. The Klan tell him not to come back down here. He taking them at their word. They say the sheriff be looking for him. Say he stole a horse. He a fool to come on back here." Lola just stood there looking at his ridiculous feet so unlike Abedegno's much smaller and efficient ones. "Miss Lola?

Don't tell nobody I told you. He don't want no one to know where he is. That way if someone be asking, you can say you don't know and mean it."

"Sure, Jamie. I won't. Thanks." She turned and headed back towards Auntie's, shuffling her feet on the road, kicking cicadas away. She felt hollow inside, like a tornado had just blown her heart away into the next county. She approached Auntie's porch and the empty chairs where she and Auntie and Abednego had spent so many evenings talking. She sat down in one, rocked, and cried. She tried to console herself by remembering the joy she felt when he asked her to marry him, his touch when he placed the daisy ring on her finger.

She rose from the rocker and went in her room, opened the dresser drawer. She lifted up her underwear to see the daisy ring. The petals were wilted, and it smelled funny. She picked it up and placed it gently in her palm.

"What's that?" asked Auntie. Lola turned around and faced her. She didn't try to hide the daisy ring.

"Something Abednego gave me," said Lola. Auntie walked over and inspected the ring, sniffed and frowned.

"That shriveled up junk? Throw it away," said Auntie. "Might make ants come inside." Lola cupped her hand protectively around the ring and pulled back her hand.

"I'm keeping it, till Abednego come for me," she said. Lola was tired of hiding her feelings about Abednego from her aunt, and now that he was gone, she felt compelled to share them.

"That boy ain't gone come back here, ever. And if he do, the Klan gonna be right behind him, that is if the sheriff don't arrest him first. Why you say he coming for you?"

Lola carefully placed the ring on top of her dresser,

behind a picture of her mother and the Bible. She turned back to face Auntie who had taken a stubborn stance. Her legs were slightly apart, her hands were on her hips, and her chin was tilted to the floor. Her dark eyes glowered up from her thick eyebrows. Maybe if Auntie knew how Abednego felt, she would help Lola figure out a way to get up North and be with him. Maybe if she knew they were engaged. With everything else in a turmoil, it was worth a shot.

"Abednego loves me, Auntie. He asked me to marry. That daisy ring was just till he get me a gold one." Aunt took two steps forward and slapped Lola hard on the cheek. Lola reeled back and grabbed her face with her hand. She tried to rub away the hurt and sting.

"You been lying to me, gal. You told me he was like your brother. Humph! You ain't gonna marry no farmer boy, and you sure ain't gonna marry no horse thief, neither."

"He not a horse thief," Lola yelled. Auntie moved in close to Lola, lowered her voice.

"Did you lay with him?" she said. She grabbed Lola by the shoulders and shook her. "You tell me gal!" Lola let her shoulders and head be shaken by her aunt and tried to think. If she answered yes, maybe Auntie would make her marry Abednego, maybe she would help her get up North.

"I'm sorry, Auntie." Auntie let go of her shoulders and once again slapped her hard in the face, and then shoved her down on the bed.

"You ruined, now," she wailed. She walked to the dresser, reached behind the framed picture of Lola's mother, and picked up the daisy ring. Holding it in her hand, she walked back over to the bed where Lola lay.

"No," screamed Lola. Squeezing her hand into a

tight fist, Auntie crushed the daisy ring and threw it to the floor. "You forget about that boy and that mess that happen. Don't nobody need to know you give yourself to him. And for what? This?" She stepped on top of the daisy ring with the squared toe of her orthopedic shoe.

"Tomorrow you gonna get up and go on back to the Buttrills. You gonna do your work and come straight back here every night. And you ain't gonna tell nobody that boy ever touch you. I'm so shame of you. You let me down, and your poor mama, not to mention our Lord and savior."

Auntie lifted her head to heaven, closed her eyes, and shook her head. She took a deep breath, turned, and walked out the door, slamming it behind her. Lola pulled herself out of the bed, went over to see what was left of her engagement ring. She stooped down to look. Her ring was now a flattened, ugly mush of green, yellow and white. She went over to the dresser, took the cardboard backing off the picture frame, and used it to gently lift what was left of her ring from the floor. She opened up her Bible to Daniel 3:23 and let the crushed ring slide in between the pages. There, it would be safe.

She reached under her bed and pulled out her largest handbag—a black patent leather purse handed down from Auntie—and one of the paper bags she had just unpacked. She placed the Bible into the purse, along with a rolled up nightgown, some underwear, and a pair of socks. She carefully folded up her favorite skirt and blouse, a slip, and an extra dress and placed them in the brown bag. She added her hairbrush, a lipstick, and her wallet. She reached in her bottom drawer and pulled out the sock where she hid her savings. She counted out fifty two dollars and some change. She needed more if she was going to follow Abednego north. She would wait to leave until she got paid on Friday. Without Abednego in the valley, she didn't belong here anymore. She only wanted to be where he was.

The next morning she rose with the dawn, washed up, and left quietly for her job before Auntie had even stirred. When she passed Abednego's cabin, she glanced at its lifelessness and shivered. At the Buttrills, as soon as she walked in through the side porch leading to the kitchen, she heard Mr. and Mrs. Buttrill talking about the Tucker's cabin almost catching fire the night the Klan visited Abednego.

"I'm thankful that nigra is out of here," said Mr. Buttrill. "The Tuckers should know better than to move one down here in the first place."

"We won't have any more trouble around here now," said Mrs. Buttrill. Lola let the screen door slam behind her to announce her presence. She wanted to say, "don't be calling my man trouble." Instead she yanked a clean apron off the peg, tied it on, and walked in after she heard Mr. Buttrill's footsteps retreat from the kitchen.

"Morning, Lola," said Mrs. Buttrill. "Did you get your friend buried?" Lola cleared off the breakfast dishes as she spoke.

"Yes Ma'am. Had ourselves a big crowd up to the funeral. Mr. Sam, he real tore up."

"I can imagine," said Mrs. Buttrill. "Did you hear about the trouble we had down here?"

"No, Ma'am," Lola lied. She wanted to hear Mrs. Buttrill's version of the story.

"The Klan, not from around here of course, paid a visit to that colored fella who lived down on the Tucker place. They say he stole a horse. The Klan straightened him out. I don't think he'll be stealing any more horses for a while." Mrs. Buttrill added a little laugh, then waddled across the kitchen.

"They say what?" asked Lola. "I hear it this way. First they took him up to the top of the ridge, beat him almost to death, and try to string him up. They tell him not to come back here no more. Then he borrow a horse to get his little sister away, so the Klan don't hurt her, too."

Mrs. Buttrill lifted a basket of okra off the pantry shelf and thrust it towards Lola. Lola quickly put the dirty plate she was holding down onto the counter. She took the basket of green pods.

"We'll have this and some pole beans for lunch. And Mr. Buttrill wants some fried chicken. Crispy." She walked over, picked up a blue ceramic pitcher and poured herself a glass of water. "And don't you worry yourself about the Klan. They don't come after law-abiding coloreds like yourself." She added that little laugh again. "Unless you plan on stealing some horses." Lola watched her walk out of the room, her wide, night-gowned hips almost filling the doorway. Almost as big as a horse's rear, almost as large as Sassy's. Lola wanted to throw the basket of okra at her but did not. She would wait until she got her pay. And once she had the money, on the way out, she would give Mrs. Buttrill a piece of her mind. A big piece. In four more days. She could hardly wait.

Walking along the road into Crystal Springs that evening, she felt a change in the air, a tension. Old folks on front porches along the way who usually waved when Lola passed by hushed up when they saw her. At dusk, she heard mothers calling in their children and warning them not to go out again. At Auntie's, it was even worse. Auntie refused to speak although they sat across the table from one another during supper. Auntie had the Bible open in front of her plate and read while she ate.

Afterwards, when Auntie retired to the front porch to visit a neighbor, Lola searched in the wooden bowl where Auntie put the mail and found nothing. She washed up the supper dishes, returned to her room, closed the door, and took the Bible off her dresser. She lay down in the bed, opened it up to Daniel. She looked at her daisy ring and saw it was somewhat drier and flatter. It did not look at all like a circle. Beneath the ring, she saw the verses that explained how Abednego, Shadrach, and Meshach had survived the furnace. She knew as she read it that Abednego would be alright, but would she?

At the Buttrills the next day, she struggled with the boys' high fevers and the baby's crying. Mrs. Buttrill begged her to stay late because Mr. Buttrill was out at another of his Citizens' Council meetings and had said he would not be home till after midnight. After what had happened to Abednego, Lola didn't want to work past sunset, but she was worried about little Coke, who seemed listless. Mrs. Buttrill thought some aspirin might help. She asked Lola to walk down to the store to buy a new bottle.

Dusk was falling as she headed to Elmwood's. She glanced up at Taylor's Ridge. Through the trees she could see a pair of headlights snaking down the side headed toward the valley. She wondered if it was the Klan again, driving back down after attacking another Negro on the ridge, or worse, stringing him up to some tree.

At Elmwood's, Lola walked past several white customers and went past the tobacco and snuff shelf to find the aspirin wedged in between laxatives and Alka-Seltzer. She also picked up a new can opener to replace one the boys had broken when they used it to dig a grave for a beetle they'd killed. She paid for her things, thanked the clerk and placed the items in her deep apron pocket. Since the house fire and the Klan attack, she made a point of only saying what was necessary, remembering what John had told her after the fire that killed Miss Lizzie. In times like this, it was best not to speak to whites you didn't know unless they spoke first. It would only bring trouble.

Against a sky darkened to a deep indigo, she walked back towards the Buttrill's at a fast clip. The cicadas' chorus reminded her of Abednego. Could he have returned to the cabin? She didn't really think so, but she wanted to check, just in case. It would only take a minute to go around back and see.

She ducked off the road by the hickory nut tree and continued towards the back porch. She smelled the scent of old smoke coming from the cabin. So it must have been true about the fire. Suddenly she felt someone grab her hair and push her to the ground.

She kicked and screamed as she felt herself being dragged along in the grass. She shoved her hand up to claw at her attacker with her fingernails. She felt the wooden stairs bump under her helpless legs as she was dragged onto the porch. She was no match for the long arms that encircled her chest. Her captor kicked open the door and pulled her inside of Abednego's empty cabin. Her feet thumped along the wooden floor as she kicked trying to get away.

"Gal, no one can hear you in here," said her captor. It was a man's voice, and it sounded familiar. A shot of fear bolted up her spine. She tried to yank away. He shoved her hard against the wood floor and threw a cloth over her eyes. "Open up them brown legs, gal." Instead she clamped her thighs together tightly. She felt his weight spread over her, felt her chest being mashed down by his weight. She felt a large hand wedge between her legs, heard the tearing of cloth. She cried out in pain.

"Shut up, you nigger whore," he snarled. She trembled all over as it happened and felt like vomiting when she smelled the overpowering stench of raw onions. Mr. Buttrill!

With his weight pressing down on her, she could not get away. She shut her eyes and tried to think of something else, anything else, except what was happening. She imagined she was outside again, walking to the store, looking up at the ridge. A pair of headlights wound down the ridge road, snaking their way into the valley. Valley of the shadow of death. Fear no evil. Deliver us from evil. Deliver me from evil. Deliver me. Deliver me. She clung to the words; her body rocked like a boat battered in a stormy sea. Her attacker grunted. All at once, he collapsed on her. She was certain she would suffocate.

She coughed hard and pushed up against him. She felt him lift off her. He reached out and squeezed her throat with his hand.

"Leave that towel on your face," he ordered. "Don't you try and look." He shoved her back to the floor. "Stay here, and don't you move. When you hear me close the door you can get up off the floor." She heard a zipping noise. "Don't you tell anyone what we did. No one would believe you anyway," he said. A hard slap stung her cheek.

Lola did as she was told and lay still until she heard the door shut. She opened her eyes and saw only darkness. She shook as she realized what had just happened. Her teeth chattered uncontrollably. She thought she might be going crazy. She forced herself to stare at the walls, covered in old newspapers. To keep out the wind, Abednego had said. What would he think of her now, lying on the ground, torn apart, broken? In less than five minutes,

Mr. Buttrill had soiled her body and her spirit. She sobbed and shivered for some time, unable to move. She wanted to go curl up on Abednego's cot and lie there until she fell asleep, or died. She could not even pull herself up off the floor. She felt the cool boards against her cheek and thought about how Abednego's bare feet had touched this same spot. The thought brought her some small comfort. Feeling an irritating wetness, she reached in her pocket to look for a tissue or a handkerchief. Instead her fingers felt the hard glass of the aspirin bottle. She remembered the feverish boy waiting up at the Buttrill's for her to return. She did not know if she could. She did not want to ever see Mr. Buttrill again.

The thought of his juice being in her made her mad. She rose up, used her ripped panties to dab off the blood and sticky mess. His seed. She wiped until it hurt. She straightened out her dress, moved her hands to rearrange her hair, then walked out the back door and stood under the big beech tree. She reached out and touched the initials Abednego had carved, traced her finger along the heart. She found a broken branch on the ground and begin digging a hole a few feet away from the big beech. She scraped away furiously, dug hard into the soil, ripping the earth open. She buried her panties, hoping she could bury the memory of what had happened.

She thought about throwing away the aspirin, too, but she remembered the Bible verse about the sins of the father. The boys should not have to suffer because of their father's brutal attack. She would walk up the driveway, check the garage first to see if his car was there. If it was, she would not go inside.

When she arrived at the house, she hid under the magnolia tree and looked towards the garage. The door was open, revealing an empty space. No sign of Mr. Buttrill. She straightened her skirt, brushed her hair away from her face, and walked inside.

"What took you so long?" asked Mrs. Buttrill.

"My head hurt so bad, Miss Buttrill. I had to stop along the road and sit down in the grass a minute. I was dizzy," said Lola.

"Your hair looks like you been rolling around in the field," she said. "You may be coming down with what the boys have. If you feel sick tomorrow, don't you come in. Send your aunt, or another girl, in your place. I can't take care of these sick babies without help."

"Yes, Ma'am." Lola nodded, took off her apron. "I may go to the doctor and get some medicine. Can you give me my pay now? He won't see me without no money." Mrs. Buttrill sighed.

"I'll have to see if I have any money in my purse," she said. As she turned to walk out of the room, Lola heard her muttering to herself. "More trouble than they're worth." Not to you, anymore, Lola thought. After Adelaide had handed her pay, Lola took off her apron and hung it on the peg.

"Good evening," Lola said. She walked out the squeaky back door for the last time.

Chapter 24

ADELAIDE

In the nursery, Adelaide had fallen asleep in the chair while rocking Emily. She startled when she heard a noise at the back door. Glancing at her watch, she saw it was after midnight. Not wanting to wake the baby, she placed her in the crib and eased out, closing the door behind her. Sewell was coming up the stairs, unbuttoning his shirt as he approached their bedroom. In the hallway they met. Adelaide put her index finger to her lips to indicate he should be quiet. They walked in silence to their bedroom and closed the door.

"The baby is finally asleep," she said. She turned on the bedside lamp and saw his face. A thin red line ran down his left cheek, a scrape of some sort. She moved closer to see.

"That's a nasty scratch," she said. "Can I get some Mercurochrome on it?" She reached out to touch his cheek. He pushed her hand away.

"Got tangled up with Clyde Greery's rose bush before the meeting," he said.

"Mrs. Greery has roses? She told me she had bad luck with them. Didn't she plant hydrangeas?"

"Would you quit prattling on? Rose, hydrangea, or just plain old briar. In the dark, they're all the same," Sewell snapped. "Now get me that Mercurochrome. I don't need an infection."

Adelaide waddled to the bathroom, switched on the light, and found the bottle in the medicine cabinet. Back at Sewell's side with cotton ball in hand, she reached up to dab his face. He grabbed the orange saturated cotton from her.

"I can do it myself. Why don't you go on back to bed," he said. She backed away and climbed into their bed without saying a word. At times like these, after his council meetings, he sometimes came home in a bad mood. She wondered why he went in the first place if it riled him up so. What happened at the meetings? And she could swear there were no roses, or thorny plants of any kind, outside the Greery's place. She would look next time she drove into town. She felt the mattress quiver as her husband climbed into the bed beside her.

"Adelaide?" he whispered.

"Yes?"

"I think we ought to get rid of that nigger gal and get ourselves a white woman."

Adelaide rolled over and propped up on her elbow.

"She's been a big help with the boys, Sewell," Adelaide replied, treading lightly so as not to sound disagreeable. Sewell sighed.

"It don't look right to head up the Citizens' Council and have a nigger employed in our home, not after all that mess with that boy stealing the Tucker's horse. We've had enough trouble down here, don't you think?"

"I don't want any trouble," said Adelaide, rolling over on her back and patting her huge belly. "I just need somebody to help right now, honey. I've got our baby to worry about here." Sewell reached out and stroked her belly.

"I'll talk to Williams tomorrow," he said. "He has

three high school daughters who might want some summer work."

"Crandell and Coke liked playing with Lola," she said. Sewell quickly removed his hand from her belly and grasped her forearm with his hand.

"I said get rid of her. No more niggers. They're nothing but trouble."

"Alright, Sewell," she answered and patted his hand with her free hand, hoping he would loosen his grip. It was beginning to hurt.

He let go of her arm and ran his hand back up over her stomach. His fingers trailed lightly over her swollen breasts.

"Good. You too tired to have a little party?" he asked. She was exhausted, but she knew what was expected. She rolled over on her side and lay still as she felt his body spoon up against her.

The next morning, after Sewell had left for work, Adelaide opened her eyes to a bright sun. It was late. The baby was miraculously asleep, and the boys must have been getting along because she didn't hear a peep from their room. She hadn't heard anyone come in, so she figured Lola hadn't been able to find anyone to help her. She'd have to do it all herself until Sewell got someone else.

She rose from the bed and went to the chair where Sewell had left his clothes from last night. She would have to take them down stairs when she went to make some breakfast. Lifting up his cotton shirt, she caught a whiff of something she recognized, not Sewell's usual masculine smell of sweat mixed with aftershave. She pulled his shirt close to her nose and sniffed the faint smell of cherries and almonds. A familiar scent. Although her sense of smell was stronger when she was pregnant, her brain felt in a fog. She could not quite place where she had smelled it before.

"Mama," we need a flashlight for our fort," Crandell said as he ran into the room. He tugged at the hem of her nightgown.

"First let's go down and get some breakfast," she answered. She grabbed the clothes in a bundle and went to tend to her son.

After making toast and hard boiled eggs for the children, she began loading the clothes in the washer while the children played in a fort they built. She really missed Lola's help.

Staring at a thin brown line on the sleeve of Sewell's dress shirt, she remembered what he had said about the encounter with the rose thorns—or not. Prudence Greery had won the Garden Club award for her hydrangeas; she had seen it in the newspaper last week. Pink and blue. She pulled the shirt to her nose and smelled again. The scent was fainter but still there. Suddenly she knew what it was.

She let the clothes fall into the washer. She walked to the spot where Lola hung her apron and yanked it off the peg. She pulled the apron close to her nostrils and inhaled. It was the same cherry-almond smell, Jergens Lotion, Lola had said when Adelaide asked her. She liked to keep her hands soft.

Adelaide turned and walked back to the washer, pulled out Sewell's baggy undershorts. She hated herself for even thinking something so ridiculous, but she needed to know. Before she could even get them close to her nose, she smelled it, the musky scent of a woman—not herself. She had not been with Sewell until after he came home. She thought about his sudden wish to get rid of Lola, remembered the way Lola had looked last night when she came in from the store, her tangled hair, her rumpled clothes, the wild look in her eyes. She claimed she had sat down in the grass. Or was she pushed? She thought about Lola's cherry-almond smell that she had always found comforting. Until now.

Dizziness overcame her. She felt herself off balance. She grabbed the edges of the washing machine and hung on, staring at her husband's soiled clothes down in the drum. Bile came up her throat. She leaned over the washer and threw up all over Sewell's clothes.

Chapter 25

LOLA

Returning back to Rome to her Mama was easy. Auntie was glad to see her go, and after the attack by Mr. Buttrill, Lola was too scared to stay. Her mind felt too jumbled up, her body bruised, to pursue Abednego up North. Going home was the safe choice.

When Auntie asked John and Rose to drive Lola down to Rome, they were glad to do so. They left the next afternoon, driving through the countryside the hour or so south to Rome, a town with seven hills and textile mills. Seeing all the cars on the road as they approached the town, John asked her if she would miss living in the quiet of the country.

"Yes, I'm gonna miss the country," she answered. "But I'm glad to be away from Taylor's Crossing. I don't aim to be the next one the Klan get a hold of." She did not tell them what had happened, how Mr. Buttrill had raped her. She was too ashamed. Instead, she spoke of Abednego.

"Did you hear anymore from him?" she asked. From her place in the back seat, Lola saw John glance at Rose briefly before speaking.

"No," said John. "Sure don't. Probably up at his mama's laying low with that knee. They say it was broke."

"When he get better, he going to let you hear. Probably all shook up still," said Rose.

"I reckon," said Lola, but she wondered. It had been

almost a week and not a word. During the rest of the ride to Rome, looking out at the pine trees that covered the mountains and hills and lined the road, she tried to imagine what he was doing, wondered if he was thinking of her.

Her mother lived in North Rome on a hill above the Five Points area. The house was aging clapboard with peeling paint. Since the road was too steep for the car's fickle transmission, Lola asked John and Rose to drop her off at the bottom. She thanked them, said goodbye, and promised she would try to write.

Carrying her two brown bags of belongings, she ascended the narrow dirt road to the house. She opened the door and found her mother ironing.

"Lord, child," said her mother. "Do that family let you go?"

"No, Ma'am," she answered, and set her bags on the floor. She walked over to hug her mother and felt her boney back as she wrapped her arms around her. "The white hoods done take over up there. They like to have killed the boy who worked at the next farm over. We was the only two coloreds in the valley. I figure I be next, so I left." Mama pulled away from her and moved over to a pile of laundry stacked up on the sofa.

"Well, I guess you had no choice. Been taking in laundry. You can help me till you find some work."

"Yes 'em," she said "I aim to return to Main High in September and finish up."

"Good," said Mama. She smiled. "Dr. Doushaun asked after you when I went in the other day for my water pills." Lola nodded, trying to act as though she still cared for the starched-shirt doctor. The idea of romance with him no longer appealed.

"He have any work?" she asked.

"Don't think work was what he have in mind. He say she a fine looking gal when he speak of you."

"Yes 'em," she said. "Let me put my things away, and I'll help you."

Adjusting to Rome was hard after the quiet of the valley. Cars seemed to be everywhere, and noise. The sounds of horns and sirens seemed to rise up to the hill where Lola now lived. The sounds of a new decade coming, she thought. The 60's. Would her life be here, surrounded by cars, mills and people, or would she and Abednego find another place in the country, perhaps a Negro community up North? Or would they go to a city?

Her mother nagged her to get out of the house some, to look for work. Lola didn't feel like going anywhere, especially places where she might run into white men. She wanted to be at home to check the mail. Every day Lola would walk to the mailboxes at the bottom of the hill to look for a letter from Abednego, but there was none. While they were working on a pile of laundry one day, her mother remarked on the change she saw in Lola.

"When you leave here, you be talking more, cheerful like," she said. "Now you so quiet."

"Yes 'em," said Lola. She pulled white undershirts out of a basket and folded them as she talked.

"You seem all growed up or something," said her mother. Lola nodded. As usual, she was lost in her thoughts, which raced from her stolen moments of joy with Abednego to the brutal attack by her boss. Her mind followed its own road map and travelled all over the place. And she could not cut up onions, refused to. They reminded her of Mr. Buttrill, of the attack.

Late one morning when her mother was dicing up onions for a soup, Lola got a whiff and was overcome with nausea. She ran outside and threw up in the yard. Her mama came running after with a cold wash cloth. She handed it over. Lola wiped her face and mouth clean while her mother gave her a hard stare. Over the next few weeks, Lola's nausea continued off and on, even when there were no onions. She begin to feel a tingling in her breasts and realized she had not had her monthly. In late September, after her breasts begin to swell and her blouse tightened around her bosom, Mama sat her down at the kitchen table for a talk.

"You think you be carrying a baby?" she asked. Lola studied the beveled edge of the kitchen table. She did not know how to answer.

"I don't think so," she said. Her mama jumped up and grabbed her arm.

"You lay with that farmer boy up there in the country?"

"Once, it was an accident." Her mother got up, walked over to the counter, and leaned against it. Lola heard her sigh. She came back and pointed her finger at Lola.

"Who do this?" she asked. Lola thought of Sewell Buttrill splitting her open and felt she might throw up again. She swallowed back the bile. She could not tell her mother what had really happened, how the white man had pumped her full of his sticky mess. Not only was she humiliated, but she did not want to dignify the rape by telling anyone about it. By not saying it aloud, it might be like it never happened. Now she was carrying a baby, she had to pretend it was Abednego's.

"We was going to marry, but the Klan run him off," she said.

"Where is he now?" asked her mother. Lola shook

her head.

"Uh, huh, that's what I thought. Just like your own sorry Daddy. He a sharecropper?"

"No, Ma'am. Abednego a dairyman. Saving for a farm. The Klan come and beat him up, try to hang him." Her mama grabbed Lola by her arm again.

"If any fool ask you, say your man was killed."

"He missing, not dead," said Lola. Mama's fingers dug hard into Lola's arm.

"He dead, you hear me?" she said. "Folks ain't gonna be asking too much about the father if he be dead. When your belly be sticking out, you gonna stay inside this house. When it time to have that baby, we'll get you a ride over to Cartersville and find you a doctor. Dr. Doushaun don't need to know your business." All Lola could do was nod.

Through the long and difficult days of her confinement, Lola both loved and hated what was growing inside her. Would the baby come out white, revealing her shameful secret? She soon quit going to the mailbox. She went no farther than her mother's back porch where the lone pine tree and its long branches brushed up against the porch rail in the wind. When she saw the dark green needles, the narrow red-brown pine cones, smelled the fresh scent, she thought of Taylor's Ridge Valley and Abednego.

There on the porch, under the shade of the loblolly pine, she began sketching. Using a pencil and drawing on old envelopes or paper scraps, she drew the pine tree and later added drawings of birds and squirrels that she fed stale pieces of bread. She looked out on the horizon and drew what she saw—the forest beyond. Another time, she drew her mother and the neighbor's cat. One afternoon when she returned from Five Points, Lola's mother handed over a bag containing a watercolor set and some paper. Looking inside the bag, she smiled and hugged her mother.

"Do we have the money for this?" she asked.

"You earn it helping me with the laundry," she said. "Worth every penny to see you smiling again."

From then on, when Lola wasn't helping with the laundry or cooking, she painted non-stop. She found solace in her art, put the bad memories aside while her child finished making himself inside her belly. When she painted, she forced herself to concentrate on the colors, the way the paint bled out when she used too much water. After a nighttime rain, she focused on figuring out how to illustrate a silver ribbon of water that meandered between the pines. Lost in brushstrokes, her mind was free from missing Abednego or worrying about the future.

In early October, the hills turned yellow, red and brown as the leaves of yellow poplar, hickories, dogwoods, maples, and sassafras acknowledged the shorter days. Her mother's brother, Uncle Hershel, a successful insurance salesman, came to visit. He presented her with a small oil painting he had bought from a Negro painter along the highway in Florida. It was a colorful beach scene painted on a canvas of Upson Board, an inexpensive construction material. A lone cocoa-colored palm tree stood by white roiling surf with a scrim of blue and green sea on the horizon. Lola loved the way the sand was a lighter shade of the palm tree, how the cocoa was blended with pink to make the storm clouds in the sky, and the way the green branches blew in the wind she could almost feel. She tried to copy the picture using her watercolors but could not capture the vivid colors. At night she dreamed of warm beaches and tropical breezes. Her uncle would soon head south for his insurance work. Lola was determined to go with him.

"Uncle Hershel, I like to get out of this cold, ride with you down to Florida," she said over dinner one Sunday. She wrapped a sweater tight against her shoulders as she spoke.

"How warm do it get down in Ft. Pierce?" asked her mama, referring to where their childhood friend, Miss Belle, ran a diner.

"Never this cold," he said. "Don't ever need much more than a sweater."

"Mama, ain't it time I be seeing a doctor?" asked Lola. Mama finished chewing a mouthful of collards, then spoke.

"Hershel, do they have good doctors down in Ft. Pierce?" asked Lola's mama. It was then that Lola knew she would get to go to Florida. Mama did not want to risk Dr. Doushaun finding out she was pregnant.

"I reckon they do. And Belle would probably put Lola up."

They left Rome the week before Halloween. When Lola saw her mother crying at the doorstep, she said she would come back home by Christmas. She hoped she wouldn't. She could already see all the vivid colors that seemed to be Florida.

With her uncle at the wheel of his '55 Ford T-Bird, they drove south. Lola peered out the window at the changing landscape. The pine forests of the mountains gave way to the Piedmont Plain where Atlanta lay. The highway turned into four lanes of traffic, and she had never seen so many cars or so many people at once.

"Looky there," said Uncle Hershel pointing at a gold-domed building in the distance. "A real gold-leaf dome."

"Who owns it?" asked Lola.

"You do, I do, the people of Georgia," he said. Lola looked at the lady standing on top holding a torch. "Some folks down in Dahlonega, where they had the first gold rush a long time ago, donated the gold."

"Who that woman up top?" she asked, referring to the lady dressed in robes with her arm raised up in the air.

"Supposed to represent Freedom," he said. "She's holding a torch and a sword. Can you see it?" Lola couldn't make out the sword. If she would have had one when Sewell Buttrill raped her, she would have stabbed him straight through the heart. Then she wouldn't have been pregnant now. She would still be up in Taylor's Crossing or heading north to be with Abednego. She still had not heard from him. She wondered why, and felt sad and hurt as she thought of him. She knew in her heart she would not hear from him. She forced herself to think of the passing landscape instead.

Past Atlanta, the land became flatter, the roads seemed straighter. With the sun streaming through the car window, she was lulled into a sleep. A few hours later, she felt the car slowing down as they pulled into the Negro state park at Cordele. After they visited the restrooms, Uncle Hershel pulled out the picnic basket that Lola's mother had packed for them. Sitting on a cloth they spread out by the lake, the pair enjoyed ham sandwiches and crisp apples.

"How long till we get to the ocean?" asked Lola.

"Couple of more hours to Valdosta," said Hershel.

"Florida?" asked Lola.

"Last city in Georgia before we cross the line," he said. "Dr. King was in a speech contest once down in

Valdosta."

"Silver rights talk?" asked Lola.

"Civil rights is how you say it, Lola, and I'm not sure what the speech was about." Hershel knew all kind of facts like this and also talked different. Lola wished she talked like that. She was going to try.

As Lola cleaned up after the picnic, Hershel told her if she was going to sleep, she might as well crawl into the back seat. He grabbed her pillow from the trunk and handed it to her. She settled in the back seat for another long nap, thinking of Abednego as she drifted off.

Chapter 26

ABEDNEGO

Abednego holed up at his mother's house up in Chattanooga for over a month fighting a deep depression. Even though he was only nineteen, he felt as broken down as an old man. His knee was smashed, and he wore a cast that covered his knee and kept his leg straight. His body was covered in painful bruises, and his neck was stiff from the beating. His savings, hidden inside one of the couch pillows, was ruined in the fire set by the Klan. He had not heard from Lola, although he had sent several letters to her down in Rome at the address John and Rose had given him. She had not responded. He wanted John and Rose to take him there, but since his entire leg was in the cast, he could not even fit inside the car unless someone lifted him into the back seat. He would have to wait. He had explained all this to Lola in the letters, and he knew she would understand.

Although Marvelous tried to cheer him up with her stories about her school day every afternoon when she came home, he saw few other people. He spent his days and nights in an upholstered green-old fabric covered chair with his feet propped up on the matching foot stool, sinking into the black hole of self-pity. So when his cousin Willy stopped by one Sunday morning while his mother and Marvelous were at church, it was easy to take his first drink of whiskey. On the way over, Willy had stopped off on

Ninth Street and picked up a bottle of Old Crow. Willy, who had been injured in the Korean War, said it would help some with the pain. Abednego took a small sip. The liquid slipped easily down his throat and gave him a warm glow that obliterated his dark mood. After Willie left, he penned a long letter to Lola declaring his love and his plans for them to move farther north. When he read it the next day, it sounded ridiculous. He didn't even know when he would be able to walk again without a cane. He tore up the letter and pulled out the Old Crow, which Willy had left behind.

"What that stink?" asked his mother when she returned from a trip to the grocer. Abednego opened his eyes to see his mother's face inches from his, inhaling his alcohol breath.

"Nothing, Mama, let me sleep," he answered. She reached in between the chair cushion and the side of the chair, pulled out the whiskey bottle.

"Nothing? I'm gonna throw this trash away." She marched off to pour the whiskey down the sink, then came back to where he sat. "You been setting in this chair too long," she said. "If you gonna drink, you go and find yourself some place else to do it."

Within a few days, and preferring whiskey to his mama's nagging, he moved in with Willie at his apartment near Ninth Street, "The Big Nine." While Willie worked at the Martin Hotel as a server, Abednego stayed in, let his body heal. His spirits were a different matter.

Every morning he woke up with a hangover and a feeling of worthlessness. After Willie left for work, he pulled out the whiskey bottle and drank his way through the hours, listening to the noise of "The Big Nine" as the crowds strolled along partying and visiting clubs. The sound of their voices, their laughter, and the whiskey, made him feel better—until the following morning. The pattern repeated every day and night for another week until Willie noticed all his whiskey disappearing down his cousin's throat.

"You gonna have to come up with some money, cousin. I can't be carrying you forever." Fueled by the liquor, Abednego responded.

"I'm heading North," he said.

"North?" asked Willie. "You ain't in no shape to be travelling."

"I can't be staying here no more," said Abednego. "Only a fool stay around in a place where any old white man's word can get you beat up."

"No one going to bother you here, cousin. They be looking for a busboy over the hotel. Why don't you come talk to the boss?"

From his spot on the chair, Abednego reached down and touched his cast, tugged aimlessly at the cotton gauze that protruded from the edges.

"The South making me crazy. I need to get away before the Klan find out where I am." He slapped his cast with his hand. "Help me get this thing off."

"Don't the doctor have to do it?" asked Willie.

"I can't be paying no doctor. Don't have no money," said Abednego. "You know they got a saw over at the hotel. You go borrow it."

"I don't know about that," said Willie. But the next afternoon, a Saturday, Willie showed up with a saw in hand. Abednego sat in one chair and propped his leg up on another. He watched as Willie lifted the saw over the plaster.

"You be careful now," said Abednego. Willie responded by taking a sip of whiskey.

"Don't you worry none," he said. "I boned out hogs before. This ain't nothing." He handed the flask to Abednego. Abednego took a sip and grimaced as Willie stroked the blade back and forth over the cast with a studied gentleness. Powdery flakes rose from the cut. Willie said, "You holler if you feel anything." Abednego raised his brows when he heard it.

A few minutes later the sawing was complete, Willie finished pulling the cast apart with his hands.

"Whew! You sure there ain't no skunk in there?" said Willie. "First thing is you need to get a shower." Abednego hopped to a standing position, mostly on one leg. Willie watched while he tried to put pressure on his weak and stiff leg. The cane helped some but not much. He showered, got dressed in some clean pants, and packed up his clothes. The next morning he had Willie drive him to his mother's place.

"Wait here," he said. "I'll be right back." Using his own key, he let himself in, and called out "hello" although he knew his mother and sister would be at church.

Entering his mother's bedroom, he took $70 from the sock drawer where she hid her savings. He knew it wasn't right, and he felt bad about it. He reasoned that as soon as he got his first paycheck, he would send the money back. He checked the pile of mail on the front table and saw nothing from Lola. It confirmed what he suspected. She had gone back home to Rome and perhaps even gone to work for that doctor she talked about. With no money and no job, Lola would not want Abednego. She had made that clear by not responding to his letters. He would have to get some money, make something of himself, and then try to get her back.

He returned to the car and asked if Willie would

take him to the bus station.

"Where you planning on going?" asked Willie.

"North," said Abednego. He climbed out of the car and limped into the bus station carrying his only possessions, Willie's battered up army duffle bag filled with a few clothes and a flask of whiskey. He sat down on a bench in the colored area, and waited for the first bus headed north.

Chapter 27

LOLA

From time to time, Lola's eyes fluttered open to peek at the passing scenery when Uncle Hershel said the name of a town. Mountains gave way to flatter terrain, down through Macon and Valdosta. Finally, a "Florida" sign appeared ahead. She perked up with the sight of gallberry bushes, palmetto, and loblolly pines. As the new landscape unfolded, her senses heightened. She thought she smelled water. She sat up in her seat and looked to her left and saw a vast expanse of blue. She cried out.

"The ocean!"

"What do you think?" asked her uncle.

"It's huge," she said. Hershel laughed.

"Yep, you want to see it up close?"

"I want to put my feet in," said Lola.

A few minutes later, he pulled to the side of the road and parked. He led her down a meandering path of sea grapes. She made him hold her hand as she timidly put her bare feet into the cold water. After a few minutes, she felt braver and waded in up to ankles. She kicked at the water with her feet, splashing out toward the ocean. Waves rolled in and splashed back at her. From the pictures she had seen, she had not thought of the ocean being so alive, so full of movement. She liked the tug of the tide against her swollen ankles, the cool embrace of the sand against her feet. She picked up shells that the surf had washed on the shore. She never wanted to leave this spot. Seeing a car of whites pull over, Uncle Hershel grabbed her hand and pulled her away from the beach, back to the car.

"This beach don't allow Negroes," he said. "I don't aim to cause any trouble." As their car pulled away from the ocean, she wondered how the view of something so magnificent could be controlled by other people. Surely this had not been in God's plan when he created the oceans; surely he had meant for everyone to share the beach.

Soon her heart was lightened by the sight of marinas where jaunty flags fluttered in the breeze and sails rumpled in the wind. The flags lifted her spirits, and she felt hopeful. The vegetation became denser—forests made up of bent pines, tall palms and short bushy palms with tangled, dense underbrush underneath. Occasional gravel and sandy side roads ran off the main highway into the forest. An old black man walked along carrying a ragged pack on his back and wearing a faded cap. On the east side of the road, fishing piers jutted out in the water. Abednego would have loved them. She smiled as she remembered the time he had tried to teach her to bait the hook with a worm, and she had talked him into letting her use a bit of Vienna sausage instead. She would never fish with him again. She did not try to hold back the sadness that washed over her, left her feeling as helpless as a shell she had seen tumbling in the surf. She leaned her head against the window, pulled a blanket up around her head, and pretended to sleep so her uncle wouldn't see her crying.

As she felt the tears sting her cheeks, she saw through blurry eyes a sign announcing a new town. Sebastian. She sounded the name out in her head.

"Uncle, where do you think that name come from?" she asked.

"Don't know, child. Been called Sebastian as long as long as I can remember."

"Suh-bas-tee-un," she said, drawing out the syllables, "Sounds distinguished."

"Well the way you saying it child, it does," said Uncle Hershel. They both laughed.

"I like it," she said.

"Don't like it too much because we aren't where we're going just yet," said Uncle. She settled back against the window and repeated the name to herself. And then she knew. If the baby was a boy, she would name him Sebastian, give him a dignified name, one that would make folks respect him. It didn't matter who his father was—if the baby had a high-class name, folks would look up to him. She prayed it would be a Sebastian.

Chapter 28

ABEDNEGO

After a long and tiring bus ride, he arrived in Pittsburgh at the bus station, sober and scared. He had less than $45 in his pocket and nowhere to stay. His knee ached from the ride. He knew he needed to lose the cane before he could find work, unless he took work no one else wanted. He visited the bathroom, a place dominated by the strong odor of stale urine, then limped over to the ticket counter. He spoke to the uniformed attendant.

"Excuse me, Sir," said Abednego. The man looked up from some paperwork.

"Where you headed?" he asked.

"Just got here," Abednego answered. "Wondering if you let me clean up that bathroom for you?" Maybe he could make a little money, do some cleaning until his knee got better, and then he could apply at the steel mills.

"The janitor comes in later." He looked away, and glanced down at his paperwork.

"I'll do it for free," said Abednego.

"Look, I don't want any trouble," said the man.

"No trouble," said Abednego. He limped away and headed for the restroom. Then he heard the ticket man's voice.

"Help yourself," he said. Abednego wet some paper towels, and using soap from the dispensers, wiped down every smelly toilet seat and the floors around the toilet bottoms. He cleaned the sinks and wiped down the door handles. With his knee still hurting, he could not get down on the floor. He was puzzling about what to use for a mop when the ticket man walked in.

"It's my break. Was going to show you the cleaning closet but looks like you already finished."

"I need a mop," said Abednego. The man motioned for him to follow. In the closet he found a bucket, a mop, and some pine-scented cleanser. He got to work and in half an hour had mopped the floors until they were glistening and fresh-smelling. He returned to the ticket counter to see if the ticket man might pay him.

"I'd really like to help you out," he said. "The restroom hasn't been so clean in months. The problem is I'm not the one in charge here." He handed Abednego fifty cents. "You might want to try down at the produce yards. They're always looking for men at the loading docks."

By the time he made his way across town to the produce yard, it was almost midnight. You wouldn't know it at the produce yard. A train had just pulled in. Workers rushed to unload pallets of boxes and crates filled with produce. Their destination was the largest building he had ever seen, a warehouse that ran the length of twenty football fields with a loading dock that ran the entire length. Hundreds of empty trucks were parked at loading docks. He stood gaping at the scene. He had never seen so many people in one place and so much activity.

"You new around here?"

Abednego turned to see a giant of a man with rock hard biceps.

"Yes, Sir. I heard they might be work down here."

"No loading till five. The buyers leave, go get breakfast and come back in when it's loading time. Come back then." Abednego thanked him and turned to look for a spot to rest. His knee ached.

He had hoed hundreds of rows, picked thousands of tomatoes. He had shoveled out tons of manure from the stable and shoveled it back into the garden to nourish the growing plants. At the end of a long day of work, he had always had a place to sleep. Looking around the produce yard, weary from thoughts of his future, he spotted two men leaving their empty truck and heard them talking about going to get breakfast.

Careful not to aggravate his bad leg, he lifted his body into a truck half full of potatoes. The earthy smell was overpowering yet familiar. An overwhelming stench reminded him of decaying fish and made him queasy. A rotten potato.

Banking his duffle bag against the back truck's back wall, he lay his head down and tried to rest. A light rain pattered against the truck's roof. As he fell asleep, he soothed himself with a memory of digging potatoes out of the warm, red ground down at the farm.

A few hours later, he awakened to the sound of voices. It was still dark, but the produce yard was coming alive. Although he was exhausted, he knew he had to get out of the truck before its owners returned. He sat up, gathered his things, and slipped out onto the loading dock, landing on his good leg. All around him he saw men with clipboards. Buyers and sellers buzzed around inside the big warehouse near the large stacks of produce. Crates of cantaloupes, bags of potatoes, sacks of onions, and flats of cherries were on pallets. As he walked towards the warehouse, a burly, dark man wearing overalls and carrying a crate of cantaloupe spoke to him.

"Wanna make a buck?" he asked. "Help me load

my truck, and I'll give you a dollar."

"Yes Sir," Abednego answered. Abednego moved as quickly as he could, and trying to hide his limp, followed the man back to the loading dock and pallets of melons.

"First we'll get the cantaloupes and melons, put them towards the front, then some onions and tomatoes." Abednego worked hard for the next hour and a half, finishing up one loading job and moving on to the next. By the end of the morning, he had a sore knee and five dollars, enough to pay for a room at a boarding house in the Hill Town area where some of the other laborers lived.

Over the next few months, between temporary jobs, he worked on his growing love affair with the bottle. At first he drank to kill his fear of the unknown, of where he would find his next dollar. He drank to put Lola and home out of his mind. And when he was lucky enough to find work, he drank to kill the pain of his leg which worsened from all the physical labor.

From some of the other men he met at the boarding house, he learned that U.S. Steel was looking for Negro laborers to work in the open hearth department. As long as he could handle the task, he was told his slight limp would not be a problem.

The first day at his new job as a third helper, the crew leader, Roll, handed him a protective helmet and goggles. Abednego put it on and followed Roll into the brick oven area called an open air furnace, a vast area filled with flames and noise. The heat overwhelmed him. Compared to this, an August afternoon in the Georgia heat felt like a picnic.

"Bet you never seen nothing this hot," said Roll. "Like to get up to almost 3,000 degrees."

"Why so hot?" asked Abednego.

"To burn out the dirt from the iron, the junk that don't belong," Roll answered.

Abednego took in the twin fires, which burned on either side of the area. Suddenly loud banging noises filled the hearth area. Abednego turned to see some of the other workers banging on beams. Roll took his arm and pulled him to the side.

"They about to tap the furnace, pour out the steel," he yelled. "Watch yourself. Sometime the steel explode, spray metal out everywhere." As he watched the hot steel pouring out, he was sure this was what hell looked like. How had all the dark men ended up in this place?

At the first break, he tossed down a handful of peanuts and asked Roll why all the men were Negro. "They pay us the lowest wage and throw us in the hot and dirty jobs," he said. Just like down South, Abednego thought. "I seen men be burn to death," Roll added.

The worst part of the job, he quickly found out, was when Roll instructed him to add manganese and carbon to the molten steel. Abednego had to pick up a huge sack of coal and run directly towards the molten steel. Aiming toward the huge ladle, some 200,000 pounds, Abednego hurled the sack into the 75 tons of scalding liquid. Flames shot up, and more intense heat. Taking a shovelful of manganese, Abednego rushed once again towards the giant ladle and added more manganese. The process of running toward fire went against his nature, and seemed as foolish as running towards an angry bull.

He did not like the work, but he needed the money. As he charged toward the white hot steel and flame, he thought of his namesake, Abednego, and how he had survived the furnace. Silently, he prayed to God to spare him as he had his Biblical brother. Jesus, you keep my brother from the fire. Please, Lord, I know you got my back. And every time the molten steel was successfully poured, he mumbled, thank you, Jesus.

After work, he drank. Upon his return to the boarding house after each shift, he checked the front table for mail, hoping to hear from Lola. After finding nothing except for an occasional letter from his mother or Marvelous, he reasoned that she must have forgotten him and moved on. He showered and returned to his room. His ears rang with the roar of the furnace; his face burned with the heat of the molten steel. Sometimes he looked out the grimy window into the gloomy sky. When he got to thinking too much about his life, he headed down to the juke joint. Drinking after work came with the territory. For Abednego, the cool beer drowned his thoughts of home and Lola, of each hellish shift. Soon, heavy drinking was part of his routine. His nights blurred into a haze of beer, juke box music, and rowdy company, while his days were heat, sweat, and prayer.

Chapter 29

LOLA

In Ft. Pierce, Florida, in an area known as "Blacktown," Lola settled in at Belle's on what had once been a back porch. Although the room was narrow and small, Lola loved the light from the many windows. Using some old sheets Belle gave her, Lola made curtains that let in the morning light to wake her up each day but gave her privacy. She would rise and get dressed for work at Belle's lunch room. There, Lola worked in the kitchen as a cook's helper, cleaning and slicing vegetables, and setting up plates with bread, buns or cornbread. The restaurant closed after lunch, so when she returned home mid-afternoon, she had the rest of the day to herself.

In the afternoons, she enjoyed sitting out back on an old chair in the warm sunshine. She liked thc sounds of the birds, the feel of the breeze that carried the scent of the ocean.

On a tablet she had purchased at the five and dime, she wrote letters to her mother telling her about Florida and her new life. She always closed with a line, "If Abednego send a letter, please send it to me." No letters ever came.

At first she simply missed him, found herself brooding over what might have been. Although they had not known each other that long, she knew he had been the only man for her. Had the Klan not kidnapped him, or the green-eyed devil raped her, how different would life be?

In the evening, she looked at the stars above and wondered if Abednego was looking at them too, thinking of her. She felt he was, but she knew she could not expect him to accept a baby that wasn't his, a baby created by someone who had taken away what was hers to give to her husband. She was determined to let the baby finish growing itself. Once he was born, she would try to find him a good home. In her heart, Lola didn't think she could ever grow to love the child—it would always be a reminder of the cruelty she had suffered that day.

One afternoon while she was deep in dark thoughts, she was distracted by laughter coming through the back fence. It sounded like a group of friends, men, working on something, talking and drinking in the back yard that bordered Belle's property. Curious, Lola got up from the chair and moved closer to the fence to try and make out what they were saying. She leaned close and listened.

"Go ahead, put some more blue here," one said to another.

"He don't know what he talking about, you need yourself some green." What were they discussing, Lola wondered? And what was that odd smell? She sneaked along the fence looking for a gap so she could see what they were doing. She found a narrow space between two boards and peered in.

Several men stood in front of a couple of paintings. Each of the men held a brush and appeared to be working on the half-finished paintings of Florida scenes—palm trees, beaches, birds –all done in bright colors. She quietly observed for a few minutes as the men took turns working on the canvases; it appeared to be a team project.

"Why don't you shut up, Lucky, and go get us some beer?" said one of the men.

"You be paying?" the man who appeared to be Lucky responded. He turned toward the fence as he said it, and caught a glimpse of Lola. "Hey, we got ourselves a spy over here," he said, and peered back through the gap to see her face. His twinkling brown eyes stared at Lola's face. "You pretty little thing, why don't you come on over?"

Almost five months pregnant, Lola was anything except little. Embarrassed, she didn't know what to say, so she said, "I'm sorry." The men laughed, and she retreated to her own yard. Later, she asked Belle about the men and the paintings.

"They painting pictures to sell along the highway to folks come down here on vacation," she said. "Like the one Hershel give you. Don't see how they be painting, the way they drink and carry on."

But paint they did. Lola continued to listen to them through the fence and sometimes when they grew quiet, she peeked through to see what she could of the paintings. The bright colors didn't match her dark moods, but she could see why their art sold so well to tourists. The colorful scenes, a red-flowered tree here, a turquoise beach there, warm-toned sands, made you want to jump right into the picture. She wanted to find out where the men had learned to paint like this. She felt too shy to talk to them, despite the fact they sometimes talked to her through the fence.

"You over there gal? Come on over and have yourself a beer," one would say, or "We won't bite you," came another. She always pretended she wasn't there. Finally her curiosity got to her. She wanted to learn more about their art. So when Belle was out one afternoon, Lola strolled around the corner and turned the block to try and find the house where the men painted out back. She spotted a house with several cars out front and saw an open gate that appeared to lead to the back yard. She approached cautiously until she heard Lucky's familiar bass voice. She walked through the open gate into the back yard.

Armed with palettes and brushes, four men worked on a row of more than half a dozen canvases nailed to boards that ran between several trees. It appeared to be an art factory of some sort. One of the men noticed her.

"Hey," he said, smiling. He glanced down at her stomach—which was huge. She looked at his face, his dark eyes, and recognized him from before as Lucky. "You the girl from the fence. You ain't so little, but I was right. You sure pretty." Lola was embarrassed by her size and felt like fleeing. Instead, she asked a question.

"Can I watch?"

"Sure," Lucky responded, and offered her a seat at a picnic table spread out with tubes of paint, containers of turpentine and linseed oil and brushes. "Want a beer?"

"No, thanks," she said.

"This is T.C., Jessie, and Shorty," said Lucky, introducing all of the men who appeared to be in their twenties. The men politely nodded hello and kept on painting.

"Get to work, Lucky, unless you want to end up back out in the orchard picking oranges."

"You wish I was out in the orchard," Lucky responded. "You know I can out paint you anytime, T.C." Using a palette knife, Lucky applied several globs of scarlet at the top of a tree. He then picked up a brush and made short strokes to fashion red into Poinciana blossoms.

From that day on, Lola would spend the first half of the day helping Belle at the lunch room and the afternoons watching Lucky and the other men paint. Their "canvases" were really Upson Board, a building material, cut into smaller sized rectangles that would fit perfectly over a sofa or on a wall. The men used shellac to prime the "canvases" and worked quickly to block out the scenes. The men's techniques varied. T.C. would first pencil in his scenes before painting. Lucky used the brush and a light coating of color to block in his scene—an ocean or river, a tree, a bird. Then, using his palette knife, he would apply more color before returning again to the brush to make the scenes come alive. Lola's favorite part was watching Lucky mix the tubes of paint to make new colors. With a little green, white and black added, the blue of the sky would turn to the blue-green-gray of the Atlantic. Each of the men worked on two or three paintings at once, painting in all the blues in all the scenes before adding the next color. They watched each other and learned as they worked, usually from their memory of the places and things they had seen: sunsets, Poinciana trees, everglades, the nearby Indian River, birds, and flowers. What impressed Lola most was their certainty and swiftness when they painted, their decisive brush strokes. Some of the paintings were more abstract than others, but most all were empty of people, allowing the person viewing to imagine himself in the picture.

As Thanksgiving neared, Lucky invited Lola to go visit a "real special lady friend" who was in the county welfare home. "She real sick, but I want you two to meet," he told Lola. He helped her into his Mercury Marquis and loaded a basket of grapefruit, oranges, apples, and some white Cape jasmine blooms in the back seat. The scent of flowers reminded Lola of her days in the pasture, and of Abednego, but she did not say so.

When they arrived, the nurse said Miss Hurston didn't need to see any visitors, she was too sick. Lucky insisted. "It's almost Thanksgiving. This will cheer her up.

Tell her it's Lucky, the painter she met up to Beanie Baccus' house." The nurse sighed, and disappeared down a corridor. Lola hoped she would hurry. The home's smells nauseated her.

In about five minutes, the nurse returned and told Lucky he could go in. "She don't much want anyone to see her like this. She asked if you already see her since the stroke." Lucky nodded.

"Sure have," he said. "I be right back Lola. Just wait here for me." Lola sat down on a tattered upholstered chair that smelled like old newspapers. She hoped he would hurry. She didn't like the faded yellow walls of the place, and she struggled not to vomit. Sweat and urine, mingled with a light pine scent that didn't mask a thing, were overwhelming. She tried to block out the noise of a woman repeatedly calling out for help. She had never been to a county home, and the place scared her. She let her hand trail to her stomach to feel the baby's reassuring kick. She hoped she or the baby never ended up in a place like this.

After a few minutes, she realized she had to find a restroom. Looking around and seeing no nurse, she wandered down the hall in the direction Lucky had gone. Soon she heard the sound of his voice coming through an open door. She approached slowly, hoping to ask him where the bathroom was. As she got closer, she found herself eavesdropping.

"You like a taste of that apple, Miss Zora Neale?" asked Lucky. She heard a low cough, then a raspy voice.

"Pull out your pocket knife and slice me a piece."

"Yes 'em," Lucky said.

"You sweet on that gal you told me about?"

"Might be, Miss Zora Neale, might be."

Lola peeked into the dark room and saw two

shadowy figures profiled against the pale light of drawn curtains. Lucky had pulled out his pocket knife and was slicing apples into wedges. She felt her bladder was about to pop. She tapped lightly on the door frame.

"Lucky?" Lola said. He stood up and came over. "I need a bathroom." He pointed down the hall to an open door about fifty feet away.

"Right there, then come on back. Miss Zora Neale want to meet you."

After she had relieved herself, she returned to the room. Lucky and the patient were chewing on apples. Lola approached the bed hesitantly. A large woman of a lighter color, Miss Zora Neale tried to beckon her over with a wave. Her arm simply quivered.

"Stroke left me in bad shape," she said. "Come on over so I can see you." Her voice was hoarse and garbled. Lola could barely understand her. "What's your name?"

"Lola James. I hope you going to be better soon."

"Me, too," the raspy voice replied. "I want to write again more than anything."

"Yes 'em," Lola said.

"You be back to writing your stories soon, Miss Zora Neale. You will. You tough," Lucky said. Zora Neale shook her head.

"Being like this, it's bad. All froze up in some places. You know what is worse than this sick body of mine? Not being able to write down my stories. No agony like bearing an untold story inside you."

"Lucky say you write books," said Lola.

"I have," said Miss Zora. She nodded as she spoke. "There's plenty more inside me. If only I could hold the pen steady to write them down."

"I'm sorry," Lola said. "Maybe Lucky can bring me

back one afternoon. I could bring some paper, write down some of your stories for you." Miss Zora Neale laughed, and coughed.

"Looks like you might be busy yourself having a baby," she said.

"Yes 'em," Lola replied. She felt a tap on her shoulder and turned around. It was the nurse who they had spoken to earlier.

"Miss Hurston needs to be taking her afternoon nap," she said. Lola and Lucky stood up to leave. Lucky leaned down and kissed Zora Neale's forehead.

"We gonna come see you again soon," he said.

"You do that. And bring your girl back with you," she said. She smiled a crooked smile.

As they left the county home, Lola asked Lucky more about the lady who, in the short time they visited, had intrigued her.

"She used to teach down at Lincoln School. Sometime this famous painter, man named Beanie Baccus, have us down to his house to talk art and drink. Miss Zora Neale, she come there too, tell us some story. Can't believe she be down like this."

"Maybe she'll be better soon, be able to write down her stories," Lola said.

"Maybe," Lucky answered. Driving home, Lola couldn't believe she had met a real author. She wished she could help Miss Zora Neale get her stories from her head onto paper. She would try to sneak away one day to do this.

By the time they returned home, it was almost dark and Belle was furious.

"Where you been?" she demanded. Lola didn't have time to answer before Belle continued. "Don't you be going over there and fooling around with those drunk painters.

We don't need no more men around here," she said, staring at Lola's big belly. Lola tried to explain about visiting Miss Zora Neale Hurston. Belle would hear none of it.

"Who you think you're fooling? The neighbors talk."

In the short time she had been in Florida, Lola had taken note of Belle's standards, which did not include men, drinking, or art, looked upon by Belle with great suspicion. It was no way to earn a living, she said. Lola did not agree with Belle's conservative stance on how the world should be run. With her growing belly, though, she was dependent on Belle for a job and housing, and was in no position to fight.

"I'm sorry, Miss Belle. I don't know it would bother you so." However, Lola did not promise not to go over.

For the next week, she tried to sit in her chair out back, to ignore her urge to visit with the painters. The dark thoughts returned, and she found herself dwelling on Abednego. Every time she opened the mail, she expected to find a letter from him. Instead, she found letters from her mother or sometimes, Hershel. Every opened letter not from Abednego brought a stab of pain to her heart. Why did he not write?

She could not stop thinking about the visit to the county welfare home to Miss Zora Neale Hurston and what the author told Lucky about the agony of bearing an untold story inside. She felt that Miss Zora Neale had been speaking to her directly, talking about Lola's own untold story. She flinched as she remembered the pain of that day in Taylor's Crossing when she was pinned down to the cabin floor, her helplessness. Maybe Miss Zora Neale was right, but she felt too ashamed to tell anyone her story. As

Lola contemplated the rape, and her growing belly, her spirits sank lower. Was not telling anyone what had really happened causing her to suffer?

Brooding under a warm sun one December day, she heard Lucky's voice through the fence.

"Hey, gal, you mad or something?" Lucky asked.

"Nah. Belle told me I can't come over no more."

"She don't have to know," he said. "Come on through." She heard the sound of boards being pried away from the fence. Lucky fashioned a passage by loosening several boards. Lola squeezed through, just barely. She was reunited with her new neighbors, and once again felt happy for the distraction. She continued to learn painting techniques. Lucky let her wield the brush—encouraged her to work on one of his canvases.

"What do I paint?" she asked.

"What do you want to paint?" he asked. She thought of the pine trees of her native North Georgia and of the beech tree where Abednego had one time carved their initials, but she was in Florida now. She never answered Lucky. Instead, she began dabbing a bit of green on the canvas. Using slow strokes, she fashioned the top of a palm tree. Lucky encouraged her and although she was slow, she soon conquered painting an entire palm tree.

In the tender days of her pregnancy, she found herself feeling like the tourists who bought the paintings, lost in the unfolding Florida scenes created by the artists next door. She begin to feel something growing inside her soul. Something full of promise and hope. It was not the child, and it was not Lucky. As 1959 drew to a close, she found herself falling in love with painting.

Every spare moment she had, Lola painted. While creating scenes, applying colors, she lost track of time. She almost forgot to send her mother a Christmas card with two five-dollar bills tucked inside.

A new decade arrived with New Year's Day, January 1, 1960. While Belle was napping, Lola sneaked off to share a pot of black-eyed peas, some collards, and ham with Lucky and the painters.

"Mama told me every pea you eat is worth a dollar," said Lola. "I'm going to make mine wishes instead." Lola speared a single pea with her fork.

"What you wishing for with that one?" Lucky teased.

"To paint as good as you."

"You coming along mighty fine yourself," said Lucky. He speared a pea and held it up for her to see.

"What's that one for?" she asked.

"I'm wishing Miss Zora Neale would get better."

"Let's go see her," she said. "I'll write down her stories." Sadly, this never happened. Miss Zora Neale worsened, and by the end of January, she had passed away. Hearing the news, Lola cried. "I feel bad I never got a chance to help her get her stories out," she said. Determined to go to the funeral, she was getting dressed in her church clothes when Belle came home early from work and stopped her.

"You not going anywhere with that wild bunch from next door," she announced.

"It's a funeral for a writer," said Lola.

"You don't even know her!" Belle said.

"She's friends with Lucky."

Belle stood in front of the door. "And that's exactly why you ain't going," she said. Lola realized she could not tell Belle she had met Miss Zora Neale, or how she spoke the truth. She had no choice but to stay at home. Later,

Lucky would tell her about the big crowd that had come to send Miss Zora Neale off, more than a hundred people, Lucky said. Lola wished she could have been there, too.

Chapter 30

LOLA

Lola woke up with a sharp contraction on a spring night when a storm threatened. Lightning ripped the sky apart. As Lola looked up at the jagged sky, she thought the pains would tear her in two. She cried out for Belle.

Soon the midwife, a trim woman who smelled like camphor, arrived with a small bag and enough confidence for both of them.

"We gonna get through this together," Mrs. Tracey reassured a tearful Lola. "I brought hundreds of young' uns into this world to women plenty scrawnier than you. Can you do what I tell you?" Lola nodded.

When each contraction hit Lola, Mrs. Tracey told her she could either breathe hard or yell, her choice. At first Lola breathed hard, remembering the kittens she had once seen birthed by an old mama kitty. The contractions built along with the lightning storm, and as the end neared some seven hours later, she found herself yelling with each wave of pain. When Mrs. Tracey directed her to push, she felt like she was in the outhouse passing a cantaloupe. The lightning storm had passed, leaving the sky in one piece. As the baby emerged, she felt herself tearing apart.

Mrs. Tracey handed the baby boy over to Lola. He was pale, looked white. Lola looked into his eyes--green, like his daddy's—and felt a flash of hate for the brutal man, but not for the baby. "Don't be worried about the color, they all born pale like that. He'll color up," the midwife said. "His daddy have them cat's eyes?"

"Yes, Ma'am," Lola answered. When the baby cuddled up against her, tried to suckle her breast, she felt his need for her. She did not want to let him go. Belle had arranged for a "nice couple" from church to come the following Sunday evening to pick up "their baby." Lola protested.

"I've changed my mind," she said. "I'm keeping Sebastian."

"Sebastian? You don't be naming this child. I made the arrangements already. How you gonna feed him and be working at the same time?" Lola did not know, yet when she held her son, when he cried, she felt her heart squeeze. She knew she had to figure out a way to keep him. While Belle was at the lunch room, Lola sneaked out and carried him over to show Lucky and the others.

"This is Sebastian," she said.

"Afternoon, little man," Lucky said, holding the baby's tiny fingers in his own. "Guess I'm gonna have to make you a crib so you can have a place to sleep while your Mama help me paint." Lola began to cry as he said it, and she told him she had to give up the baby.

"That ain't right," he said.

"What can I do, Lucky? Belle said if I keep him, I can't stay with her." Lola started sobbing again. Lucky reached out and put his arm around Lola.

"Let me think some."

On Sunday after lunch, while Belle was taking a long nap, Lola sat in the back yard cuddling her baby and counting the hours till the people came to take him away that evening. She had never felt so miserable, even after the rape. She was humming "Sleepy Time Down South" to the baby when she heard a whisper through the fence.

"Lola?" said Lucky. "You and that baby boy gonna come live with me."

"I can't do that," said Lola.

"Why not?"

"Belle would kill me, and you too."

"We gonna marry," said Lucky. "Then she can't be telling you what to do no more." Cradling the baby, Lola stood up and walked over to the fence. She pushed open the "gate," so she could see Lucky.

"Marry?"

"If that what it take to keep your boy," said Lucky. Lola gazed at his wide, open face, saw he was not joking. He was not Abednego, but Lucky was here, right in front of her. Lola nodded, and handed the baby through the fence to Lucky.

"I'll pack up my things," she said. Although she liked him, she did not love him as she had loved Abednego. With all that had happened in the last few months, she was learning to be a practical young woman.

Lucky moved Lola and the baby into his two-room apartment, already crowded with his painting things: Upson Board, oil paints, brushcs, turpentine, and easels. Lola barely had room to turn around. She quietly stored her things under the bed and helped Lucky set up a second-hand crib they borrowed from a neighbor. She felt grateful Lucky had taken her in, and she wanted Sebastian to have a father. She would work to make the space more efficient, to make Lucky glad he asked her to be his wife. Exhausted after moving in, she fell asleep on the sofa nursing the baby.

The next afternoon, they were married by a justice of the peace. Lucky took her to buy a hamburger and Coke after. Back at home, after she had tucked the baby in his crib for a nap, she turned around to find Lucky unbuttoning his shirt.

"Come here, Mrs. Banks," he said, moving toward her. She knew what he wanted.

"We can't, it's too early," she said. "I'm still tore up from the baby."

Lucky looked disappointed. "Well, you come lie down with me, why don't you?"

"As long as we don't fool around or nothing." Lola followed him to his narrow bed and lay next to him. He kissed her shoulder, pressed his chest up against her back. She took his hand and pulled it around her waist, then closed her eyes and pretended to fall asleep. Soon his breathing eased into a steady pattern, and she felt relief. In her rush to keep her baby, she had not given much thought to what Lucky would expect in their marriage. She had only had sex once, and she had hated it. She did not look forward to having it again.

A few weeks later her new husband approached her again.

"Lucky, I ain't been but with one man. One time," she said, holding up her index finger. Lucky looked surprised.

"Once? And you got yourself a baby?" Lola shrugged. Lucky pulled out a small foil package and held it up for her to see.

"What's that?"

"This will keep you from having a baby. Come here, baby girl. That's what be scaring you," he said. That, and the fact she wished it was Abednego. Lola took his hand and let him lead her to the bed.

There, she closed her eyes and let herself be taken.

Lucky was gentle and sweet but she did not really want to be this close with him. She did not know what else to do. She had married him, and it was his right. She felt him inside her, imagined it was Abednego, the only man she had ever loved. She felt bad for Lucky, who she could not make herself love. She lay there quietly. She did not love him back the way she thought a good wife should.

As one day led into another, Lola tried to make up for their lackluster sex life in other ways. She swept and dusted their small apartment, cooked for him, cleaned his brushes with turpentine, and mixed his paints. At night when Sebastian cried, she got up and cared for him so Lucky could sleep.

Like all newly marrieds, they had their struggles. On days when Lucky went to paint with the others, he would return late with alcohol on his breath and in a foul mood. He snapped at her about the smallest things, an unwashed dish in the kitchen sink or the smell of the diapers soaking in bleach. Lola wanted to snap back at him, but she was determined to make their marriage work. She kept her mouth shut. Even if it was dark outside, she would put Sebastian in a stroller and take him out for a walk so Lucky could cool down.

Through Lucky, she learned that Belle was furious and had threatened the painters repeatedly for "kidnapping" the baby. Nothing ever came of the threats, and after a time, Belle settled down. Lola never went back to T.J.'s back yard and the painting parties again. She did not want to risk Belle seeing her and trying to persuade her to give up her son for adoption.

When he went to sell his work by the side of Highway A1A and sometimes U.S. 1, Lucky liked to take Lola and the baby along. She and Sebastian squeezed into the passenger seat of his Mercury Marquis which was packed with his colorful paintings. With the window letting in a breeze, intoxicated by the smell of fresh, damp oil paint and the sweet scent of the baby, she felt happiest on those days that she went to sell with him. At the end of the day, Lucky would pull out a beer and drink on the way home. This made her uncomfortable, and she said so. One day he pulled over to the side of the road and announced it was time she learned to drive, so he could drink his beer in the car. He traded places with her. Holding the baby tightly in his lap, he told her how to steer, brake, and shift gears. She caught on quickly and was soon driving the big Marquis on her own, especially when he wanted to drink.

Most of the time Lucky was good to her. The longer they were together, the more they learned to get along. He played with Sebastian and treated him as his own. By their first anniversary, Lola had grown to care for her husband, not in a romantic or passionate way but as a best friend she could count on.

She felt closest to him when they worked on his paintings. He encouraged her to paint in a tree, or clouds, whenever the baby napped. She quickly learned his style and enjoyed the work, the feeling of the brush rubbing against the canvas, the concentration required to make nature come alive in a scene. Sometimes she would catch him watching her. She would smile back.

Together they watched their son take his first step, speak his first word. They shared their dreams. Lucky wanted to take her to Miami to see the Art Deco buildings.

"You got to see them pink flamingos on the walls," he said. She told him she would like to go there. Secretly, she hoped they would one day travel to Georgia. She missed her mother, the pines, and Abednego. She thought about him sometimes, wondered where he was. Even though her mother said no mail came from him, Lola thought if she were in Georgia, she might somehow see him again. She imagined one day showing off her little family, Lucky on one arm, and her son on the other. Abednego would beg her to leave Lucky for him. She would refuse. When she thought all of this, she realized that she had more anger for Abednego than love. After all, he had never sent her a single letter. Was he even still alive?

In their second year together, when Sebastian had mastered short phrases like "Daddy home" and "play ball" and the space in Lola's heart had opened up to her husband, she lost him. It was a wet October night. She was rocking her son back and forth when she heard a knock at the door. Carrying the baby in her arms, she opened the door to T.J., who looked shaken.

"Lucky been in a wreck," he said. "Slid on a curve, hit a wall." Lola reached for the umbrella that was propped by the front door.

"Take me to the hospital." T.J. stood still. He shook his head back and forth.

"He didn't make it, Lola," he said. Lola screamed, and the baby began to cry. T.J. took her arm and led her to the sofa to sit down. "I'm sorry." She sobbed uncontrollably and gasped for air. She could not believe he was really dead.

"I want to see him," she said. "Can you drive me to the hospital?"

"Not tonight, Lola. Not till the funeral home fix him up." She screamed again. She was too young to be dealing with funeral homes or her husband's death.

"Did he suffer?"

"No, the police say he dead the minute the car crash

into the wall. When you see the car, you gonna know that. Totaled." Lola put her hands over her face and tried to block out what she saw—Lucky lying in the twisted wreckage. She moaned. Seeing his mama upset, Sebastian wailed. T.J. took the baby from her and steered her toward the bedroom, helped her onto the bed. "You lay down now. My gal gonna come sit with you tonight. She can watch the baby. You rest some." Lola reached out for Sebastian. T.J. passed him into her arms.

"I need my son to sleep with me tonight," she said. T.J. nodded. He left the room and returned a few minutes later. He handed her a glass filled with amber liquid, some kind of whiskey. Although she normally wouldn't drink, she gulped it down and let the warm sensation calm her. Cradling Sebastian, she fell back on the pillows that still smelled like her husband. She tried to block the thought from her mind, but couldn't. Lucky would no longer be there to love her and her son.

For the next few days, she alternated between falling apart and feeling numb. The other painters somehow raised the money for a simple pine coffin and purchased a plot. The service and the burial seemed to pass by in a blur. After the funeral, left with only her memories and $40 in her purse, Lola did what she had to. She pulled Lucky's favorite paintings off the walls and gave six of them to T.J. to sell. She would have liked to have kept them all, but she needed money to feed the baby and gas for the drive north. She tucked a small painting, one of a Poinciana tree, into her suitcase and then packed up more paintings and the rest of her things into an aging Chevy T.J. found for her at a used car lot. Since they had so little money, she and Lucky hadn't accumulated much.

T.J. returned the next day with $500. She knew the

paintings couldn't have sold for more than $200. The other painters must have chipped in. She thanked him and took the money. T.J. helped her map out the route.

The next morning, she put Sebastian in the back seat between two large mounds of blankets and sheets and climbed into the driver's seat. Using T.J.'s directions, she drove north all day and into the night, only stopping to sleep by the side of the road for a few hours when she felt sleepy. She had heard most motels didn't allow coloreds and not knowing the area, she didn't know where the Negro motels were, or even if they existed. She was afraid to stop and ask. Exhausted, she arrived back in Georgia on a Sunday afternoon. Once again she was in her mother's house, near her beloved pine trees, so very far from Florida and the life she had come to know with Lucky.

Chapter 31

LOLA

When Lola's mother opened up the door, she embraced her daughter and the baby who she had wanted her daughter to give away.

"Look at them green eyes," she said, and took the baby in her arms. Lola was surprised to see how frail her mother had grown in the last two years, how she stooped over. She sounded out-of-breath when she spoke. "It's a blessing you here, child. Doctor say I can't clean no more houses. My heart carrying water. You can take over my jobs while I watch this boy." Although Lola had planned on going to work for her and the baby, she hadn't expected to support her mother, too, and certainly not so soon. She was still reeling from Lucky's death and wasn't yet ready to face the work world. She told her mother.

"I've got enough to live on for a couple of months. I want to just hold Sebastian and look at the pine trees. Maybe paint some."

"Opportunity don't be growing on them pine trees, or money. My boss ladies going to find someone else to clean while you be setting out in them trees. You ain't in Florida no more, child, and now you a widow." Lola looked at her mother's swollen ankles, at Sebastian's innocent smile and felt heavy with the burden of responsibility. She had just turned twenty-one and now had to make enough for herself, her young son and her disabled mother as well. She did not have a choice—in this small family of three, she was the only one capable of earning a living.

"Okay, Mama. Let me put my things away while you play with Sebastian. Tomorrow you can tell me all about these ladies I need to see." Lola unloaded the car and carried her things back to her old room. She closed the door behind her, sat down on the bed, and wept.

After a few minutes, she rubbed her eyes and stood to look out the window. The old pine tree was taller than ever. Its branches reached up proudly to the sky. She felt stronger just looking at it.

With new resolve, she unpacked her things. She looked at Lucky's picture with the pink flamingo. He had never had a chance to take her to Miami. And although she did not realize it at the time, her life with Lucky in Florida had been a charmed one. She had been around the world she loved--art-- and felt the safety of a man loving her. She hoped Lucky had known how much she cared for him, even though she realized she had not often shown him. She propped the picture up on the dresser, touched the letters where her late husband had signed the painting. L-u-c-k-y. She was the one, after all, who had been lucky. She had not seen it until now.

She went to bed and dreamed not of flamingos, or Lucky, but of Abednego and the big beech tree where he had carved her name under the light of the moon.

The next morning, she rose just after sunrise and went out back in the cool stillness. She opened up her paints, made a light blue wash. Strokes of gray and brown formed a beech tree and into its bark she darkened the initials "L.J. and A.H." She felt a twinge of guilt when she realized she had not put her late husband's initials. Lucky was gone, though, but perhaps Abednego was still alive. With thoughts of him, there was hope.

Over a breakfast of grits and sausage, her mother shared the quirks and habits of her first client, Mrs. Knolls, who had a penchant for cleaning only with vinegar and water in most places. Lola kissed the baby goodbye and set off for her first day working in the three-story Victorian where Mrs. Knolls lived with her husband, a doctor.

When Mrs. Knolls opened the door, she was surprised to see Lola but quickly assessed the arrival of the younger woman as an opportunity.

"Maybe we can finally get to the attic," she said. "Your mother couldn't make it up those steep stairs."

"Where would you like me to begin, Ma'am?"

All day as she dusted, swept, and mopped, Lola thought of her painting and things she would add when she got home. A man, a woman, dark like her and Abednego. She was so absorbed in her thoughts she did not hear Mrs. Knolls come in to ask her to make lunch.

"Girl, where has your mind wandered off to?" Mrs. Knolls asked. Lola looked up from her sweeping.

"A new pastime," she said. When Mrs. Knolls asked what, Lola knew better than to answer truthfully. She had just dusted Mrs. Knolls' paint-by-numbers oil paintings and knew she might be threatened.

"Gardening," Lola lied.

"Gardening's good and practical for a person of your station," she said. Lola flinched inwardly when she heard it and followed Mrs. Knolls to the kitchen.

"I'd like a roast beef sandwich," said Mrs. Knolls. "And you can eat those leftover beans. I think they're still good." As directed, Lola served Mrs. Knolls in the dining room and ate her beans in the kitchen using, as she had been instructed, a different set of silverware and plates. When she had to pee, she was referred to the outhouse in the back of the house, although inside there were two bathrooms she had just cleaned.

By the time she returned home after dark, Sebastian was asleep. Lola ate the cold supper her mother had made for her, went to her room, and felt the tiredness wash over her. That night, she was too exhausted to paint. Instead she thought about what she would like to paint: the way she thought the world should be.

Chapter 32

LOLA
Rome, Georgia 1962-1970

Over the next decade, while everyone else in the world seemed to be fighting for change, Lola was busy pushing a broom, mopping floors and dusting, in order to provide for her little family. She had taken over her mother's cleaning jobs and worked as a custodian at Floyd Community College.

She had heard that a Negro woman attended the University of Georgia down in Athens in 1961. A few years later, some Negro students appeared on the campus where she worked. One day she came face to face with one of them, a serious young man wearing glasses and a tie. Lola gave a simple and slow nod to let him know she was glad he was there. He nodded back at her and spoke. "Ma'am," he said. She was happy for him and the other students, for their opportunities. She was content to be a spectator. The idea of returning to classes, trying to work and study all at once, and caring for Sebastian and her mother, seemed overwhelming. For the most part, she stayed in her part of town, an area of modest homes and colored people. She taught Sebastian to do the same. Always keeping her past in mind, she forbade him to go down certain roads and made sure he came home before dark. With desegregation of Rome's schools in the late 60's, and not wanting her son to be a target, she chose to keep him in the Negro school near their neighborhood.

During these busy years, she painted in her mind. Every time she intended to pull out Lucky's paints, some new bit of work popped up—Mama or Sebastian needed driving somewhere, the laundry needed washing, or the supper cooked. Mama's heart weakened and she was in and out of the hospital. In between hospitalizations, she would retire to her favorite chair, a worn out piece one of her "ladies" had given her twenty years earlier. Lola was going to surprise her with a new one for Christmas. She had already put a new pink wing chair on layaway.

One frigid winter day, Lola came home to make lunch for herself and her mother. "Hi Mama," she said, hanging her scarf up on one of the hooks Sebastian had helped her screw into the front wall by the door. "I thought I'd heat up some soup." She poked her head around the wall and saw her mother sitting with a fixed stare. She rushed to her and took her hand. It felt cold and stiff. Her knees buckled, and she fell to the floor. She laid her head against the side of the chair and wept. Mama was gone.

Lola was left with the funeral expenses, medical bills, the title to the old house, and a new wing chair that made her feel guilty she hadn't been able to do more for her mother. She was only thirty-one, and already she had lost her husband and her mother.

In the summer of 1970, Sebastian went to visit Atlanta with a school friend and his family. For the first time in years, Lola found herself with time to paint. She opened up Lucky's art case to discover the paints had all dried out. On the way to her jobs, she saw an art store in the white shopping district. She stopped in to see about buying some new paint. The white clerk spoke down to her and asked her what she wanted the paint for.

"My boss lady want to take up painting," she answered.

"Why doesn't she come in herself?"

"She crippled," Lola lied. The clerk's attitude quickly changed.

"There's oils," he said, leading her to the aisle filled with tubes of paint and jars of turpentine and linseed oil. "They can be expensive." He handed her a tube, and seeing the price, she sighed. Noticing, he pointed to another shelf.

"This is something cheaper, and it's water based. Quick to dry and the latest thing," he said. When Lola saw the price she was convinced. She bought the primary colors, white, black, a mixing tray, and an art pad. The clerk tried to sell her brushes.

"She already have brushes," Lola said.

"I thought you said she was just taking it up," he said.

"She is," Lola responded. "Her husband died, he painted with oils."

"Well, I think it best to buy new ones. This is water based, not oil." She let him pick out a range of brushes, although it cost her every dollar in her wallet.

At home, she went outside to the old picnic table where she had painted when she was carrying Sebastian years before. She set up her paints, brushes, and several cans of water.

Using water to thin some blue and white paint, she applied a pale wash across the top of the page. Remembering how Lucky had left room for clouds, she left some white space. She laid in a darker blue across the middle--an ocean--and a pale yellow-tan wash across the bottom--sand. Using a light brush stroke of gray, she fashioned a tree trunk, and switching to red, some

Poinciana blossoms. She stood back and assessed her work. The Poinciana appeared to blow in the wind and the waves of the sea looked ready to break. Not bad, not at all, but not her style. Her painting, she realized, looked like one of Lucky's. It made her sad to think of him.

She had not really gone out with anyone since Lucky died. She had been too busy and tired from caring for her mother and her son. And the truth was, all the men her age seemed to be married or bachelors stuck on themselves. A friend from work, Anita, dated some of these single men and called them "fool's gold." Although Lola sometimes felt lonely, she would rather spend her time alone and remembering Lucky, and sometimes Abednego, than to spend time with "fool's gold."

She put the beach painting aside and went to bed. She dreamed of her time in Crystal Springs and Taylor's Crossing, the time she spent with Abednego. The next morning, she woke up early before work and went out back, opened up her paints, and started to paint. She laid in a green wash for summer pastures, a pale blue for the sky, and left the white of the canvas for clouds. She was about to add some people when she realized it was time to rush off for work.

All day as she folded laundry, cooked and cleaned at her first job, she thought of her painting and things she would add when she got home. That night, when she returned from her second job at the college, she added herself and Abednego, and a host of white people alongside them. All together, all getting along.

Chapter 33

LOLA
1988

By the late 80's, Lola was well into her forties, and Sebastian had earned a business degree at Morehouse and was working in Atlanta. For the first time in her life, Lola found the time to paint. After work, she spent hours at the easel creating bright and bold, colorful landscapes populated with black and white people living and working side-by-side. By this time, a diverse society was not unusual. What made her pictures unique was the period frame they depicted, the 1950's. She always put a clue into every painting—a girl in a poodle skirt, or bobby socks, a '58 sedan—some hint to let the viewer know he was looking back in time to a reality that had never existed, at least not down South where Lola had lived.

Her confidence in her work had grown after she painted in acrylics for a few years. She kept her talent to herself. One day at work when she was sweeping the art studio floor, she stopped for a moment to stare at the students' art work hanging on the walls.

"What do you think?" a man asked her. She turned to see the familiar face of the art teacher, a bespectacled man with ruffled hair. Could she be honest with him? Seeing the cookie crumbs dotting the front of his maroon t-shirt somehow made her feel as though it were safe to proceed.

"I think," she said, pointing at a landscape, "that the artist painted it at several sittings and didn't cover his paints up—the colors are different." The professor laughed.

"You are absolutely right," he answered. "What about his technique?" She stared at the trees—straight up and stilted.

"No movement, no feeling, in the trees."

"I agree," he said, and introduced himself.

"Chuck Cramble." She saw his hand rise slightly, as though he expected her to shake hands. She offered her hand, and he took it with his, dry and warm. Even though she had born a white man's baby, she could not remember ever shaking hands with one.

"Lola, Lola Banks."

"I suspect you must paint some yourself," he said. She nodded.

"Watercolors?"

"No, acrylics," she said. "Mostly landscapes, some people." He asked her to bring some of her work. She hesitated. He was an art teacher, and she had no formal training. And she was not a college student.

"It's just a hobby," she said, and went back to sweeping. She tried to avoid him. She didn't want to risk his judging her work. For the next several weeks, he kept finding her in the hallway, asking her to bring something in. He was relentless. Finally she gave in.

Deciding which ones to share was difficult. To be safe, she planned to bring in a couple of landscapes. At the last minute, she decided to bring in two 50's scenes instead. She found him in the studio at his desk. He motioned for her to set her canvases on two empty easels that stood side-by-side. She placed them there and stood back, waiting for his reaction. He crossed his arms and moved closer to view her work.

In one, a black couple walked next to a white couple on a country lane. They carried picnic baskets. The women both wore bobby socks and saddle shoes. In the other painting, four teenaged boys leaned against a 1960 Ford, their fishing lines thrown into a lazy creek. Two were black, and two were white.

Uncrossing his arms, Professor Cramble stepped back and continued to stare at her work. He still didn't speak. Lola felt jittery. She knew she shouldn't have brought them in. He hated them.

"Your subject is excellent. Reminds me of Rockwell. He paints the world the way he wishes it was. And you manage to make your viewer feel like he's in the painting."

"Thank you." Lola stepped forward to retrieve her canvases. He held his hand up.

"Do you sketch first?"

"No, I just paint what's in my head."

"Your style is full of energy, bold," he said, and turned to face her. "I want you to enter both of these in the spring student art show. You'll have to enroll in one of my classes to participate." Lola hesitated.

"I can't afford college."

"You can't afford not to, Miss Banks. I've never seen anything like these!" Encouraged by his remarks, a few weeks later she walked through the registration process and even secured a scholarship to cover her tuition.

Thus, in the spring of 1989, at forty-seven years old, she found herself in a college classroom standing at an easel painting alongside students of all ages. With Professor Cramble's encouragement, she painted a series of the country scenes with a black and white population enjoying themselves.

Her work was hung along with the other students at the art show. Viewers crowded around her paintings. Some of the students and many of the locals asked if they could purchase some. Professor Cramble helped her price some of her pieces, and the very next week she sold two of her 50's-era paintings.

With the business degree he had received at Morehouse, her son Sebastian saw something she didn't: an opportunity to make a business from her art. He researched all the art shows within driving distance and encouraged her to go. He helped her buy a van to carry her inventory. Every weekend she traveled to shows in Tennessee, Georgia, and Alabama. People were drawn to her paintings, and her sales flourished.

In order to keep up with the demand for her paintings, she eventually had to cut down to only one job, her cleaning work at the college where she had health insurance in place. A year later, Sebastian further encouraged her.

"Mama, you don't need to work at the college anymore," he said. "If you work on your art business full time, you'll make a good living." He pulled out her sales records to prove his point. When she heard his suggestion, she felt excited, and scared.

"What if it doesn't work?" she asked.

"What did you send me to college for, Mama? I've run the numbers through, and it will work." With a leap of faith, she turned in her resignation. Within a year, she was making enough money to live on from the sales of her artwork.

In the South, her work became well known and sought after. She had been on regional TV talk shows and was featured in magazines and newspapers for her "retro idealistic" scenes. Despite her success, her growing reputation, and the requests for interviews, she never heard a word from the one person who she thought of every time she painted scenes from Taylor's Crossing. Abednego had never contacted her.

Chapter 34

XYLIA ELMWOOD
June, 2009, Taylor's Crossing, Georgia

Although it was almost 6:45 a.m., and she should have opened her store by 6:30, Xylia Elmwood found herself poking around her bedroom on the warm June morning. As she fastened the buttons on her flowered blouse, she wondered what her son Ernie was doing at this moment. Would he be awake yet, having breakfast? Did a bell summon the campers to activities? Would he make her a pine cone bird feeder? Did Ernie like being there? She hoped so. He was thirty-one, autistic, and away from home for the first time in his life, or hers, for that matter. At the camp, her son would work on daily living skills, communication, and socialization for the next two weeks. The social services worker had assured her it was the right thing to do, and she knew in her heart it was. At seventy-one, she was realistic about how many years she had left, and she wanted Ernie to be ready to function better in the world, if possible. Although he'd been gone for less than twenty-four hours, Xylia really missed her son, the sound of his voice counting cars, the movement of his hands as he colored on his sketch pad. She even missed things that usually annoyed her like his repetitive rocking motion as he watched TV. For as long as she could remember he'd been in the background keeping her company, especially since her husband Leo had died. But she knew it wasn't fair to hold him back when he might be able to have a more productive life. Thinking of background noise, she walked across her bedroom and turned off the radio, which had been set to an oldies station and was playing Dean Martin's version of "I'm So Lonesome I Could Die." No wonder I'm moping, she thought. Enough of this self-pity. I've got a store to run. She brushed back her silver-streaked hair, secured it into a ponytail. She looked in the mirror at her wrinkled, pleasant face, her clear hazel eyes and spoke aloud.

"Xylia Elmwood, I believe you have empty nest syndrome." She glanced at the clock—6:50 a.m.--and headed out the door to Elmwood's store.

She walked across the yard and saw the stump of the old dead oak tree she had chopped down the year before. One of these days, she intended to plant a new tree, but she hadn't gotten around to it. Next time Mr. Hank or old man Porter came in, she'd have to ask when was the best time for planting a sapling.

Rounding the corner of the old rock building, she saw no cars in the lot and thought no one's here yet, thank goodness. But when she headed for the store's front door, she saw someone already seated in the sun-bleached plastic chairs she had placed out front so customers could enjoy the late afternoon breeze that sometimes picked up. Her first customer of the day was an older African-American man seated next to a little black dog, looked like a terrier of some sort.

"Good morning. Hope you haven't been waiting too long. Late start this morning. My years are starting to tell on me," Xylia said. She unlocked the door as she talked.

"Um, hum," the man agreed. Using his cane, he rose from the chair to follow her inside. The little dog tagged along behind.

"Come on in, but you'll have to leave the dog outside."

The man pulled out a leash from a duffle bag he had brought along and tied the dog to the chair leg. Xylia went inside to brew coffee. As he entered, she offered him a seat.

"Thank you. First I need to get something for Daisy. Can I buy a piece of lunch meat or something? Time for her pill. The old gal won't take it unless I hide it."

"Reckon I can find something," she said. She walked over to the cold case and pulled out a fat roll of bologna, sliced off a thick slice and handed it over to him wrapped in waxed paper. "Will that do?"

"Thank you," he said. "And a paper cup for some water." She motioned him towards the restroom in the back of the store.

"There's cups and water in there," she said. "Help yourself." While he was in the restroom, she opened the safe, counted change into the cash register and poured two cups of coffee.

"Cream and sugar?" she asked.

"Yes, thank you," he said. He appeared to be about her age but with less hair. He walked out the back door to feed his dog. Xylia finished preparing the coffee and handed him a cup when he came back in. She gestured to the old school desks that ringed the room. He sat down while she stood at the counter, sipping her coffee and straightening out the clutter by the cash register.

"You're up awful early," she said.

"If I can get ahold of my man John, we're going fishing. Could I pay you to make a phone call? Local number?" The man fumbled in his pocket, pulled out the paper with phone number, and limped over to the counter to take the phone from Xylia.

"No charge." He took the receiver, dialed the number. There was no answer.

"Probably stepped out for a while," he said. "Should be back soon." The man handed back the receiver.

"Good day to be out. My bones tell me there's no rain in store," she said. She looked at his cane, thought about his slow, shuffling gate.

"You're not traveling on foot, are you?" she asked.

"Nope, caught myself a ride. Car broke down up near Ringgold. They have to order the part. Might take a few days."

"Make yourself at home," she said. She moved over to a chalkboard placed in the back of the room and began erasing the words: "Even God cannot change the past."—Agathon. The man watched her.

"What's that you're erasing?"

"My sayings board. I put up a new one every week. Gives folks something to talk about. Lately they've been getting more sophisticated." She retrieved a jar from behind the counter and walked over to hand it to the man. "Would you do me a favor and select the next quote?" she asked, holding out the jar. He hesitated.

"Go ahead. Don't be shy. It's either you or Mr. Hank, and he's been known to cheat. He spots his own quotes and pulls them out of the jar every time. You'd be doing me a favor, Mr.—what did you say your name is?"

"Ben," he said, and hesitated. "Shepherd." He drew out a slip. She took it from him.

"Well, Mr. Shepherd, thank you for putting randomness back into Elmwood's quotation system."

Mr. Shepherd had the hint of a smile on his face when he answered. "You welcome."

Xylia unfolded the quote and begin writing on the board. "History is a set of lies agreed upon."—Napoleon Bonaparte. She copied the phrase out in big letters while her lone customer watched. The door burst open and Earl Williams barreled in. He headed straight to the tobacco products to get snuff for his wife, Cottie.

"Mornin', Mr. Earl," she said.

"Mornin', Miss Xylia," he replied. Then he spoke to the stranger. "That your dog out there?"

"Daisy Bates? Yes, she mine," Mr. Shepherd said.

"Never seen one like that around these parts. What kind is she?" Earl asked, looking up at the black man occupying his usual spot.

"A mix. Part Manchester terrier, part Jack Russell terrier," said Mr. Shepherd.

Although he wasn't an educated man, and pretty near ignorant, Earl Williams could spot a Yankee accent when he heard one. This black fellow's voice didn't sound exactly Yankee, but it wasn't pure southern, either.

"You passing through?" he asked.

Xylia, who didn't like anyone to feel unwelcome in her store, answered for Mr. Shepherd. "He's waiting for his fishing buddy to show up."

"Well, them fish ain't been hitting round here. Why don't you head up to Chickamauga Lake?"

"Don't know," he said. "My friend in charge of all that." Earl poured himself a cup of coffee and went over to pay Xylia.

"Your friend from round here?"

"Over to Crystal Springs," Mr. Shepherd answered, referring to the area that back in the day was primarily an African-American community.

"You been down this way before?" Earl asked. He

took his coffee and remained standing, facing Mr. Shepherd.

"What is this, Mr. Earl? Twenty questions?" Xylia asked. Earl scowled at her.

"Not been down here for a long while," said Mr. Shepherd.

"We don't have too many strangers around these parts," said Earl. Xylia was embarrassed at his not-so-subtle prejudice against outsiders. She wanted to shove him out the door. There was no easy way to get rid of Earl Williams, she'd learned. He was like a grease stain that wouldn't come out. "What's your buddy's name? Maybe I know him." Mr. Shepherd glanced at this bulky powerhouse of a man who asked too many questions and hesitated before he answered.

"I doubt it," said Mr. Shepherd. Xylia jumped in to change the subject.

"Mr. Earl, before I forget, could you take a look at that leaky faucet around the side of the building?" she asked. Since her husband Leo had died, Earl had acted as her unofficial handyman. She steered him to the front door, leaving Mr. Shepherd with his coffee and peace of mind.

She was outside with Earl when Mr. Hank pulled up in his classic town car. He climbed out, adjusted the overalls strap that he always had trouble keeping on his frail shoulders. After he tipped his Georgia Power cap at Xylia and said good morning, he headed into the store.

Leaving Earl with the faucet, she followed Mr. Hank inside and poured him his usual cup of black coffee while he rooted around looking for the perfect Honey Buns. He picked up two of them and pulled out his money to pay Xylia.

"Mr. Hank, you must be hungry this morning," she

said.

"Nah, one's for Sewell Buttrill. Now his wife is dead, he don't eat much. His kids all went on a cruise somewhere. Figured I'd take him something. Since that heart attack he don't get out much. Says them heart pills make him dizzy."

"That's right nice of you," she said. "I know he'll appreciate it. That visiting nurse wouldn't be bringing him anything as good as a Honey Bun." She tucked the Honey Bun into a bag and handed it over. Mr. Hank took a seat at one of the school desks across from Mr. Shepherd, and tore off the bun's cellophane wrapper.

Chapter 35

ABEDNEGO

Before Mr. Hank showed up, Abednego had been nursing his coffee and peering around the room at the shelves full of canned goods, at the antique candy counter, and at the chewing tobacco and snuff. He walked to the cooler and picked up a carton of worms. Some things never changed. Same old rednecks asking too many questions. Maybe he should never have planned to stop here on the way to New Orleans. Why had he wanted to come back? What did he hope to find here? Did she even live here anymore? His musings were interrupted by the man who had appeared across from him.

"Going fishing are you?" Mr. Hank asked, pointing at the worms.

"Planning on it," Abednego answered. He wondered if he was in for another round of questioning from another cracker. "My friend down to Crystal Springs be picking me up soon." Mr. Hank took a bite of his Honey Bun, chewed contently, and spoke.

"Best spot's down by the bridge over little Chickamauga Creek on the old Tucker farm. Course you all will have to be careful down there. My great grandson was down there a few weeks ago and sat hisself down on one of them ant mounds. Fire ants it was, stung him all over. Lordy you should have seen them blisters." Abednego nodded agreeably, which Mr. Hank saw as an invitation to continue. "Brown grazes his cattle down there and you'd want to watch out for that mean spotted bull."

"Tucker? They still live around here?" Abednego asked.

"Back in the 60's, Tucker sold the farm and moved up to Chattanooga near Mrs. Tucker's folks. Their girl, can't recall her name, some flower or such. She lives up by the river. Runs herself an inn up there. I can't remember her name to save my life."

"You talking about Iris Tucker?" Xylia asked.

"That's it!" said Mr. Hank. "Little gal used to ride horses all the time." Abednego knew he was talking about his sister Marvelous' childhood friend but didn't say so.

"My friend had a cousin used to work for the Tuckers in the dairy," Abednego said. "Quite a while back."

"Dairy shut down in the early 60's, before they moved away. Your friend, was he a colored fellow?" Abednego nodded.

"Lived in the cabin down by the branch, along Ridgeview Road. I remember that boy. He had some muscles, yes he did. Right quick around them animals. Had me a bull mean as fire. Must of weighed a ton. I asked Henry if the boy could come over one afternoon to help me put a copper ring in the bull's nose, so I could handle him better. Henry agreed and told me he'd mention it to the boy. Well, he must've misunderstood cause he went ahead and penned that bull on his own and stuck that copper ring right in that bull's nose hisself. I imagine that bull was shocked. I know Henry and I was. Never heard of a man handling no bull by hisself like that before, no Sir-ee."

Abednego nodded and wondered if Mr. Hank could hear his heart beating hard.

"I heard about that," Abednego said. Once Mr. Hank got wound up, he couldn't stop.

"Now another time, there was a colt wilder than tarnation. Everyone in the valley knew that boy had a way with animals. I asked Henry if he thought the boy could break him. He arrived late one afternoon at my place, and we went out to the pasture where I kept the colt. He asked if I could bring a bridle and a bucket of sweet feed. He took the feed bucket and bridle and went out into the pasture and had that colt eatin' out of his hand in no time. While the colt had his head down in the bucket, the boy moved quick as lightning and slipped his arm over the colt's neck and slipped the bit into his mouth and the bridle over top of his head. While the colt was tryin' to figure out what had hit him, the boy jumped up on his back and hung on. You never seen a colt buck like that one. It run and bucked all over the place, tried to run him into a barbed wire fence. That boy tugged hard on them reins and turned him away at the last minute. They went on like this for hours—they both was trying to out stubborn one another. Must have been midnight by the time that colt had tuckered hisself out. He was real thirsty and hungry by that point. The boy called out for me to bring over some more sweet feed. I sat it down by the trough and that horse wandered over nice and easy, not carin' whether or not the boy was on his back or not. When he lowered his head for the oats, the boy slid off real easy and fed him out of his hand, petted him all over. That colt was so derned tired and hungry, he didn't flinch none. The boy came back out every evening for a week and worked with that colt. Made him into the gentlest ridin' horse I ever had."

"A fine riding horse," Abednego muttered, just as another gentleman opened the door to Elmwood's and walked in. The man nodded hello.

"Hello Porter," said Mr. Hank. Old man Porter nodded in greeting, and moved over to pour himself a coffee. He came and sat in the circle of school desks with the other two men.

"You talking about a fellow named Abednego," said Abednego. "He could break any colt in the valley."

"That's it, Abednego, his name slipped my mind."

"Ain't all that's slipped," Old Man Porter said.

"You ain't too far behind," Mr. Hank shot back." Porter ignored the comment and continued.

"Abednego was quick and strong, always willing to help out when needed. One time we had no lights at the ball field. Kids shot out them bulbs. We got some new ones from the store here, and one of the fellows drove home to get a ladder. Abednego was there that night. He took the bulbs from me, said he didn't need no ladder. Shimmied right up the pole and changed them light bulbs hisself. That Abednego, he was a good one." Xylia, who had busied herself dusting shelves, looked up.

"Now you all have talked him up so, I have to ask whatever happened to the legendary super-strong, bull master, horse-taming Abednego?" asked Xylia. Mr. Hank and Mr. Porter looked at each other for a moment, then Mr. Hank spoke.

"Reckon he left around the time the dairy closed, don't you think, Porter?" Old man Porter nodded.

"Reckon he did," Porter replied. Abednego scrutinized the two older men before speaking.

"With all that horse breaking and pole shimmying, he be a fool not to stay on," Abednego said. He wanted to hear what they had to say about the Klan kidnapping.

"Abednego, he wasn't no fool," said Mr. Hank.

"Things was different then. Not a lot of opportunity down here for the coloreds back then." Mr. Porter added, "He up and left right quick one evening. Never heard from him again. Some said he headed up North. Don't blame him. There was a lot of trouble down here in these parts in those days." At this, Abednego leaned back in his desk and twisted his face into a puzzled expression.

"Trouble?" he asked. Once again, Porter and Johnson looked at one another, communicated in their silence.

"Well, not here in Taylor's Crossing, no Sir-ree. Up to Chattanooga and down Atlanta way, might have been a little trouble with Jim Crow laws and such. Down here, we got along fine." Mr. Porter nodded too eagerly.

"We sure did."

"I see," said Abednego. There was an awkward pause until Mr. Hank got up and shuffled over to the chalkboard to study the quote.

"Xylia, I see you went and changed the der-gone sayin' without me. Wasn't it my turn to draw the slip from the jar?"

"Sorry, Mr. Hank. I thought I'd give someone else a shot, for a change," Xylia said. Hank moved in to better see the quote. Porter joined him.

"History is a set of lies agreed upon," said Porter.

"Napoleon Bonaparte," added Mr. Hank. "Heck, Xylia, your customers are gettin' too fancy."

"And it don't make no sense," said Porter.

To Abednego, sitting quietly at the school desk, it did.

Chapter 36

ABEDNEGO

The morning passed quickly at Elmwood's after Mr. Hank and old man Porter left. Customers had come and gone, each one more curious than the last. All had advised Abednego on what type of bait to use, from mini-franks to cheese balls. One of the customers even told him the worms wouldn't be any count if they got too warm, so he eventually returned them to the cooler. It had gotten so hot he'd had to move Daisy Bates around to the shady side of the building near the store's back door.

Abednego glanced up at the clock again, saw it was noon. He stood up and went over to dial his fishing buddy's number on the phone. Still there was no answer. As he hung up the receiver, he wondered if coming here had been a stupid idea. His friend John had to be seventy-five by now. Maybe John's memory was slipping, maybe he had forgotten this was the day he was passing through, maybe he had forgotten he'd even called. What would happen if he never reached John? He had planned to sleep at John and Rose's place, or possibly even Lola's, if he found her. Now there was a thought…but what would his late wife have said about that? Sarah wouldn't have liked it.

Over the long years of his marriage, he had mentioned Lola a few times, saying he hoped to look her up one day. Sarah had bristled. Even after all their years of marriage, she had remained jealous of her husband's first love. He had tried to explain that it was nothing more than curiosity that made him want to find Lola, and that he wanted to say a proper goodbye. Of course he had loved Sarah, and she had given him many happy years and three children. Now she had been gone for a year, he saw nothing wrong with finally searching for Lola before he moved to New Orleans. He might never pass this way again, as the song said. Even if Sarah could somehow see him from heaven, weren't you supposed to forget about earthly concerns, leave them to the living?

And what could there possibly be between him and Lola for Sarah to be jealous of? Who was he kidding? He had just turned seventy, and Lola would be at least sixty-eight by now, most likely a grandmother, and she probably couldn't care less about an old man like himself. She might not even remember me, he thought, straightening his shirt collar and running his fingers through his still thick hair, now silver. Even as he tried to arrange himself to look more presentable, he lied to himself; I am simply looking up a friend from a long time ago.

Another customer, Lawson, dropped by to get a Moon Pie. He told Xylia he was just passing through on the way to Dalton, and like the others, he asked too many questions. Where was Mr. Shepherd from? Up North. And what kind of job had he worked before he retired? Melting crew at a steel mill. Lawson didn't appear to recognize Abednego at all.

Abednego learned that Lawson had just retired from the carpet mill and seemed to have too much time on his hands. Finally Lawson left when he remembered he was supposed to pick up a tractor part down in Dalton.

Abednego looked up at the clock and sighed. He'd

never seen people as snoopy as these folks in Taylor's Crossing.

"How'd you like me to scare us up some lunch?" Xylia asked.

"Seeing how my friend is still missing in action, that might be a good idea," he said. She pulled out a loaf of whole wheat and listed the possibilities: bologna, cheese, ham, pimiento cheese, and tomatoes.

"Pimiento cheese be great. Hadn't had one for years. You can't get it up North." From underneath the counter, she retrieved a toaster and put in the slices. When the bread popped up, she dabbed on some pimiento cheese and sliced up a homegrown tomato. She put the sandwiches on paper plates, got a couple of Cokes out of the cooler, and carried all to the old school desks. They sat across from each other, eating and talking.

"The day's wearing on, and it's getting too hot to fish," she said. "I know that much, even though I admit I don't know the first thing about fishing."

"You be the only one round here who don't," Abednego said. "Everyone else claim to be an expert."

"I love all my customers, but some of them know quite a bit about nothing. They like to hear the sound of their own voices," she said. She explained that her friend Jolene was coming in shortly to watch the store while she drove in to Chattanooga for an appointment. He needn't worry, she said, the store didn't close until seven. And Jolene was good company.

"Surely your fishing friend will be here by then," she said. He shrugged his shoulders.

"I hope so."

"Maybe he'll be back home at the end of the day."

As he chewed on the salty, rich pimiento cheese, the

cool sliced tomatoes, and the crunchy bread, he couldn't help thinking of Iris, who had introduced him and Marvelous to "menta cheese" as she called it. Then he had an idea.

"Mrs. Elmwood, you going anywhere near where that Tucker girl live?"

"You mean Iris' bed and breakfast? That's right up near the river, in the Bluff View Arts district. Not too far from downtown and my doctor's office."

"If it not too much trouble, maybe you could drop me off there? I can visit with her while you at your appointment."

"Do you want to call and tell her you're coming?"

"No, been a long time since she saw me. I'm gonna surprise her," he said. "When you done with your appointment, I'll drive back down here with you and try to reach my friend again. I been thinking about it. Bet he thought I was coming in this evening. When them fish start to hit."

A half hour later, Abednego and Xylia were headed north up the Old Alabama Highway towards the interstate. Abednego looked out the window towards Taylor's Ridge, which ran alongside the road all the way to Ringgold.

"It's beautiful, isn't it?" asked Xylia. "Especially in the fall when the leaves turn orange and gold." As Abednego stared at the dense forest, his thoughts weren't nearly as pleasant.

Even though it had been half a century, he remembered the bumpy journey up the dirt road that led to the crest of the ridge. He remembered waking up in the trunk of the car. He remembered the gas smell of the gag that kept him from screaming when he thought of his baby sister caught in the flames. He looked up towards the trees that covered the ridge, wondered which one of the Klan men had pulled him out from the car trunk? He remembered lying in the dark listening to the sound of their voices discussing how to dispose of his body. He remembered playing possum while he tried to untie his hands before they could realize he'd come to.

He glanced around to see his dog. Daisy Bates was happy, too, riding in the back with her head hanging out the window, sniffing in the country air. He envied her. She had it easy.

Chapter 37

XYLIA

Xylia looked over at Mr. Shepherd and wondered if she should tell him what she'd always heard about Abednego. On the one hand, Mr. Shepherd seemed perfectly content to stare out the window at Taylor's Ridge, no doubt caught up in his own thoughts. On the other hand, she felt it wasn't right that Mr. Johnson and old man Porter had conveniently forgotten to mention the truth. Perhaps, she reasoned, the men had been embarrassed to talk about what had really happened back in 1959 down in Taylor's Crossing. Being from up North herself, and not having arrived in the valley until the mid-sixties, Xylia bore no responsibility for what had happened back then. Reared as the daughter of a Methodist minister, she felt the only thing to do was to tell the truth, even if it might be awkward.

"Mr. Shepherd, you know when you asked what happened to Abednego?" she said. He nodded. "Well, I've heard a lot of talk over the past years since I've been running the store, some of it idle gossip, for sure. I've heard several different stories about why Abednego left so suddenly. All of them involve him being kidnapped."

"What do you hear?" he asked.

"Some say Abednego heard someone knock at the door and had time to escape through the floorboards of the cabin where he lived. He sneaked out back and slipped into the creek and followed it a mile or two away from where they were. I've also heard that a group of white men took him up on the ridge and tied him to a tree. They went back to their car to discuss how to get rid of him but while they were gone, he somehow managed to cut himself free, and then he escaped by hiding in the woods up there. Others say a gang of men broke through his front door with ax handles and knocked him out. They tied him up, threw him in the trunk, and drove him up to the top. He acted like he was unconscious when they unloaded him from the trunk. While they went back to the car to get their rifles, he got up and sneaked off."

"Funny," said Mr. Shepherd.

"You mean that there are so many different versions of what happened?"

"No, I mean no one want to talk about it, but everyone seem to know."

"Things have changed a lot since then. I imagine folks aren't proud about the past. They'd rather not talk about those ugly times."

"At least not with no black man. They ever say who was do it?"

"Folks have speculated. No one's ever said for sure. Some claim it was the Klan from Chattanooga."

"Cause we don't have no trouble down here in the valley," Mr. Shepherd said in a perfect imitation of Mr. Johnson's drawl. Xylia laughed.

"What I like to know is how anyone be knowing what Klan it was, or wasn't, if they wasn't there that night?"

"Like I said, there's a lot of speculating over the years," said Xylia. Mr. Shepherd nodded and turned around to look at Daisy Bates, who whimpered a bit.

"Hate to trouble you, Miss Elmwood. I see Daisy

Bates needs to do her business. She get like this in the car sometimes. Think you could pull off somewhere before we get to the interstate?"

"Sure," said Xylia. Seeing a small church ahead, she swung into the parking lot. "You can take her off in the grass there," she said. "I've got some paper towels in the trunk if you need them." Mr. Shepherd reached down and grabbed his duffel bag.

"I've got something in here," he said. "I be right back." He opened the back door, and the little dog followed him out into the parking lot. Xylia watched them in the rear view mirror as they walked behind the car and disappeared behind a tall oak tree.

Chapter 38

ABEDNEGO

Hidden by the tree trunk, Abednego reached into his bag for his bottle. He took several sips of whiskey, felt the hot burn on his throat, felt the wash of warmth calm him. All the talk about the Klan had made his head feel like it was going to explode. He wondered, once again, why he had come back to this awful place. "Lola," he said out loud to Daisy Bates. The dog looked up at him and wagged her tail. He tucked his flask back in the bag and returned to the car. They continued north on the highway, toward Tennessee.

"How long since you were up this way?" Xylia asked.

"Too long," he answered. He hadn't seen downtown Chattanooga for five decades. When they exited and headed into downtown, it wasn't as he had remembered it. The streets were wider and looked cleaner, and the town had so many more buildings. Xylia drove out of her way to point out the new stadium, the IMAX Theatre, and the aquarium. Then they headed up 4th Street towards High Street and the Hunter Art Gallery, which overlooked the Tennessee River.

"This is quite the tourist spot now," said Xylia "They restored some old buildings, put in some shops and restaurants. Now it's called the Bluff View Art District." They parked in a lot behind several ivy-covered buildings.

With the dog in tow, Abednego and Xylia walked around the corner towards a gray and white Victorian style home.

"This is the place," she said, opening the gate to a yard filled with hydrangeas and hedges. Abednego followed her to the front door, which was in the center of a large covered porch populated with wooden rockers and an old-timey swing. A sign next to the door simply said, "Bed and Breakfast." A lavender iris was painted at the bottom. Xylia rang the bell while Abednego stood by the swing waiting.

The swing reminded him of the one at the old Tucker place. Would Iris recognize him? Probably not. He was all broken down, like an old gnarly tree on the outside and today, on the inside, too. He could feel the many rings of the passing years to his core.

Sometimes being old had its advantages. He now travelled the world hidden inside his broken down exterior, a façade not remembered by those who knew him in the energetic days of his youth.

Chapter 39

IRIS

Iris' morning had been unpredictable thus far. The housekeeper had called in sick, and the man in the small room at the back of the house was complaining about an odd smell emanating from the toilet. Iris had agreed to move him to an upstairs room as soon as a couple checked out, which they had about an hour ago. She had just finished changing the linens and was dusting when she heard the buzzer. It was probably the plumber arriving early. She ran down the stairs to let him in but was surprised to see her old friend Xylia Elmwood standing at the door.

"Xylia, what a treat to see you," she said, and gave her a hug. "Come on in." Xylia hesitated at the door, probably because Iris looked disheveled. Her hair was tied back in a ponytail, secured with a rubber band. She held a dust cloth in one hand and a roll of toilet paper in the other.

"I'm sorry I didn't call first."

"No, it's alright. I've just finished making up a room. This place is a madhouse. I'm missing a maid and the plumbing's making a smell."

"I've brought someone to see you," Xylia said. She stepped aside, revealing a silver-haired African-American man. "He showed up this morning to fish with an old buddy who's missing in action. He wanted to meet you, has a friend who used to work at your family's dairy." Iris stepped forward and shook his hand. The man had a strong grip. As Iris stared into his deep brown eyes, she felt a strange familiarity but didn't say so. "Why don't you both come on in, and we can talk over some iced tea," she said. Xylia explained she had to leave for her doctor's appointment right away but would come back later.

"I like to stay and visit, if that's alright," said Mr. Shepherd.

"Why sure," said Iris. She waved goodbye to Xylia and ushered him inside. He followed her to a small parlor furnished with overstuffed chintz chairs and a rolltop desk. On the wall were paintings of hunt scenes filled with horses. A grandfather clock, antique lamps, and a pile of art books lying on the end table gave the parlor the feel of a country home.

Iris urged him to sit down in one of the fat chairs. When he did so, his small dog—a terrier of some sort?—curled up on the hardwood floor next to his feet.

"I want to hear all about your friend but first things first. Want a sweet tea?" she asked.

"No, thank you, just had me something to drink," he said. "Daisy Bates, she might be thirsty." He nodded his head toward the dog.

"Sure. I'll get her some water, and I'll bring in some tea, just in case you change your mind." Iris excused herself and left Mr. Shepherd with his dog.

In the small kitchen off the parlor, Iris put ice cubes into glasses and racked her brain trying to remember why the dog's name sounded so familiar. A character in a book? No, that was Daisy somebody else. Someone in history? A school teacher? In Arkansas? And then she remembered. Mrs. Bates had helped get those black students into the all-white high school in Little Rock in the 50's. A civil rights hero. Iris put the glasses and a small bowl of water on the tray and returned to her guest. She set the tray down and put out the bowl for the dog.

"Here you go, Daisy Bates," she said. "That's a great name. Did you know the real Daisy Bates?"

"No, but you the first one who know the name without me explaining," he said. She took an iced tea in her hand and sat down across from him.

"I'm a bit of a history buff," she said. "So tell me about your friend who worked for my father."

"Name was Abednego Harris. You may remember him," Mr. Shepherd said. "He work there round fifty-eight, fifty-nine."

Iris smiled. "Of course I remember him. He broke my mare, Gypsy, took us fishing, his sister and me. Marvelous was her name." Abednego nodded. Iris continued. "We two rode horses all the time. We were like sisters. Did you come here to see Abednego?" she asked. "I'd like to see him too. I haven't seen him since I was a child."

"I be looking for a friend of his. Do you remember a young lady used to work for the Buttrills?"

"You're talking about Abednego's girlfriend?" she asked. "Of course I remember. She was a tall girl with a beautiful smile. Lots of dark curls. She came over to fish with us sometimes in the creek behind Abednego's cabin. And she and Abednego used to laugh and whisper while Marvelous and I fed stale bread to the snapping turtles. Lola, wasn't it?"

"Lola," Mr. Shepherd said, "Lola." The name rolled off his tongue slow and sweet. "Do you ever hear what become of her?" Mr. Shepherd asked.

Iris tapped her fingers against the side of her glass

as she tried to remember.

"I think she moved to Atlanta and went to work down there. Doesn't her cousin John live down in Crystal Springs?"

"That's what I thought. He the one I'm going fishing with. He don't answer his phone."

"Excuse me," said a heavy set man who appeared at the doorway. It was a guest wanting to know when his room would be ready. Iris handed him the key to the new room and returned to the seat across from Mr. Shepherd.

"You're welcome to use my phone to call him," she said. "Maybe his phone is out. Or, when my night person comes in at five, I could drive you down there myself."

"You could. Mrs. Elmwood, she planning to take me back down when she come back, around six, I think. I wouldn't want to be no trouble."

"Oh, it's no trouble," she said.

"I imagine you got more important things to do than chauffeur an old man around all evening. It'd be like *Driving Miss Daisy*, only in reverse." He chuckled as he said it. She laughed.

"You're funny. No, I'd love to have an excuse to drive down to the country. I'd like to see John, too. Maybe he'd know what happened to Marvelous."

"You don't know what become of her?" he asked. Iris shook her head.

"No, I don't. The Klan kidnapped Abednego one night. They beat him with baseball bats and threw him into the trunk, took him away." Mr. Shepherd leaned forward to hear better.

"Where you hear that?" he asked.

"My daddy. The FBI investigated. Never could come up with any answers. Everyone knew it was the Klan, but no one seemed to know where they came from. Daddy got so mad he eventually moved us up to Chattanooga." Telling it made her feel agitated. She opened a drawer in the desk and reached for a pack of cigarettes. "It makes me sick to think of it. Mind if I smoke?"

"Go ahead," said Mr. Shepherd. She scraped the match alongside the cover and lit up, inhaled deeply, and sighed. She walked over to the window, opened it a few inches to let out the smoke.

"I have to hide my smoking from the guests. We're officially a no smoking place. Anyway, as I grew older, I got madder and madder about the way things were down here back then. In junior high, I was the only one who wanted Kennedy to be president. The other kids called me a communist because I wore a button showing a Catholic whose election would surely bring on the end of the world." Mr. Shepherd laughed. Iris went on.

"Crazy, huh? But remember, it was the South in the sixties. By the time I reached high school, I was furious with a lot of what was going on down here. Daddy wouldn't let me participate in the sit-ins, but I did what I could get away with. One of the local high schools used 'The Rebels' for their mascot. A lot of people, including me, thought that this was all wrong. The worst part was after pep rallies. The students formed a caravan of cars and drove around town waving their Rebel flags. I hated this custom but didn't tell anyone. One night I played along like I was one of them. I joined the caravan along with another friend who also secretly hated the whole Rebel mascot thing. We drove our car out first, screaming and waving our flags. All the other cars fell in behind us. I led them through the usual friendly white neighborhoods, and folks clapped and cheered as we passed. At one point I took a 'wrong turn' into a black neighborhood where some of my friends lived. Hiding behind shrubs, they waited for us and threw raw eggs and water balloons at all the cars except mine. Silly, I know. My way of getting back." Iris stopped to take a breath and noticed Mr. Shepherd look down at his duffel bag.

"Do you have a restroom I can use?" he asked.

"Sure," she said, and pointed him down the hall. She wondered why he took the duffel bag with him, but thought it would be rude to ask. She returned to the parlor and petted Daisy Bates, who let her scratch between her ears.

Chapter 40

ABEDNEGO

In the bathroom, Abednego pulled the flask out of the bag, gripped it in his hands, and took two sips, waited for the warm feeling to take over. He wrapped the flask up inside an old jacket, zipped up the bag. Iris was intense. And her true telling of what the Klan had done that night had hurt to hear. He thought about telling her he'd been there, too. He couldn't. She'd want to contact Marvelous at once, and Marvelous would be furious with him for disappearing. No, he wasn't ready for all hell to break loose. Besides, what was wrong with wanting to leave Abednego the way Iris had remembered him? A strong man who was in his prime? Wasn't this a better way to be remembered? It was starting to get complicated. All he had really wanted to do was find Lola. That's what he would do. A low pounding began in his ears. Demon drums. He looked in the mirror and stared at his eyes, starting to get a little bloodshot. He turned on the faucet, leaned down, splashed his eyes, and rinsed out his mouth with the fancy, mint-flavored mouthwash by the sink.

When he returned to the parlor, he announced that it was time for Daisy Bates to take a walk. Iris wanted to go with him, but she had to wait for the plumber. Thank God, he thought. He needed a few minutes to recover from all she had said.

"Why don't you wait in the sculpture garden on the

bench and I'll be right along?" she asked. "It's not too far."

"I move a little slow," he said, "but I can walk just fine. Suppose I can wait a spell on that bench."

Chapter 41

IRIS

Iris stood on the far end of the bed and breakfast front porch and glanced around the corner to make sure Mr. Shepherd and his dog were safely pointed in the right direction. Making sure no guests were in sight, she lit up a cigarette and sat down on the porch swing to wait for the plumber.

The man's sudden appearance had gotten her to thinking about something she had rather not. Of course she fondly remembered the good times with her childhood friend Marvelous, exploring the farm together, riding horses, and hanging out with Abednego at the creek. Thinking about that last night together disturbed her, churned up a host of bad feelings: remorse, sadness, and most of all, guilt. The night rides had been her idea; at eleven, she had been a full year older than Marvelous and should have known better.

The first time it had happened was their second summer together, June, 1959. Iris awoke to a soft blowing noise outside her bedroom window. She rose and walked over to the open window where her mare Gypsy beckoned, her white fluffy body outlined by the moon's silvery light. Hearing no noise in the house, Iris knew her parents were asleep. She quietly pushed against the window screen and eased out onto the mare's wide back, passed under the rustling leaves of the crabapple tree, and headed for the fence that enclosed the yard.

Although it had been a hot day, the evening had given way to a nighttime coolness. Iris wore a thin nightgown and liked the warmth of her horse against her bare legs. At the edge of the yard, she leaned down low over Gypsy's neck and unlatched the gate. They trotted down the lane into the moonlit night.

Not much moonlight reached the windows of the cabin where Marvelous stayed with her brother, Abednego. Built in a low place near the stream, the cabin was mostly hidden by trees and bushes, sheltered from the harsher weather and the prying eyes of neighbors who mostly didn't like folks who looked different, like Abednego. He worked at the dairy along with Iris' uncle, and was allowed to stay in the cabin for free. Iris had heard some men down at the store make fun of "that stupid nigger living too close to the hundred year flood line," but she knew they were wrong. Her daddy had said that any plain fool knew a cool stream was better than air conditioning.

Hearing Iris' tapping noise at the window, Marvelous woke up, came to the window, pulled back the old flour sack curtains, and saw Iris' pale grinning face. Carefully timing her steps to her brother's inward snores, Marvelous tiptoed over the creaking floorboards. Once outside, she took Iris' hand and was pulled up behind her onto Gypsy's wide back.

"Won't we get in trouble?" Marvelous whispered.

"Be quiet and hang on," Iris instructed. "And don't let go." Although Iris was only a year older, and both were horse crazy, Iris had more riding experience. Marvelous put aside her fears, wrapped her slim arms around her friend's waist, and hung on.

The girls cut across the road to Iris' grandmother's

field. Atop the horse, they moved like a paddleboat, cutting a wake in the silver green grass. The wind blew in their hair as they cantered along, moving together to the horse's up and down rolling gait. Marvelous began to hum the tune, then sing the words.

"Bringing in the sheaves, bringing in the sheaves," her high voice sang into Iris' ears. Iris joined in.

"Bringing in the sheaves, we shall come rejoicing, bringing in the sheaves," they sang together as the mare's hooves rose up and through the sea of grass, leaving behind a wide, circular path. They were giggling their way through the second chorus of "Bringing in the Sheaves" when it happened. The horse stumbled in a gopher hole, causing the two riders to spin forward like a Ferris wheel knocked off its foundation. The twosome tumbled forward and landed all at once in the soft grass, knocking out their breaths. Gypsy recovered and bolted away. On the ground, Marvelous still clung to Iris, as she'd been instructed. As soon as Iris caught her breath, she spoke.

"You can let go," she said. Marvelous hadn't even realized they were now safe. She loosened her hands, sat up, and saw nothing but grass walls.

"Where Gypsy?" she asked. Before Iris could give her an answer, both girls heard a nearby rustle and a low growl. They reached for each other's hands and stood up to face danger together. The faces of two ugly German Shepherds appeared through the blades of tall grass, less than four feet away. Iris had seen those dogs before and remembered how mean her daddy had said they were. One of the dogs lunged forward, snarling. There was no point in running—the dogs had outrun and killed a terrier last year, her uncle said.

"Go away," Iris screamed and flung her arm out in a

hitting motion. The larger more aggressive dog only briefly recoiled, then moved in closer, lowering its head. She pushed Marvelous behind her, prepared for the worst. She felt her heart beat hard and strong. The ground seemed to vibrate. The pounding of hooves signaled Gypsy's arrival. The curs turned their heads to look around and saw nothing but the high grass before a pair of sharp hooves came down hard on their heads. They yelped and cowered and ran away as quickly as they'd appeared.

The girls began to shake and laugh with relief. Iris reached out to stroke Gypsy's silky muzzle, whispered thanks. Marvelous simply flung her arms around the horse's hot, damp chest. Iris bounced into a jump, then hoisted herself up on the mare's warm back. She pulled Marvelous up behind and set off across the field. They arrived back home well before the roosters begin to stir.

When she returned to her own bed after that first night ride, Iris fell asleep thinking of riding through the tall grass, high on her horse, safe from the world. In the mornings, she remembered the dogs and wondered if they were out roaming by themselves, or was someone out there? Around Grandmother's supper table with her father, mother and uncle talking all at once, she had often heard about the ignorant fools who tried to hurt Negroes. She heard about the cross burnings and bombings, always "up the road a ways" or "down yonder a piece." She worried about Abednego and Marvelous. Her grandmother assured her that no one would bother "our colored friends." The Tuckers were well respected and her granddaddy and his sons, William and Henry, were powerful men known for their strong tempers. They had once caught a horse thief trying to steal one of the foals. The man begged for them to call the sheriff, but the Tucker menfolk had already pulled out the horsewhip. The thief's screams echoed across the valley that night. Everyone knew not to cross the Tuckers. Iris had a hard time imagining someone would do so.

So her friendship with Marvelous grew that summer. Their nighttime rides remained their secret, bringing them closer as the summer of 1959 passed, until that last ride that Iris was certain had caused the calamity with Abednego and the Klan.

Chapter 42

ABEDNEGO

Abednego thought of Iris as he walked the circular path of the sculpture garden. She had the same quick smile, the dimple in her check, and lived the same charmed life she always had in some fancy house.

He glanced down below, saw an abundance of trees and the gentle curves of the Tennessee River. A few boats traveled up and down the water while above, cars sped over a bridge lined with flags. So much movement everywhere, not at all the way he had remembered it. What he really wanted was to find a nice quiet, private space to sit and rest. When he had almost completed the circular walk, he took a path that switched back to the right and led to a secluded courtyard area with a bench next to a sculpture.

He sat down on the bench, pulled Daisy Bates up to sit beside him, and studied the bronze of two people embracing. The shorter one's arms encircled the taller one's back. It made him think of Lola in the hay barn one July afternoon.

He had just finished unloading a truck of hay when he heard Lola call his name. He turned to see her coming under the archway. The light was behind her, penetrating the thin cloth of her white dress to illuminate the slender lines of her body. At the time, he thought she looked like an angel. He brushed off the hay from his shirt, walked towards her. She was carrying a pail.

He took it from her hand and set it down on the ground. He took her in his arms, pulled her in close until their bodies met as one. He cupped her head in his hand and kissed her long and deep, searched for her nutty flavor but tasted only blueberries. A voice called out for him, Henry. Lola pulled away and reached for the pail of berries.

"You can eat them right out of the bucket they so sweet," she said. Henry came around the corner and saw them together, oblivious; it seemed, to what he was interrupting. Lola said hello to him, then left in a hurry. Flustered at almost being caught in an embrace, Abednego had offered Henry a handful of berries.

"Blueberries," he said aloud. Daisy Bates pushed her head down against his lap. With the late afternoon sun caressing his face, and a shot of liquor in his belly, he decided to lie down to rest. Daisy scrambled to lie next to him, placing her head on his chest, so, he figured, she could hear him breathe. He stared at the sky for a few minutes, remembered the times he and Lola lay near the creek on a blanket watching the changing shapes in the clouds. He drifted off to sleep. Hearing her master's light snoring, the dog soon followed.

"Mr. Shepherd?"

Abednego opened his eyes and saw Iris.

"It's getting late," said Iris. "Xylia will be here before too long." Abednego yawned and stood up. He picked up the bag and Daisy's leash and followed her up the path towards the Bluff View Arts District. Daisy Bates trailed behind.

"I always felt my being friends with Marvelous might have caused the Klan to come for Abednego," said Iris. Although at least an hour must have passed, the woman was still talking about the past.

"They come for the man, not the girl," said Abednego. "Most likely they think he take a job away from a white man. That the way it was back then, down here."

"If Marvelous had been there at home with her brother, maybe they would have left him alone," Iris said.

"You fooling me?" asked Abednego. "They don't care nothing about no black child." Iris nodded.

"Like those young girls down in Birmingham they killed in the church bombing in sixty-three," Iris said. "I thought of Marvelous when that happened. And that was when I realized riding around with her after dark might not have been too smart."

"What?"

"Marvelous and I would sneak out and ride my horse at night. I didn't think anyone saw us until this one night. Someone set some mean dogs on us."

"Nights don't be safe down South back then for black folks," said Abednego. "Things happen." And what a fool you were to take my baby sister out in the dark, he wanted to say, but didn't. They continued in silence up the hill, which seemed much steeper going back up. She breathed almost as hard as he did, probably from all that cigarette smoking.

When they got back to the inn, Xylia was waiting on the porch in the swing. Iris insisted on taking them both to an early supper at the nearby restaurant. Before they went, Xylia called to check in at the store and learned that Mr. Shepherd's friend had not yet stopped by. Using Iris' phone, Abednego tried John's number again, but to no avail. The long afternoon, liquor, and talk of the past had left him tired and hungry. He let the two women lead him over to the Italian restaurant.

Over plates of steaming pasta and glasses of wine,

the women caught up with each other while he remained, for the most part, silent, lost in his own thoughts and a glass of burgundy. He was angry with himself for seeking out Iris. He had thought seeing her would bring back warm memories of his days on the farm with her, Marvelous, and Lola. Or perhaps she would steer him to Lola somehow. What he hadn't planned on was re-living the horrible night the Klan had ruined his life. He hadn't anticipated having her unload her guilt on him. And he hadn't expected to feel so irritated with the girl, now a woman, as he was at this very instant.

"Mr. Shepherd, would you have room for some dessert?" Iris asked. "Or we all could split one." Mr. Shepherd looked up from his spaghetti and shook his head.

"No, thanks, y'all go ahead. I'd like to try some of that Irish coffee, though." Iris ordered some tiramisu and coffees and turned to Mr. Shepherd.

"You've been so quiet all during dinner. Are you alright?" she asked. "I know it was a long walk."

"Feeling fine," he said. "I been thinking about what we discussed during our walk." She nodded eagerly.

"Yes?" she asked, displaying her annoying dimple.

"What would you be telling Abednego if you ever do see him?" he asked. She looked puzzled for a moment, and then spoke.

"I imagine I'd tell him I'm sorry for being friends with Marvelous." He nodded and took a sip of the Irish coffee the waiter had set on the table. The warmness of the drink soothed his throat. Xylia reached out and patted Iris' arm.

"You shouldn't have to apologize for your friendship," she said.

Abednego took another sip of the hot drink and

nodded in agreement. Either it was hearing Iris' apology, or the liquor in the coffee, but he began to feel better towards her.

After dinner, they went back to the inn where Abednego tried once again to reach John. There was no answer. He had never showed up at Elmwood's. Iris insisted that Mr. Shepherd and Xylia had to spend the night; she had two free rooms and she wanted them to stay for her blueberry pancakes the next morning. Xylia felt she had to get back home in case Ernie called. She urged Abednego to stay the night at the inn. After all, he didn't have to get up and open the store the next day.

Later, after Xylia had driven off, Iris showed Abednego to a room on the first floor. She tried to tell him something about a painting, and he struggled to appear like he was listening. He was simply too tired for her incessant talking. Saying he was exhausted, he wished her a good night and closed the door.

He reached into the duffel bag for his flask and sat down on the faded green, satin brocade upholstered chair to enjoy a nightcap before turning in. Daisy Bates curled up at the foot of the bed when her master climbed into the Lincoln-style bed.

Abednego lay between the cool, clean sheets, looked up at the high dark, wooden headboard. He let his hand linger on the smooth surface of the satin-trimmed bedspread. He glanced up at a painting above the bed, a pleasant blur of colors from his perspective. The warm, familiar feeling brought on by the nightcap washed over his chest. With a big grin on his face, he fell asleep.

Chapter 43

XYLIA

When Xylia returned home, the house seemed emptier than ever. So when her phone rang shortly after she got in from her evening with Iris and Mr. Shepherd, she hurried over to pick it up, thinking it was Ernie calling from camp.

"Hello?" she said, but no one spoke. "Ernie? Is that you?" Ernie had never been good on the phone, so she stayed quiet for a moment, allowing him a chance to speak. Perhaps his counselor was there coaching him along. A few moments later, she heard a voice, not Ernie's. A muffled male voice spoke. "Stay away from the nigger."

Xylia was stunned. She didn't have a chance to reply before the line went dead. After she hung up, she got angrier and angrier the more she thought about it. She sat by the phone daring the anonymous caller to ring her up again. She'd spend her time with whoever she wanted, especially Mr. Shepherd, who had been nothing but a gentleman. How dare anyone call her like this! Perhaps it was a prankster, but she didn't have to put up with it. She would call Sheriff Young the next day or maybe not. In her heart, she knew it was most likely Earl Williams. Always making trouble. She would ignore it.

Chapter 44

IRIS

Up in Chattanooga at the bed and breakfast, while most of her guests slept, Iris sat awake thinking of her days as a girl with Marvelous. Sitting in her small second floor apartment over the B &B, Iris pulled out a box of pictures from her days in Taylor's Crossing. She found one of Marvelous and her aboard Gypsy.

Always petite and spunky, Marvelous was behind Iris, facing the opposite direction. Her hands were on her hips, and she was trying her best to look puzzled. Iris remembered that day. They were trying stunt moves on the horse and had asked Abednego to snap some shots. In another photo, Marvelous was on the horse, lying down with her hands clasping the horse's neck, her dark curls mingled with the mare's mane. Their childhood days at the farm had been good ones until the night the Klan had ruined it all.

Afterwards, Iris' father speculated as to why the Klan had gone to the trouble to get rid of a single, colored man who lived in their community. Iris always felt it was because of her friendship with Marvelous. Her brother had tried to warn her. She had ignored him.

She had not really thought much about her and Marvelous being different colors until one afternoon in Ringgold when they had ridden along with Abednego and Henry to pick up some feed. While they were waiting in the truck, they both got thirsty and climbed out to find some water. The fountain marked "colored" was broken, so Iris encouraged Marvelous to drink out of the "whites" fountain. After some urging, and since no one was around, Marvelous did so. Someone inside the feed store must have seen her; later Abednego scolded her and told her not to cause trouble. And the next day, Iris's older brother Lawson had lectured her on keeping her distance from Marvelous in town. His friends had teased him and called him a nigger lover. He urged her to stop hanging out with Marvelous. Once again, she didn't listen.

She snuffed out her cigarette, picked up the photo of her and Marvelous doing the backwards stunt on Gypsy, and pinned it to her bulletin board. Yes, she had loved her friend Marvelous, and always would.

Chapter 45

MARVELOUS
New Orleans, Louisiana

It was going to be another hot, sultry day in New Orleans, Marvelous thought as she opened the back door of her townhome. It was only eight in the morning, yet the humidity and heat pressed down on her.

She had spent the night tossing and thinking what nerve her brother Abednego had not checking in with her. So typical of Abednego.

Putting on her tee shirt, Bermuda shorts and walking shoes, she scolded herself for sending her older brother off on a road trip. She locked the door behind her and set out for her morning walk down Freret Street towards Tulane and Audubon Park. New Orleans would now be their new home, thanks to her plan for the two of them to move south to warmer weather, mostly for Abednego's benefit since he suffered in the cold winters up North. She didn't know what was worse, the pain in his knee, or the pain in his heart. His grown children avoided him on account of his years of drinking and his uneven temperament. On some days he brooded for no apparent reason and was quick to anger. She had always thought it was because of what the Klan had done to him. His wife, God rest her soul, had tolerated him and stuck by his side until she died of cancer a year ago. He had cut back on his drinking but had not quit, despite Marvelous' warnings about his high blood pressure and alcohol. In the last several months, he seemed lost in his thoughts most of the time and had, blessedly, even lost his terrible temper somewhere along the way. She was the only one who noticed; his own children didn't seem to have time for him.

When she'd heard about the job opening in New Orleans, she'd applied immediately and been hired. She was an experienced and skilled surgical nurse, and she had never had trouble finding work. In her early sixties, she was compact like her brother, but unlike him, she was in top shape. She planned to work as long as she could. She had to save for retirement. Her new job didn't begin for another week, but she had flown down ahead of her brother to meet the moving truck at their new place. She cleaned up their new townhome and was already half unpacked.

The road trip had been her brother's idea. He said the plane ride would be too much with his high blood pressure and knees. And there was that dog—he was afraid she would be miserable in the airplane carry-on bag. Ever since his wife had died, he treated that dog of his like a baby. She worried it wasn't a good idea to send her brother off in a relic of a car, but he finally convinced her when he offered to carry her breakable box of collectible china horses safely in the trunk. After all, the movers couldn't be trusted with some things. God only knew where Abednego was now and when he'd get to New Orleans. Wasn't it just like a man to be running off somewhere, never being where he was supposed to be?

Even under the shade of the live oaks at Audubon Park, Marvelous found herself wiping the sweat off her forehead with the back of her hand. It was getting hotter, so she decided it was time to head back to her air-conditioned home.

As soon as she got in, she made herself a cup of tea and some whole wheat cinnamon toast and sat down to unpack some of her brother's things. He'd never get around to it. She cut through the tape to open one of the boxes. Inside were some fishing magazines, some old watches, a box of photos, and a wire ring notebook. She picked up the notebook and flipped it open. It appeared to be some kind of fishing diary. Fish caught, time and place, and bait used. On the last page there were two words: Lola and Taylor's Crossing. And then she knew where he was.

Thinking of that last night in Taylor's Crossing, she remembered it all, and shivered. Why on earth would Abednego want to go and stir up trouble? God only knew. She grabbed up several changes of clothes, threw them into a suitcase, and headed outside to her car.

Chapter 46

ABEDNEGO

He awoke to the smell of coffee and some muffled voices out in the hall. Until Daisy Bates whimpered from underneath the bed, he couldn't exactly remember where he was. He pushed away the fancy bedspread and swung his legs around to the floor.

"You'll have to wait a minute, Daisy Bates, my bladder's worse than yours," he said. After going to the bathroom and slipping into the same pants he'd worn the day before, Abednego snapped on Daisy's leash and took her out the door leading directly from his room to a small side yard filled with lavender hydrangeas and purple irises. He watched his dog sniffing around under the bushes and tried to let the fog lift off his mind. He wasn't much of a morning person and wanted to get a shower before having to face the day, not to mention the talkative Iris. After Daisy had done her business, he returned to his room and stepped into a steaming shower. It was only when he finished and sat down on the bench at the end of his bed to put on his pants and shoes that he really saw clearly the framed print on the south wall that Iris mentioned the night before.

In the picture, a black man faced an angry bull that had been captured in a narrow bull pen. In his left hand, hidden behind his back, the man held a copper ring, anticipating the right moment to put it into the bull's red nostrils.

Astonished by what he was seeing, Abednego got up from the bench, walked closer to study the picture. He stared at the man's face, his compact body, and the muscles in his forearms and biceps. The young man in the picture had no fear. He was confident in his ability to carry out a job meant for several men, a job that many men would not attempt, even with help. The man in the picture was like the bull, full of himself. Unbroken. And then he knew. He was seeing himself as a young man, at nineteen.

Whoever had painted it had known him then, the person he was before the Klan had tried to humiliate him. Looking at the picture, seeing his old self, Abednego stood a little taller, threw his shoulders back, and felt reinvigorated.

He quickly finished getting dressed, left the room and went down the hall tugging Daisy Bates along behind him. He found Iris in her office on the phone taking some reservations. He waited impatiently until she hung up.

"Good morning, Mr. Shepherd. I trust you slept well," she said. He didn't even bother with the pleasantries.

"Who painted that picture in my room?" he asked. "The one with the bull?" She smiled.

"I thought you'd like it. I don't know, but you can ask at the gallery a few doors down. They don't open till ten. Why don't you let Daisy Bates rest right here in my office while you go into the dining room and have some of those blueberry pancakes I promised?" He nodded and followed the aroma of coffee, bacon and pancakes into the dining area where several other guests were already enjoying their breakfasts. The hostess seated him alone at a table with a view of the Tennessee River.

While he drank his coffee and waited for his food,

he looked around the room at his fellow travelers. A middle-aged black couple looked over tourist brochures while they talked and ate. A pair of white women discussed biscuit recipes with the intensity of men talking football teams. When the young waitress delivered his food, he was surprised to find himself eagerly digging into the steaming stack of pancakes and warm maple syrup. He hadn't had much of an appetite lately. He gazed out on the river where a barge floated by and let the buttery cakes melt in his mouth. For the first time in many months, he felt full of purpose.

After giving Daisy her heart medicine, Abednego was antsy to get over to the art gallery Iris had pointed out. She still needed to check out some guests and urged him to go ahead and walk over alone. She didn't think pets were allowed.

He left Daisy with her and returned to his room. He glanced at the grandfather clock in the corner. It was nearly ten, almost time to take a nip. When he turned to get his duffle bag, his eyes drifted up to see the painting of himself. He hesitated.

As a young man, he tried alcohol. He never really drank much, partly because he couldn't afford it. He also found he was sharper without it, and he liked to keep his head clear and alert when he dealt with the farm animals. Horses and cattle could be unpredictable. He liked being able to think on his feet when he was around them. Of course back then he hadn't had much need to drink. Life on the farm in the 1950's had been simple and clear cut. He was expected to work long and hard hours, which he did, in exchange for a meager salary, enough to cover his expenses and save a little for the future, which he'd hoped one day would include a woman. And once he'd found Lola, his head and heart had been so full of her he never even thought about drinking. Being with her left him heady; she was enough.

After that night up on Taylor's Ridge, he started. At first, during the weeks when he wore the cast and lay on the couch at his mother's home, he drank to kill the pain. After the cast came off, and when he was finally able to walk again and take the bus north, he drank when he had the money. When he was hired on at the steel mill to work on the melting crew, drinking came with the territory. He joined the other men at night when they gathered at a nearby bar after work. By the time he met and married his wife, drinking heavily was part of his daily routine.

Now, staring at the confident young man facing the bull, he wanted to be that person again. He wasn't foolish enough to expect he could suddenly be nineteen again, but cutting back on his drinking was a start. He put the duffle bag away, took one last look at the painting, and headed out.

Leaving the inn, he walked down the sidewalk up the slight incline that led to a row of shops and galleries in the ivy-covered, two story buildings. The one he was looking for, The Wandering Artist, was in the center of the block. Its display windows were filled with regional scenes: the Tennessee River, Lookout Mountain, Missionary Ridge, and the Great Smoky Mountains. He stepped inside and was greeted by the owner, a heavyset, bearded gentleman who asked if he needed help. Mr. Shepherd described the print over his bed at Iris' inn.

"Oh, you must be referring to the prints by Miss Banks. She's one of our best known regional artists," he said. "You'll love this." He led Abednego toward a narrow room in the back of the shop. When Abednego stepped over the threshold, he had to stop and take a breath.

The entire room was filled with farm scenes that looked exactly like Taylor's Crossing as he had remembered it from the 50's except for the people who populated the scenes. Black and whites appeared side-by-side engaged in life. In a meadow, families picnicked together under the trees, laughing and sharing food. In another scene, three little girls, two black and one white, sat by a stream watching turtles surface. In another print, two young couples walked down a dirt road; one pair was black, the other white. The women wore flowered button-up dresses with narrow waists, the kind he had remembered Lola wearing. The girls in the painting appeared to be laughing, happily oblivious to the Jim Crow world in which they lived. Taylor's Ridge loomed in the background. The picture that most drew his eye was a larger one featuring a single subject. A young, dark woman stood in the center of an immense flower field, an ivory cloth bag filled with flowers slung over her shoulder and riding on her hip. She wasn't picking anything, but instead stared off into the distance at something outside the realm of the picture. Abednego only had to look at it a moment until he was certain it was Lola. He turned to the gallery owner.

"Can you tell me where to find the woman who painted these pictures?"

"Miss Banks? She's usually at her studio in the Southside area."

"Where's that?" asked Abednego.

"Down near the Choo-Choo. She won't be there today. Most of the artists are up at the art festival in Gatlinburg. Today's the last day. Were you interested in purchasing one of the prints? I have them framed and unframed." Mr. Shepherd pointed to the one of Lola in the cotton field.

"Unframed. I'm traveling," he said. While he waited for the owner to wrap up the print, he thought about his last conversation with Lola's cousin, John, and remembered he'd said something about an art show. He hadn't paid much attention because he didn't know Lola was an artist. It all made sense: her slender, delicate hands, always too fine for outdoor work, her eyes always focusing on something that caught her eye.

When the shop owner told him it would be $75, Abednego did not hesitate, even though that left him only $30 in his wallet. If it had cost a hundred, he would have bought it. He paid the shop owner for the print, got him to write down the phone number and address of Lola's studio. If he couldn't see her, he could see where she had re-created an idealized version of the world they had known together.

When he returned to the inn, Iris was busy supervising the housekeeper and checking out guests. She had but a brief time between chores, explaining that Xylia was coming to pick him up at noon. She apologized for being so busy and said she'd try to come down to Taylor's Crossing a little later.

He went back to his room and dialed up John once more, to no avail. He collected Daisy Bates and his things, stopped by the office to turn in the key. He got a city map from Iris, told her where he was headed, on foot.

"That's too far. I'd take you but the plumber is coming back later. Why don't you wait for Xylia? She'll be here in a little while."

"Time is something I don't be having much of," he explained. "Tell her she can pick me up at Southside Studios." Despite her protests, he turned and walked past a couple waiting to check out.

"It's almost two miles away," Iris called after him. Abednego turned and waved as he walked out the door.

"I'm fine. Thanks for everything," he said.

Abednego moved slowly down the hill, passing over the hot sidewalks and streets, stopping occasionally on the pretense of letting Daisy Bates rest. He thought about picking up his pace but decided against it. It was just too hot. He could feel the pressure in his head, hear his heart beating in his ears. He might be old, but he was no fool. He didn't want to keel over with a stroke when he was so close to finding Lola.

He finally reached Broad Street. Two young black women coming out of a coffee shop stopped to coo at Daisy Bates. He asked them how far it was to the Southside Studios, and they offered to take him.

Of course he should have known better, he scolded himself once inside their compact "Jesus Mobile." Gospel music blared from the speakers, and they talked about a revival their church was having that evening. He was just fine with reading scripture on his own time, which wasn't too often. He didn't do revivals. The one time he had, he felt his head spinning and had to go out back of the tent and turn to the comfort of his bottle. He wondered what the preacher would have thought about that turn of events.

He let his hand slip into his bag and run along the hard edges of his flask. He wanted to take a nip. He did not. They would probably smell it and lecture him on the evils of alcohol. When they pulled up outside the warehouse building that was the gallery, the girls made no move to let him out. They both turned around in their seats and stared at him.

"Are you saved?" asked the one with the lip-glossed

mouth who sat in the passenger seat.

"If you're not, we'll help you get saved," said the driver, the one with the intense, dark eyes.

He could fight fire with fire.

"I like to be," he said. "Give me some of them papers. I'm going to bring all my friends to your meeting." They shrieked "hallelujah" and handed him a handful of flyers. After he and Daisy had climbed out, the two women yelled, "Goodbye, brother, see you tonight." He nodded, waved jauntily at them with his left hand, keeping his right hand behind his back with fingers crossed.

Using his cane and pulling Daisy Bates along behind, it took a full five minutes to negotiate the three flights of stairs that led to the loft—three to force his troublesome knee up the steep stairs, two to stop and take a shot. The Jesus freak sisters had made him nervous, and he sought some peace and quiet—about an ounce of it, just enough to get him through today. After the warm flush had passed over his chest, he continued upward until he reached the third floor.

At the top, he opened a fire door and entered into a huge open area filled with daylight from a battery of windows along two walls. There appeared to be several stations set up in the room with glass brick walls in-between to allow the light to wash over all. He had not a clue which area was Lola's space and stopped to ask the room's sole occupant, a young mustached man who was working on a charcoal still life.

"Lola's not here," he said.

"I see that," said Abednego. "I just want to see where she works. Lola and I, we go way back. You know her?" The mustached man nodded.

"What she like?" Abednego asked.

"I thought you said you know her."

"I do. Hadn't seen her in a while. Which spot she work in?" The man pointed to the cubicle at the end of the room.

"Over there. She's probably not going to come here today. She usually shows her stuff on the weekend."

"Thank you," Abednego replied, and headed towards her cubicle with Daisy Bates trailing along behind him.

"Hey mister, dogs aren't really allowed up here. You should tie her up outside. The landlord will fine us if he sees her." Abednego leaned down and scooped up Daisy, plopped her into the duffle bag, and zipped it up, leaving her head showing.

"You see a dog?" he asked.

"Yes."

"No, what you seeing is a stuffed animal in a bag." The artist shook his head and turned his back on Abednego.

When he walked into her work area, Abednego went over to an easel where she had sketched out a scene—a weathered barn he recognized from Ridgeway Road. Three girls fussed over a white pony, braiding its mane and tail and combing its coat. A black man stood over to the side, observing. Abednego placed his bag containing Daisy on the floor along with his cane and went to Lola's chair. He sat down in front of the easel he knew was hers. He allowed his fingers to trail over the lids of the acrylic paints—he'd never seen so many yellows, greens, blues and reds--before coming to her collection of brushes. Between his thumb and forefinger, he stroked the bristles of the plumpest brush and thought of her. He closed his eyes and felt he was with her again sitting on his back porch. He imagined her encircled in his arms and hummed their song,

"Sleepy Time Down South." Absorbed in his memories, he became unaware of time. At first he did not hear the voice that spoke.

"Abednego? Abednego?" He opened his eyes, turned around, and saw her. The afternoon sun played on the softened angles of her face, which she quickly covered with her hands—her long, delicate artist hands that he remembered from the last time he had held them in his, more than fifty years ago.

Chapter 47

LOLA

Lola looked at the worn out man sitting in her cherry wood chair and could not believe it was Abednego. The silver curls, the look of sadness on his face, this was not how she had thought of him over the passing years. She wanted to scream, where did you run off to, but all she said was, "Abednego Harris, what are you doing here playing with my brushes?"

Abednego laughed, the full, rich sound that she remembered, a laugh that seemed out of place coming from such a tired-looking man. He rose up and slowly moved toward her, held out his arms. And although she was not sure she wanted to, she hugged him.

"Lola, Lola, Lola. You sweet as ever," he said. She smelled the alcohol and quickly stepped back. No wonder he had aged so much.

"What are you doing here?" she asked

"Just passing through," he replied. "Had to look you up."

"What's your hurry?" she asked.

"Hurry? Ain't in that big a rush."

"I'll say. You waited half a century to look me up." Her voice had an edge to it when she spoke. She saw him clinch his fist when she said it. Perhaps she had hurt him, but not as much as he had hurt her so long ago by leaving her behind and never sending her a single letter. "How'd you find me?"

"The bull painting." She nodded.

"I always hoped you might see it somewhere one day," she said. Out of the corner of her eye she saw something moving by her chair. She glanced down to see a wriggling duffle bag with a dog's head poking out.

"Who's your friend there?" she asked.

"Daisy Bates," Abednego said. He moved over to the bag, reached down and unzipped it to pull out the dog, inadvertently revealing the silver flask in the process. Daisy jumped out and ran over to sniff Lola. She stooped down to pet her, and the dog licked her hand. Lola caressed the dog with her long fingers. Abednego reached into the bag and pulled out the flask.

"Care for a drink?"

Lola shook her head no.

"You know I never drank, Abednego Harris. And from the looks of you, you shouldn't either."

"Little nip is all," he said, and took a sip. As she watched him drink, she saw his shoulders let down. He tucked the flask back in the duffle. Lola walked over to a cabinet under the windows and pulled out some papers. She tucked them into her canvas briefcase.

"We left the show early when I sold all my prints. I've got a few minutes till Sebastian comes. Let's go downstairs, and I'll get a drink. A Coke." Gathering his bag, dog and cane, Abednego followed her down the stairs to the cool lobby.

As she watched his labored steps, she could not believe this was the strong man who had been the talk of the valley in his day. She caught him glancing at her. To be fair, she wondered what he was thinking of her rounded, fuller body, the furrows that had etched into her brow. The puppet lines that had appeared below the corners of her lips? She was, after all, almost seventy. So many years had passed since she'd seen him!

They walked over to a soft drink machine where Abednego fed in a dollar and change to buy her a Coke. It clattered down the chute, and he handed her the cold bottle.

By the soothing water sculpture in the lobby, they sat across from each other in two comfortable chairs. As she sipped delicate sips from her Coke, he smiled at her. She smiled right back.

"What happened to you, Abednego Harris?" she asked. He shrugged.

"After the Klan beat me up, and I had to leave the valley, I headed up North and went to work in a steel mill. Worked the melting crew."

"What's that?"

"The most dangerous work, pouring molten steel," Abednego said, pointing to a scar on his left arm.

"You were a dairy worker, good with animals. No experience with steel. Why'd they hire you?"

"Reckon on account I was black, strong, and easy to replace. After a while, I married and had myself three kids. Worked there all my adult life, till my luck turn."

"Your legs?"

"Yes, the steel spill and burn right through my pants." Abednego rubbed his knees as he spoke. "Between them burns and the Klan breaking my knee, I had myself four surgeries. Me and pain, we know each other on a first name basis. This help." He lifted up his flask but did not take another drink. "A year ago Sarah pass. Now I be headed south to live with my baby sister. You remember Marvelous?"

"Turtle girl? Yes I do."

"Anyway, that's what happen."

"All fascinating, Abednego Shepherd. All I really was asking is what happened to you back in 1959? I never heard a word from you, not one word."

"I wrote you letters. Plenty of them. Sent them to the address John gave me."

"I never got a single one," said Lola. "Sounds like he gave you the wrong address."

"If I find him, I give him a piece of my mind about that."

"You'd have to go to Chicago. John and Rose are up there visiting their daughter."

"He told me to swing by on the way to New Orleans. Maybe he forget?'

"Maybe," said Lola. "Like he forgot to give you the right address in Rome."

"I know they was afraid for you after I tell them what the Klan say when they beat me up." Abednego remembered the ugly words spoken from behind the white hood that night. "They tell me, if you care about your little nigger gal stay away from the valley." Abednego was silent for a moment. His face grew grim. "They call you a whore. Say they kill you if I return." He put his head down, let his shoulders slump, a gesture that spoke to Lola. He was angry, defeated and hopeless, all at the same time. She rose from her chair and bent down over him. She brushed his hand with her fingers, took his hand in hers.

"Oh Bing. You went away to keep me safe."

Chapter 48

ABEDNEGO

Abednego grasped the warm hand, the artist's hand, of the girl he had long ago left behind. He looked up at her face. She smiled right back with confident eyes he hadn't remembered from before. He saw the lines etched into her skin, markers of all she had been through in a lifetime. Still, she stood tall, and to his mind had mellowed into a softer, rounder version of the girl he had known. Time had only made her more beautiful. No wonder she was married to this Sebastian fellow. Why had he assumed she had no man? He heard a deep voice coming from behind them.

"Mama?" Lola pulled her hand away from Abednego's. He looked up to see a tall, mocha-colored man, who looked to be in his late 40's. "I've loaded up everything. The van is parked in a temporary loading zone, so we have to hurry."

"Abednego, this is my son, Sebastian. Son, remember my bull painting? This is the man." Abednego could see Sebastian's mind working to make the connection between the old man standing before him and the bull handler in the painting. Abednego stepped forward and offered his hand.

"Good to meet you," he said. He squeezed the young man's hand extra hard to show his strength. He stared into Sebastian's eyes, green. With those eyes and his skin, his father could have been white. Sebastian stared right back.

"You from Taylor's Crossing?"

"Lived there when I was younger," Abednego replied.

"Sebastian, what time did you tell the Whittakers we'd be there?" Lola said. Sebastian let go of Abednego's hand.

"Six thirty," he answered. "I'll wait in the van. I don't want to get a ticket. Nice meeting you, Sir." He nodded his head and walked out the door.

"Abednego, we have to head up the mountain for an artists' reception," Lola said. "I'm afraid I have to go home and change first." Abednego had just found her. He was not ready to let her go.

"What about supper?" he blurted out, and then he felt foolish. She was probably going to dinner with her husband, Sebastian's father. She smiled at him.

"Not tonight. The Whittakers are some of my best patrons."

"Your old man, he don't like you eating with other men?" Abednego said. She laughed.

"I don't have an old man," she answered. Abednego felt his body lighten as she said it.

"When can I see you?" he said.

"I've got to work with Sebastian to choose the paintings for the fall show in Gatlinburg."

"You have to eat, don't you?" Abednego said.

"I usually take a half hour for lunch. I go grab a sandwich down the street at the Deli," she admitted.

"I'll meet you right here at noon tomorrow and we can go together."

"Twelve thirty," she said.

"Just the two of us," Abednego said. Lola nodded.

"As cute as she is, I think Daisy won't be allowed in a restaurant." She tossed him a wave with her still lovely hand and headed for the door. Abednego sat down in the chair and pulled Daisy Bates out of the bag and into his lap. He petted her furry head.

"Well, gal, look like I have a date." She wagged her tail. He stroked her back and whispered a prayer.

"Sweet Jesus, thank you for bringing me back to Lola." Daisy sat up and licked his face. Sometimes he could swear the dog knew exactly what he was saying.

Chapter 49

LOLA

On the winding road leading up the mountain, Sebastian asked Lola about Abednego.

"Bing, he was the one I had hoped to marry," said Lola.

"Wasn't he too old for you?"

"At the time, he was nineteen, and I was seventeen. He just looks older. He's had a hard life compared to me."

"He didn't have his son for his manager." Sebastian winked as he said it.

"True," said Lola. "Someone's got to handle the business end while I focus on my art." Lola felt grateful for his help, although sometimes she wished he would spend more time on his own life. He had still not found the right woman to marry.

They arrived at the circular driveway of the Whitakers' French manor-style home, a mansion really. By the cars parked on the road, she could see a crowd was already gathered. Sebastian dropped her off at the front door. She exited the car and stood waiting for him on the front porch so he could escort her in, which was just as well. She needed to collect her thoughts about Abednego before she had to meet and greet.

After all these years, she had assumed her first love was dead or uninterested. She was surprised at how their worlds were so different. He had spent his life doing one sort of physical labor or another while her painting took her to the world of the moneyed, those who appreciated her work and could afford to pay for it. Oddly enough, she found herself intrigued by Abednego. She was not sure, though, if it was just her memory of him. The current version of her old boyfriend--silver curls and melancholy expression--was not someone she would normally find herself attracted to. To be certain, his body showed the age of a man who had experienced a difficult life, yet this was not the issue. She was not sure she wanted to reconnect with him, or the painful past she had long ago put behind. These days, all of her energy was channeled into her art. She had not had the time or the inclination for a man for at least a decade, and certainly not one who would open a Pandora's Box of bad memories. But hadn't there been good memories too? Like the daisy ring he slipped on her finger when he proposed? The thought of it brought a smile to her face. She still kept it in her Bible, although now it was mostly disintegrated, dried flakes.

A cacophony of voices interrupted her reflection. The front door had opened, revealing Ginger, Mrs. Whittaker's perky assistant.

"Come on in Miss Banks," said Ginger. "Mrs. Whitaker wants you to meet the new chairman of the Arts Council."

"I was waiting for my son," said Lola.

"He'll find you, they're all dying to meet you," Ginger said, taking her by the arm and leading her inside to the foyer where an elegant candelabra flickered candlelight against a seaside mural. Ahead she saw a crowd waiting to shake hands with "Tennessee's most revered artist" as the invitation had read. She lifted up her head and flowed into the waiting crowd of well-wishers and potential buyers.

Later that night, back in her Missionary Ridge cottage, Lola contemplated the day's events. Although the evening at the Whittakers had gone well and resulted in two commissions for paintings and sales of other works, she felt restless and unsure. She paced the hard wood floor of her small home, threw on a light floral robe, poured herself a glass of milk, and grabbed a shiny red apple and a paring knife. Carrying her snack, she retreated to her small screened-in porch.

The night air and its scents played against her thoughts. The sweet fragrance of shrubs reminded her of blackberry blooms and summer nights with Abednego in the pasture, of the countless stars in the indigo sky. How naïve she had been, how she had worried about Bing hurting her with his "snake" when the real threat was the "gentleman" she worked for.

She had never told anyone the truth about Sewell Buttrill, not even her son. She had let him believe Lucky was his father.

She took a sip of the cool milk and sliced the firm apple into four quarters. She thought of Lucky and his pocket knife, of the time they had visited Miss Zora Neale Hurston. He'd given her an apple slice. What was it Miss Zora Neale had said that day about being sick? Lola crunched down on a crisp slice of apple, felt its satisfying snap against her front teeth. She could almost see Miss Zora Neale outlined in the dim light filtering through the gauzy curtained window. She had spoken in a raspy and low voice. "No, agony like bearing an untold story inside you." Meeting Miss Zora Neale that day had inspired Lola to follow her passion. Perhaps she needed to mine these words for more meaning. Why would they have come to her now, when Abednego had come back into her life?

She walked back inside and dialed her son on the phone.

"Sebastian, change of plan for tomorrow. One of the commissions is for a scene of Taylor's Ridge. Could you postpone that meeting with the gallery owner? I need to drive out to Ringgold to do some field sketches."

Chapter 50

ABEDNEGO

As Xylia promised, she picked up Abednego from Iris' bed and breakfast that evening. Since the B & B was full, he would have to sleep at his friend's place, he told her.

"Okay, just tell me how to get there," said Xylia. "Down in Crystal Springs, isn't it?" Abednego nodded.

"Only one problem, I think he out of town." Xylia exited off the interstate and turned left towards Ringgold.

"Want to try again?" she asked as she pulled out her cell phone and handed it to him. "I need to get a few things at the drug store." While she went in to shop, he tried the phone number he had. There was no answer. Xylia returned carrying two bags.

"Any luck?" she asked.

"No," he said. "Maybe just drop me off at the little motel on the right, the one with the yellow sign."

"And let you spend perfectly good money when I have a spare room? Ernie's at camp. You can stay in his room." She smiled as she spoke.

"I don't know, Miss Xylia," he said. "Hate to cause trouble."

"You won't," she said matter-of-factly. "We're both too old." They laughed at the same time.

"Ma'am, folks talk," he said, thinking about the overly curious men who had asked too many questions at the store when he first arrived.

"Let them talk," she said. "Maybe it will get more customers into the store. Elmwood's new marketing plan."

"Might could work," he said. "Daisy and I gonna stay with you."

As soon as they arrived at Xylia's house, and as she was unlocking the door, she hastened to answer the sound of a ringing phone. "Yes, he's here," she said. She handed the receiver to Abednego. He was surprised to hear Lola's voice.

"What time? Sure. I be at Elmwood's right on the highway. I guess you remember. See you then. Night." He gently placed the receiver on the cradle. Xylia stood in the doorway putting a clean case on a plump pillow.

"Want to see your room?" she asked. Abednego and his dog followed her to Ernie's room. The walls were plastered with his crayon drawings. She handed Abednego the pillow and some clean towels. "Your friend can sleep over there in the corner." Abednego took the pillow and towels from her.

"Thank you, Ma'am. I need to tell you something."

"You need some water or something? You hungry?" she asked.

"No, I'm fine," Abednego said. "You been real good to me. I think you deserve to know the truth, as long as you keep it a secret."

"I'm good with secrets."

"Them old men yesterday? Remember they talk about the boy who was good with bulls and colts? That was me, Abednego Harris. The Klan run me off in fifty-nine. I don't want to let on who I am. Some of them Klan could still be alive."

Xylia lowered her eyes, shook her head back and

forth. Abednego knew his lying had disappointed her. He felt ashamed.

"What they did to you? It was a terrible thing," she said. "I'm sorry."

"You're not mad?" he asked.

"No. I wondered why anyone would come all the way out here just to fish the creek with the lake just up the road. Guess your fish story was just that," Xylia said. Abednego chuckled. "So why did you come back here?"

"To see my friend John. Thought he help me find a gal I know."

Xylia nodded. "The one who just called?"

"Yes, Ma'am."

"Then you'll be needing to get your beauty sleep, Mr. Shepherd. Or shall I call you Harris?"

"Let's keep it Shepherd for the time being," he said.

"I'm all tuckered out myself," she said. "Good night." She pulled the door closed behind her.

Chapter 51

LOLA

The next morning in the shower, Lola shaved her legs and washed her hair, something she usually did on Wednesday and Saturday nights. Wrapped in a towel and standing in front of a mirror, she scrutinized her face. The lines looked deeper this morning. Perhaps they really weren't. She carefully applied a moisturizer and topped it off with some matte powder and a rose-toned lip gloss. She put a generous dab of Jergens lotion on her hands, and spritzed on some orange-scented cologne. Going to her closet, she chose a light aqua sweater and darker teal pants that complemented her skin. Now that she had decided to see him again, she might as well look good.

Driving down the road to Taylor's Crossing, she looked up at the ridge and remembered summer nights when she had seen white orbs of light zigzagging down the ridge road to the valley. She never thought much about the car headlights until after the Klan attack on Bing. After that, she always imagined the headlights were from Klan caravans on the way home after one of their hate missions. She hadn't been back to the valley in several years except in daylight, and only to sketch scenes for her work. To be on the safe side, she'd always brought along her son. This time she had not. She knew with Abednego, she'd be safe.

Chapter 52

ABEDNEGO

As he climbed into Lola's van, Daisy Bates in tow, Abednego glanced back to see Xylia peeking through the store window. She gave him an airy wave. He waved back and turned to Lola. He inhaled her scent. The almond smell he remembered from days past, and oranges?

"Good morning, Queen of Oranges," he said. "I like me a slice." Lola responded with a light slap to his wrist.

"Don't you get fresh with me, Bing Harris." He laughed.

"Why not, Miss Lola? Yesterday I feel like I had a foot in the grave. With you today, my feet be dancing."

"You stop it, now," she said, in a low serious voice. He knew she didn't mean it.

"Okay, I gonna try to act like a man who ain't just seen the woman he been thinking of most of his life."

"A woman who right now needs directions. Is this where we turn?" She pointed left towards the next intersection. "Last time I was down here it looked different. They put some new houses up."

"Right here turn left, then down here a ways, turn left."

"One step at a time," Lola replied. As they drove past a row of cedars, Abednego stared at the end of a long driveway.

"Slow down right here. Ain't that where I first saw

you picking daffodils? That the old Buttrill place?"

"Some of the trees are gone, but the driveway looks the same, except it's paved," she answered. The van continued its slow crawl down the road. Lola pointed to a two-story house on the right that sat just beyond a towering hickory.

"Look, wasn't your cabin there?" asked Lola.

"Pull up the driveway," Abednego said. Lola slowed down and steered the van to the side of the road. She turned on her flashers.

"I'll leave it in the road. These folks down here like to shoot first and ask questions later," she said. "You go ahead and get out and look." Abednego opened the car door and almost stepped off into a ditch. He stumbled and nearly fell down. He quickly recovered and started to limp in an exaggerated fashion.

"Won't nobody shoot a cripple," he said.

"Ha," said Lola. "Don't bet on it. You're in stand-your-ground country now." Leaving Lola behind, and using his cane, he limped down the driveway past the front porch, an area covered with kids' toys and cans of paint, and a fat white kitten curled up in a ball, oblivious to all except the warm sun bathing its back. Abednego passed under the broad limbs of the tree where he'd carved their initials a half a century before. He moved closer to the wide trunk and searched. He pulled his eyeglasses out of his pocket and ran his fingers along the tree bark. One part of the tree was smoother, like a scar grown over a patch of skin. He was certain this was where the initials had been.

"Lola, come over here," he yelled out. "I see it." He continued to hold his hands over the spot, remembering the days they had spent near this very tree, fishing and talking and playing music. Lola came up behind him.

"Bing, we shouldn't be here," she said. Abednego took her hand, and together they moved closer to the tree.

"Looky here. See that smooth spot. Most likely grow over the markings right here." He guided the palm of her hand to the tree trunk. "Feel this, Lola." He placed his hand over hers. "Fifty years and still there." He moved closer, felt the warmth of her body. Together, they let their hands linger on the scarred bark. When she turned her head back towards him, he let his lips brush against her cheek. She did not pull away.

"Could I help ya'll?" It was a woman's voice. Still holding hands they both turned around to see who. A dark-haired woman held an open can of paint and a paint brush covered in yellow.

"I use to live here," said Abednego. "A cabin set right where your house be."

"Really? Must have been a long time ago. My landlord told me this house has been here since the 80's."

"See this tree here? I carve her and my letters here," said Abednego. The woman, who had mischievous blue-gray eyes, set down her paint can and brush, and came to look. "Here, see?" he showed her the smooth area. She inspected the bark.

"I hadn't noticed before. Too busy painting furniture here in my garage. My kids like to swing in that tire swing, though."

"Creek still run out back?"

"More like a stream now. Muddy. Want to come and look?"

"No," said Lola. "We're parked in the road. Don't want to get hit." Abednego tugged at her hand. She pulled away and turned to head back to the car. Abednego thanked the young woman and followed Lola.

After he closed the door, Lola released the emergency brake, put the van in gear, and eased off. He could tell she seemed too quiet.

"You mad I kiss you?"

"No."

"Something wrong?"

"I didn't want to be there any longer," she said. Abednego sensed something was bothering her and knew enough to stay quiet till they arrived at the picnic spot. In silence, they drove over the bridge into the Crystal Springs area. Very few of the houses looked the same as Abednego had remembered. Most were newer. What really was different was not a soul sat on the front porches as they had in the past. In the midday heat, air conditioning had lured folks inside.

"The holler be up on the left, just past that graveyard," he said, pointing to a sloping road, part gravel, part weeds. Lola turned onto the road which was surrounded by a jungle of fescue and Johnson grasses at least three to four feet tall.

"Where we gonna put the blanket?" he asked.

"Blanket? At our age I thought folding chairs would be a better idea." Abednego thought so too, especially since on some days he found it difficult to get up and down with his bad knees.

"You the smart one. We can look for a clearing to set down our chairs." After she shut off the engine, they both got out to search for a spot. Surrounded by walls of grass on both sides, they meandered toward a grove of trees and stopped under a towering magnolia.

"Lola, ain't this the spot where we sat at the fish fry?" She inhaled the sweet scent of magnolia.

"Looks like it," she said. "Doesn't look like anyone

picnics here anymore. Looks like a haying field."

"That need cutting," he added. Lola swatted a mosquito off her arm.

"I have an idea," she said.

Back in the car with cool air blowing from the air conditioner, Lola pulled out a big basket filled with cheese sandwiches on wheat bread, celery and carrot sticks, and jars of cold sweet tea. Abednego unwrapped the wax paper from his sandwich and was about to take a bite when he heard Lola clear her throat. He looked over to see her eyes were closed.

"Let us rejoice and be glad," she prayed.

"And Lord, thank you for bringing Lola here today."

"Amen," said Lola. They dug into the feast while Daisy Bates sat in the back seat with her ears pitched forward, hoping for a scrap to be offered.

"I remember the day of the picnic," said Abednego. "You the tallest. And prettiest."

"And you were a fresh one. Called me Sugar. All the ladies were watching you. I was so embarrassed I could of hidden under the table." She reached in the back to pull out a plate wrapped in foil. "I have a surprise. Can you guess?"

"Dessert?" he said. She nodded.

"You're getting warmer. It's what we had that day."

"Pecan pie?" he guessed. Lola pulled back the foil revealing two generous slices of pie.

"You win," she said. Abednego pulled the plate away from her.

"Two pieces for me. What you gonna have?"

"One of those pieces is for me!"

"Nah, not unless you let me feed you," he said. He

dug into the pie with a fork and cut off a nice bite. He held it up, and she leaned in, wrapped her lips around the fork, all the while looking at him with playful eyes. She chewed slowly, as though she was tasting all the flavors in each bite—the sweetness and thickness of the amber filling, the crispiness of the pecans, and the flakey light crust. The way she ate the pie reminded him of those sexy women in those TV commercials.

"Um hum, this is the best pie I ever had. Give me another bite," she said. Slowly, he moved the fork through the firm slice and lifted it to her mouth. She opened her lips for another bite.

"If you close your eyes, gonna taste better," he instructed. She let her eyes fall shut. Her lips were open and waiting. So tempting. Too tempting. He moved the forkful of pie aside and moved in for a kiss. He placed his lips firmly against hers, not lightly as before. He tasted her sweet lips, pecans, and pie filling. He placed his free hand on the back of her head and held her close. He did not want to let go. She pulled away. He looked into her eyes, and thought he saw her beginning to tear up. He wrapped his arms around her to comfort her.

"Now I done it," he whispered. "I'm sorry. Most of my life I been waiting to kiss you again. You so pretty, I couldn't help myself." He felt her sobbing. "Oh Lola, I don't mean to scare you."

"It's not you, Bing. It's me. I had this plan all figured out. I was going to bring you out here and tell you something I never told anyone before. And now I don't want to. I want to sit here and be with you. I want to laugh and eat pie and kiss you all afternoon. I can't. Not until you hear what I have to say."

"I promise you, gal, whatever it is won't make me

want to stop kissing you," he said. Apparently the wrong thing to say. She shook as the tears came down her cheeks.

"You won't want to touch me once you hear how he ruined me."

"Who?"

"Sewell Buttrill. After they ran you off, he followed me back to your cabin. He forced himself on me."

"Sewell Buttrill who you work for? When?"

"After you left for Chattanooga, I stopped by your cabin. I was missing you so bad. He dragged me inside, pushed me down on the floor. His breath stunk like onions. He called me a nigger whore, said I'd never had it so good. I'd never had it at all Bing. You know that." Her sobbing started up again. He cradled her in his arms, rocked her back and forth in a soothing motion.

"It's alright now, Lola. You wasn't no whore. You was just a young girl. What he did was wrong." And he's going to pay for it, he thought.

After Lola had calmed down, she said she wasn't hungry at all, and in fact she felt sick to her stomach. He didn't feel well either. The thought of that overbearing man holding her down and forcing himself on his Lola. The more he thought about Sewell Buttrill, the hotter his face felt. His heart pounded.

"There's more, Bing," she said.

"He do it again?" he felt his neck tighten. A pain shot down his jaw.

"No, only once. Enough to make a baby."

"You carry his child?" he asked. Lola nodded.

"Sebastian is Sewell Buttrill's son." Abednego remembered the green eyes he had noticed when he met her son.

"Do he know?"

"I never told him. He thinks Lucky is his father."

"I mean do Sewell Buttrill know he have a son?" She shook her head no.

"I tell you what. Why don't we go back to the store and get you something for your stomach. Some Alka-Seltzer." And me a swig from my flask, he thought, but didn't say.

Chapter 53

LOLA

She waited in the car while he went into the store. After Abednego brought a bubbling cup to her, and made her drink it, she told him she had to go home. He didn't want her to leave, but she explained she needed to return home and compose herself, to see how she felt about sharing her secret with him. He made her promise to see him as soon as she felt better. She said she would, but she wasn't so sure. He gave her a kiss on her forehead and waved goodbye.

As she knew it would, telling him what happened had set off a chain reaction of emotions. She breathed in deep and tried to concentrate on her driving, to ignore the ugly thing that now had returned to dwell inside of her. She rode along in silence, but inside her head, the chatter continued.

After that one violent act in the summer of 1959, she had tried hard to put it all behind. Her salvation was through her art. In her paintings, she re-wrote her past, creating scenes of her youth as she wanted to remember. The majority of her work depicted scenes of an idealistic North Georgia countryside, with views of black folk going to church, wearing hats, right alongside white folk. Children played together, colorful families walked side-by-side down dirt roads. All so very civilized, so perfect. Her paintings were well-received and big hits with both the art collectors and the general public who, with all the violence and mayhem in the world, needed to reminisce about happier days gone by.

Of course those happier days had not really been so happy. She knew that. Last year an art critic had slammed her work and said it was pure fantasy, although her technique with impasto was flawless. She hurt for a few months, walled herself away in her studio and could not paint another of her idealized scenes. In her heart, she knew he was right. She dabbled with her paints to pull herself out of her funk. Letting her brush go where it wanted to, she found herself once again painting, returning to her first subject, pine trees, and the scenes around them. Ridges, streams and creeks and paths appeared on her canvases. And if any person was depicted in her paintings, it was with only the back of his or her head showing. The people who populated her paintings wore hats, or scarves, so you couldn't tell who they were, black or white. Just a suggestion of some generic human, Sebastian had called it.

Of late, she felt better about her work and about herself. She could not be accused of perpetuating a fantasy time or place, as the critic had suggested. (Oh why did one stinging review remain so clearly in her mind, while countless positive reviews were never remembered?) In addition to feeling authentic to her true history, her new focus allowed her to paint nature scenes, which she liked better than humans of late, particularly acrid art critics. After seeing Abednego, she now understood why. She didn't want to get close to humans, to get hurt again in some way. Although Bing hadn't intended to hurt her, and in fact she had wanted to be kissed, it had opened up all those feelings. She didn't want to do that again. She would see him one more time and explain why it wouldn't work between them. She had her passion, her art. She did not need a man, even him. She would continue to channel herself into her craft. She had been wrong to go on the picnic with him, and doubly wrong to tell him about the rape. After all, her son Sebastian had come from it. Surely on some level the attack was meant to be, or at least that's what she always told herself.

Back at her cottage, after she slipped into her favorite flannel pajamas, she pulled out her sketch pad and furiously began sketching scenes of what had really happened that night in the cabin with Sewell Buttrill. A dark girl lay on a hard floor with a white cloth covering her face, a monstrous hulk of a man on top of her body. She pressed the pencil so hard against the sketch pad that the tip broke off. Lola grabbed a fresh pencil and started to work on the second scene. The girl lay on the floor afterwards. Her face was free of the white cloth but full of anguish. Her eyes were opened wide, her mouth was pulled back in a grimace, her arms were wrapped around her body in a hug.

The next sketch showed the attacker standing alone outside and touching a long scratch on his neck. His face was full of ugliness, and to anyone who might know him, it was the face of Sewell Buttrill. That arrogant turned up nose, those jade eyes and blond hair, could not be mistaken.

She sketched into the night, her tears dripping as she worked. It wasn't the first time she'd taken her feelings out on canvas, and she was sure it wouldn't be the last.

Chapter 54

ABEDNEGO

Sitting on Ernie's bed, Abednego took a big sip from his flask, felt the comforting burn coat his throat. He wanted to stop, but now was not the time. He had to do something to quench his anger. He opened up the phone book for Taylor's Crossing and looked under the "B's." He ran his finger down the page and found it: Sewell Buttrill. The address was right there in black and white. He really didn't need to see it—he had driven past the place today. He would never forget where that monster lived.

Leaving Daisy Bates behind in the room, he walked over to the store. Xylia was inside putting cans on shelves.

"Mind if I buy some them rubber glove off you? Daisy Bates done made a mess out back." He pointed to a box of gloves by the area where Xylia prepared sandwiches.

"Sure, just take as many as you like," Xylia said. "No charge. I buy them in bulk." He pulled two gloves out of the box.

"'I'm gonna take a walk when it cool off. Maybe head over to Crystal Springs to see if any John's family know when he be back. That is if they still lives there." Xylia set down a can of beans and turned around.

"It's a couple of miles over to Crystal Springs," she said.

"I could use me a good walk," he said.

"I would hate to see you go that far in this heat," she said. "If you give me a while, I can give you a ride."

"I can walk," he said. "Do me good. Would you mind checking Daisy a little later?"

"Sure," she said. "You be careful though. Folks fly down Ridgeside, and not many folks walk on the side of the road in this heat."

Back in Ernie's room, through the window on the west wall, Abednego watched the sun lowering in the sky over the rolling ridges across from the store. He reached into his duffle bag and pulled out his Buck knife, which was inside its sheath. He attached the knife to his belt and patted Daisy Bates on the head.

"Just stay here and rest. I gonna visit Mr. Buttrill. Him and me? We got lots of catching up to do." He walked out the door and passed the store window. He heard voices inside, probably Xylia talking to a customer.

He crossed the Old Alabama Highway and walked along the left shoulder of Ridgeside Road so he could see cars approaching. Breathing heavily, he finally reached the end of the Buttrills' long driveway. Although it was dusk, when he looked up at the two-story house he didn't see a single light on. Maybe Sewell had gone to bed early, not so unusual for a man who had to be close to 80 and lived alone. What he wondered was how Sewell's conscience let him sleep.

Not a single car passed by as he moved towards the long tree-lined drive leading up to the house. He slipped into the shadows under the trees and was lost in darkness. His heart quickened as he thought about confronting the man who had hurt Lola.

Moving slowly, he walked under the big magnolia and headed to the utility porch. He pulled the rubber gloves out of his pocket and slipped them onto his hands. He had a hunch the screen door would be unlocked. It was. He eased open the door and found himself on the back porch facing the kitchen door. He tried to turn the handle. It wouldn't budge.

Anger flashed through him. For a moment, he thought about busting out one of the glass panes and breaking in. He wanted to surprise Sewell Buttrill, so that wouldn't do. He took a deep breath and allowed himself to think like the man who owned this house. He would have hidden a key somewhere for the help.

Abednego ran his hand along the top of the door frame. Nothing. He turned around and faced a wall covered with jackets and hats hanging on pegs. He rummaged through the pockets of the jackets. Nothing. He felt his heart beating harder in frustration. He stood still and breathed slowly. Think. He stared at a pair of old muck boots in the corner. From the looks of the dust that coated them, not worn for quite some time. He reached down into each of the boots, found a key in one.

Before putting the key into the lock, he listened. He didn't want to be blasted to pieces by the old man's shotgun, at least not until he had a chance to talk. He eased the key in the slot, turned it, and unlocked the door. He pushed open the door and felt the cool stillness of the room. Quietly, he pulled the door closed behind him.

In the center of the kitchen sat a small round table. A bowl atop the table held two Vidalia onions, just as Lola had said. How he hated the man! He pulled his Buck knife from its sheath and held it at his side. He would move through the house till he found him.

Clutching his knife in his right hand, he walked softly through the next room, a larger dining area with a long rectangle table and a number of chairs. He fumbled around and found a door handle, and listened. He slowly pulled the door open and smelled moth balls. A closet. He ran his hands along the garments--some felt like wool, while others were smoother. Cotton. He wondered if the old man had kept his white hood and robe. He shut the closet door and moved across toward another door where light shone underneath the bottom.

Standing there, he listened, heard the sounds of a TV. Grasping the knob, he turned firmly but gently, and opened the door a few inches wide so he could see through. He was rewarded with the sight of a black leather recliner tilted back. He opened the door wider. Holding his knife low in front of his right thigh and crouching, he slipped through and moved toward the recliner. His knees were killing him, but he persisted.

Along with TV voices, he heard loud snoring. He tiptoed around beside the recliner to see who was making all the racket. By the light cast from the television's glow, he saw a shriveled up, bald-headed man who bore little resemblance to the man known as Sewell Buttrill. He watched the elderly man stop breathing, then rattle to life again with a fit of snorts. In his hand he clutched a balled up Kleenex.

Abednego slid his knife back into the sheath. He couldn't kill the old man. He was already half dead. If it was actually Buttrill.

"Buttrill. Wake up," he said. The old man stirred.

"Huh?" Buttrill looked confused. "You from the home health care? I told that bitch not to send out a nigra," Buttrill said.

Abednego bristled as he heard the words.

"That right Mr. Buttrill. I am a black man. Not just

any black man." He grabbed Buttrill by the shoulders. "Look at me." Buttrill blinked his tired eyes and tried to see the man just inches from his face. The smell of onions soured the air between them. The man deserved to be killed.

"What makes you so special, boy?"

"You tell me, Buttrill. Do you remember?" Buttrill shook his head no. Then Abednego had an idea. He clutched the old man's arm to try and tug him out of the chair.

"Where the car key?" Although frail, the old man tried to pull away.

"You're here to steal my car? You can have it. The keys are in it."

"I don't steal nothing. I'm no thief. We going for a little drive. You able to walk to the car?"

Buttrill responded by grabbing at the handle of his walking cane. Abednego snatched it away. The last thing he needed was this old man trying to beat him over the head.

"I'll help you walk." Abednego offered his arm. The old man refused. "Alright, we gonna do it the hard way." He seized Buttrill's elbow and pulled him up in a standing position, an easy task since the man couldn't be more than 135 pounds. "We gonna take a little walk out to the garage." Buttrill moved slower than a turtle trying to cross the road, and although Abednego hated touching the man who hurt his Lola, he was determined to get him to the car. They talked as they moved across the room. "Your car run good?"

"Why you care?"

"Can it make it up the ridge?" Abednego asked. Buttrill halted.

"Why you want to go there?"

"You oughta know." Suddenly Buttrill stopped and planted his feet. Abednego knew then that Buttrill remembered.

"I'm not going up there with you."

"Yes, you is." Abednego grabbed his arms and dragged him along the hardwood floors, not too difficult a task since he was light. The socks he wore made his body glide over the smooth boards, for a short time. Soon Buttrill was kicking and cursing, trying to wiggle free. He was a feisty old man, and mean. Despite his years, his injuries, Abednego was younger, stronger, and more determined. He had wrestled bulls. Sewell Buttrill was a mere man.

In the musty smelling garage, he opened up the door to the car, an aging Lexus. He strapped Buttrill in.

"Where you keep your rope?" he asked. Buttrill stiffened at the question.

"Don't have any."

"You kind always has rope. I look for myself." Abednego opened the trunk and found a coil of white rope under a blanket and next to a crow bar. He carried it back to the front seat and lay it down between him and Buttrill.

"What you need that for?" Buttrill asked.

"You tell me," Abednego said. The old man replied with a clearing of his throat and otherwise remained silent.

The car started up easily. Abednego left the lights off as he steered out of the garage and down the driveway. At the road, he looked up toward the darkened ridge. A sliver of a crescent moon was mostly obscured by clouds.

Chapter 55

IRIS

Iris went into the room where Mr. Shepherd had stayed to check the fresh flowers in the vase. She dumped out the cloudy water and filled it up with fresh water, something she always did herself between guests. These flowers were still good, so she would leave them for another day.

Nina, the new housekeeper, had done a good job on the surface. The corners were neatly tucked on the bed, the pillows fluffed. Iris moved over to the headboard and ran her index finger along the top. Not a speck of dust. She got down on her knees and pulled up the bed skirt to see if underneath the bed was clean. She saw lines in the carpet, indicating it had just been vacuumed.

The last place she always checked was the closets and drawers. She'd found even the best cleaners sometimes forgot to look there. Iris wanted her guests to enjoy an empty room, bare spaces they could fill up with their own belongings, a feng shui concept she had read about. She opened the closet door. All the hangers were neatly in place, and the carpet was clean. The dresser drawers were bare, too. She opened up the bedside table and looked at the Gideon Bible. It hadn't been touched. She started to close the drawer, but then she saw the tiny corner of a paper jutting out from underneath the Bible. She picked it up, glanced at the slip of paper. It was a receipt for a purchase made by Abednego Harris. From the art gallery.

She'd only ever met one man named Abednego. She caught her breath and jammed her hand into her pocket to find her cigarettes. Bing had stayed in this very room, and she hadn't even recognized him!

Chapter 56

ABEDNEGO

When Abednego reached the highway, he flipped on the headlights. He turned up East Nickajack and started the climb up the ridge.

"Folks still be dumping stuff up here?" he asked. He glanced over at Buttrill, who sat with his arms crossed over his mid-section. "Old washers, dryers, refrigerators? Black men?" Buttrill wasn't saying a word. "Want to see how it feel being toss out on the ground like someone garbage?" Buttrill coughed.

Abednego glanced over and saw Buttrill's hand gripping the edge of the beige leather seat. In an odd way, he felt sorry for the old man, until he spoke.

"Should've killed you myself."

"You right. Cause now I'm gonna cut you up, old man. For what you did to Lola."

"Who?"

"The gal you attack in my cabin after you run me off."

"She liked it."

"Like hell she do." Abednego pushed the accelerator to the floor and sped up the final climb to the ridge top. He switched off the lights and steered the car across the road into a clearing. He turned off the engine, got out, and went over to open the passenger door where Buttrill sat. He heard the locks click shut. Not really a problem since he had the key in his hand. He clicked the locks open again and jerked the door open. He reached over and grabbed the coil of rope, then pulled Buttrill out. He dragged him along the ground.

The old man kicked and struggled to get loose. Abednego held on tight. His eyes had adjusted to the darkness. He looked for a place to tie up Buttrill and scare him some more, just as he had been scared. He halted at a sturdy trunk that was about the circumference of the old man's body.

"Stand there against that tree. Put your hands in front."

"No," Buttrill pleaded. He began to moan. Abednego grabbed his shoulder and felt him shaking. He thought of Lola, how she might have felt the same way, full of fear, when she was trapped underneath this man.

"You scared, old man?" he asked. Buttrill's reply was a piercing wail that rose in the night, a noise that reminded Abednego of a bobcat's cry that he had once heard on the farm. "The way you feeling right now, this is what you do to my gal, my Lola." Buttrill started shaking uncontrollably. If he wasn't going to kill him, there was nothing more to do. Abednego had made his point. Now Buttrill was the victim. He clutched the old man's arm and guided him toward the car. With each staggering step Buttrill took, Abednego's anger and hate seemed to evaporate.

"Get back in," he told Buttrill. Still shaking and weeping, the man half fell into the passenger seat. "I'm gonna let you go this time," said Abednego. "You ain't worth going to jail for." Abednego closed the door behind him. "When you wake up tomorrow, this going to be like a bad dream. No one gonna believe you when you tell them about our trip up the ridge." Abednego walked around to his side of the car and stopped to look up again at the moon. The clouds had moved away and a slice of silver hung above.

He climbed in the car, switched on the headlights, and backed out onto East Nickajack. He turned the wheel, and eased the car down the road. Buttrill had quieted down as they headed off the ridge, back toward the valley. Abednego inhaled and felt his chest fill with the night air, a mixture of pine scent and honeysuckle. From the thick forest, an occasional lightning bug winked as the car descended.

After they pulled into the garage, Abednego walked around the car and opened the passenger door to get out the old man.

"You home," he said, touching Buttrill's boney cool wrist. Too cool. "Wake up." He tried to jostle Buttrill awake. He instead succeeded at tilting him over on the seat. He put his hand under the nostrils and felt no air. He felt the frail wrist for a pulse. Nothing. Sweet Jesus! The old man was dead. Abednego sighed. He'd only meant to scare him, not kill him. He grabbed under his shoulders and pulled him out of the car, dragged him across the cold cement floor of the garage. He let him down gently on the floor and opened up the door leading into the house.

Dragging him through the open doorway, he thought Buttrill somehow felt heavier than he had before. Abednego breathed hard as he tugged the limp body. He felt rapid thumping in his chest. He stopped, put his hand over his heart. He paused to rest till it slowed down again. He didn't want to die himself, especially not right here next to Sewell Buttrill. You couldn't choose where you would die, but if you could, this would be the last place he'd pick.

Wouldn't it be funny what folks might say when they found the old Klansman laid out alongside a black man? Abednego smiled at the thought.

Renewed from his own musings, he bent over and grasped the limp body in his arms, pulled it along towards the living room. When he arrived by the recliner, he used the side to steady his tired, wobbling legs. He pulled Buttrill back into his chair. Reaching alongside the chair, he pulled back the lever to put the chair in a reclining position.

He walked over to switch on the light and checked over the old man. Seeing pieces of dried leaves on his pants, Abednego realized he should have checked before putting him back in the chair. If only he had a vacuum cleaner.

He searched the closets again and finally found a vacuum in a closet tucked under the stairs. On the shelf, he saw a number of attachments and had trouble deciding which one would do the job. Finally he chose one with a narrow opening—at least this one wouldn't suck the clothes right off the man. He pushed the contraption into the living room and plugged it in. He switched it on.

"Vacuuming a dead man," Abednego said to the room. "Imagine that." Sewell did not reply, even when Abednego turned him over to clean off bits of leaves and dirt from his shirt, pants and socks. While he had Sewell rolled over to one side of the chair, he also vacuumed the chair and between the cushion. He didn't want to leave any clues.

He rolled Sewell back to a supine position in the center of the chair. Abednego felt his heart thumping again, sighed, and stopped to rest. "Sewell Buttrill, you a lot of work. You could kill a man. That is if he ain't already kill you."

When he felt certain that Buttrill looked like he had an hour earlier, well, except for his paleness, Abednego placed a blue flannel blanket over his legs and stomach. He left him reclining in his favorite chair looking like he had died watching TV. Perhaps a detective show like the one playing now, or…. Abednego picked up the remote and flipped through the channels, found an X-rated channel with lots of bare skin and heavy breathing. He set the remote down in Buttrill's lap. He turned away and headed for the door, pausing to look back one more time at the old man. Whoever found Sewell Buttrill would see he had died watching a sleazy porno channel.

Chapter 57

LOLA

Lola was in her bedroom getting ready for bed. She went to her dresser and pulled out her Bible, the same one she'd had since she was a little girl. When she turned through the worn pages, it opened up at her most read verse, Daniel 3:23. She looked at the remnants of the flower ring Abednego had placed on her finger the day he asked her to marry him. The flakes of flower had almost turned to dust. So long ago.

Her cell phone rang. It was almost midnight. Was something wrong with her son? Had he been in an accident? She answered on the second ring. It was Bing, and he wanted her to come pick him up right now.

"Are you sick?" she asked.

"No, I explain later," he said. His voice sounded different—jittery. She wondered if he had been drinking.

"Why don't I come first thing tomorrow? I have to drive to Atlanta to talk with a gallery owner, and I want to get an early start."

"I need to see you, gal, to tell you something."

"Bing, I will come tomorrow. Early."

"What time?"

"Before you see the sun come up over the ridge, I'll be there."

Chapter 58

MARVELOUS

Exhausted after driving all night, Marvelous pulled off the Ringgold exit and steered into the nearest McDonald's to grab some coffee and a bite before continuing to Taylor's Crossing. She had not been back there since the day she woke up to find the sofa on fire in her brother's cabin.

She sat at a table drinking her coffee and eating a yogurt. She looked around at the other customers, all white. She caught one staring at her, a beefy man wearing a Bull Dogs cap. He didn't look friendly. She focused on her coffee cup and sneaked a peek at him. He continued to stare at her unabashedly. Another man, his father perhaps, joined the staring one at the table. He set down a tray with breakfast sandwiches and drinks. The staring man looked away from her and began to eat. And talk.

"Daddy, I wanted a Happy Meal," the man said with a lisp.

"Son, it's too early. They don't have it yet." The younger man's lips drew down in a pout.

"You promised," the boy-man whined. The older man reached out and patted his son's sleeve. So the young man was mentally challenged—not a menace as Marvelous had assumed.

Things had changed. It had been almost half a century, or more. She was educated. She didn't need to be afraid. She finished her breakfast and with her coffee cup in hand, left for the drive alongside Taylor's Ridge.

Chapter 59

IRIS

It was almost nine by the time Iris pulled into the parking lot at Elmwood's. Xylia had a garden hose pointed at a potted plant of some sort. Iris swung the car into the parking lot and climbed out.

"Good morning, Xylia," she said. "Doing some gardening today?"

Xylia looked up and smiled.

"Not by choice. One of my customers found this little red leaf maple on sale and he swears he's going to plant it later today, right here where my big oak used to be." She pointed to the oak stump. Iris went over to inspect the little tree.

"Isn't this a Japanese maple?"

"I don't know, Iris. All I wanted was an oak. Mr. Earl said this was a real steal, meaning either he got it on sale or left a big hole in someone's back yard." Iris laughed.

"Is Mr. Shepherd awake yet? He left something behind at my B & B."

"Hadn't heard a peep out of him yet. You're welcome to walk around back to the house and tap on the door. That dog of his will bark and wake him up." Iris nodded and headed to the door. Xylia continued watering the potted tree.

After knocking for a couple of minutes, and hearing

no dog, Iris tested the door handle. It was unlocked. She opened the door and stuck her head inside to call out.

"Mr. Shepherd? It's Iris. Are you up yet? I've got something for you." She peered into the hallway, expecting to see the dog. There was nothing. Perhaps he was in a deep sleep. She didn't want to disturb him if he was; on the other hand, she couldn't stay long. She had to do the payroll this afternoon. She headed down the hallway, calling his name.

She arrived at an open bedroom door and peeked inside. Crayon drawings covered the walls. This had to be Ernie's room where Mr. Shepherd--Abednego--had slept. The bed was made up. A piece of ruled paper lay atop the pillow. She walked over, picked it up.

"Miss Xylia. Had to leave in a hurry. Thanks. Abednego Harris." Reading the note, Iris felt a chill pass through her. She hoped everything was alright.

Returning to the parking lot and Xylia, she spotted a blue SUV pulling up next to Xylia, now preoccupied with rolling the garden hose into a coil. A dark woman with voluminous curls climbed out, a woman about Iris' age. She called out to Xylia, now hanging the coiled hose over the faucet.

"Excuse me, have you seen an older man around? With a little black dog?"

"You mean Mr. Shepherd?" Xylia asked.

"Mr. Harris," said Marvelous. "Abednego Harris. He's my brother. " Iris stared at this compact woman, at her abundant curls, and knew.

"Marvelous?"

Marvelous looked up at Iris, her face a question mark.

"Do I know you?" she said. Iris walked towards her old friend.

"It's Iris Tucker."

"Iris? I wouldn't have recognized you," she said. Then she smiled. "Except for those freckles and that silly grin." Marvelous reached out to Iris and looped pinkies, their secret handshake. Wiping her hands against her apron, Xylia approached.

"Will someone tell me what's going on?"

Back inside the store, sitting at the school desks and over cups of steaming coffee, Marvelous and Iris told Xylia of their girlhood adventures, of their mutual love of horses.

"We used to sneak out at night," said Iris.

"In the moonlight," Marvelous added.

"Until this one night, someone set their mean dogs on us."

"And we both fell off the horse," said Marvelous. "Remember how I held on and wouldn't let go?"

"What were we? Ten?"

"Too young to know better," Marvelous said.

"How long has it been since you saw each other?" Xylia asked. Marvelous looked down at her paper coffee cup.

"Not since Abednego left here," said Marvelous.

"After the Klan came and tried to kill him," said Iris. "I always wondered if it was me and you, our being friends, that set them off."

Marvelous shook her head.

"I don't think so, Iris. It was the times. They were angry about Dr. King and the progress being made all around. Abednego was an obvious target because he was the only African American living down here at the time."

Xylia got up and went to the coffee pot.

"Speaking of your brother, why don't you take him a cup of coffee?" Xylia asked.

"He's gone," said Iris. "He left a note for you, Xylia." Iris reached in her pocket and pulled out a piece of paper, unfolded it and handed it to Xylia. "When I looked in Ernie's room, I found this on the pillow."

Xylia looked at the note. "Had to leave in a hurry, it says."

"For what?" asked Iris. "You think he found his fishing buddy? The one he said he was looking for?"

"I think it was a woman," Xylia said.

"Lola," said Marvelous. "He wanted to see her again.

"I remember her," said Iris. "I was sure they would marry." Suddenly the front door of the store burst open and Earl Williams marched in.

"Home health gal found Sewell Buttrill dead," he said. "About half an hour ago. Looks like a heart attack. Coroner's on the way."

"I'm sorry to hear it," Xylia said. Earl stepped over to the coffee pot and helped himself.

"Who's your visitor?" he asked Xylia.

"A friend of mine," Iris answered. She reached out to put her arm around Marvelous' shoulder. Seeing, Earl shook his head, grabbed a Honey Bun and walked toward the door.

"Add it to my tab," he said to Xylia. "I gotta go up there and tell the coroner what I saw with my own two eyes." He lowered his voice. "Looks like Sewell was watching one of them sex channels when he died."

"Too much information, Mr. Earl," Xylia said. "Too much information." She waved him out the door.

"I wonder where Bing went?" asked Marvelous.

Chapter 60

ABEDNEGO

Before the sun had even begun to peek over the ridgeline Abednego had gathered up his things, fed and walked Daisy Bates, and was ready to leave. He pulled the door shut behind him as he left, feeling not a little guilty about leaving so suddenly. That's when he thought to write a note for Xylia. He left his duffle bag and Daisy outside, returned back to the bedroom to pen a note. He didn't want to say much, just to thank her. She had opened her home to him, more than he might have done with an almost stranger. She was a good woman.

In the dawn light, he waited, and thought too much. What would Lola say when he told her what he'd done? What if she got upset? He needed something to steady his nerves. He walked over to pick up the duffle bag. He unzipped it and felt for his flask. His fingers clutched the familiar metal, cool as the copper ring he had snapped into the bull's nostrils. He remembered the young man in Lola's bull painting. All that power and not a drop of alcohol for fuel. He lifted the flask from his bag and walked over to the wet spot where Daisy had just done her business. He unscrewed the flask lid, tilted the container, and let the liquor trickle onto the ground, mingling with Daisy's urine. He twisted the lid back on and reached into his bag to find a white plastic bag he kept for his dirty laundry. He tucked the flask into the bag, tied a knot, and walked over to put it in the garbage dumpster behind the store. He turned and walked back toward the road.

In the dawn light, he saw headlights approaching on the highway. A flashing turn signal. Lola. She pulled into the Elmwood's parking lot. He opened the passenger side door.

"Morning. Mind if I set the dog and my bag in the back seat?"

"Where you think you're going?" she asked. "I thought you needed to talk. I can't stay long. I have to get on the road."

"I know," he said, lifting his bag, and then Daisy, onto the leather seat. "I'm gonna go with you." He closed the door, and climbed into the front passenger seat. He looked over at her. She had her head cocked to the side. Even in the semi-darkness, he could sense she didn't appear too happy.

"You just as bold as ever," she said. "You didn't ask me if you could come along."

"Lola, do you mind if I do? We need to talk." She shifted into reverse.

"Suppose it wouldn't hurt to have another pair of eyes when I need to change lanes down in Atlanta. Those carpool lanes get confusing," she admitted. She wheeled the vehicle around, turned left on East Nickajack and started the climb up the ridge.

"I hoped you go this way," Abednego said. "I drove Sewell Buttrill up here last evening."

"For what?" The car had reached the first curve in the road. They were a short way from the top.

"I take him up where the Klan take me. To kill him."

"What? You didn't!"

"No."

"You didn't hurt him, did you?"

"Not exactly. You don't have to worry no more. He dead." Shaking her head, Lola steered the car off the road onto a pullout area near the ridge's peak.

"What are you saying, Bing?"

"Scare him real good. He have a heart attack and die."

"And now you're running away? From the law? "

"No, everyone know he was doing real poorly with his heart. I'm running away with you." He reached for her forearm and gently placed his hand there. They sat in silence for a moment. He pointed to the valley below, to the flickering lights of a dusky dawn, to a place now rid of one wretched soul. "That's where it all start, and where it end."

"I'm sorry, Abednego Harris, I can't be happy about you scaring someone to death. I'm more of a turn your cheek kind of woman."

"I don't mean it to happen that way, Lola. I just try to shake him up a little. God must of want it that way."

"God? Don't bring him into this!"

"You right. I do it for you. And me. The old man get what he deserve. He don't get beat, or rape. He get off easy." Abednego suddenly became aware of the wash of headlights from behind. "Let's go," he said. "Don't want nobody calling the sheriff." He pulled his hand away from Lola's arm as a car passed. She shifted the car back in gear and steered it onto the pavement.

"He had them Vidalias setting on the kitchen table, like you say he do. Almost brung you one." She reached out and gave him a light slap on the arm.

"Abednego Harris, you're a mess." Abednego

nodded his head in agreement.

"A mess that love you. Love you then, love you now. That's all that matter, Miss Banks." As he spoke, the car rounded a curve and began descending towards the East. Sunbeams filtered through the trees. On the farthest ridge, towards Dalton, the sun was beginning to rise.

"Look at that big old ball coming up over there. What you thinking, Lola?"

"I'm thinking this is the day the Lord has made," she said. She glanced over and smiled at him.

"Let us rejoice, and be glad," he said. He reached for her hand, covered her long delicate artist hand with his own rougher one.

The road stretched out before them. It was a new day.

ACKNOWLEDGMENTS

I am grateful to the many people who have helped me along the road to publication. For workshopping my manuscript and helping me find my story, thank you Connie May Fowler. For her invaluable support and for reading my story, thank you Rose Davis. For talking with me about the Florida Highwaymen artists, thank you to artists Mary Ann Carrol and Robert Butler, and to Lee Drake, who also gave me the grand tour of Ft. Pierce and Miss Zora Neale's old neighborhood. A special thanks to Rita Dove who, at the Southern Literature Conference in Chattanooga a few years back, told me I could write this story as long as I found something within the characters with which I could empathize. To the Southern Women's Writers Conference at Berry College, thank you for choosing this manuscript for workshopping, and for your support of writers. Thank you to Dean Watts, Waymond Watts, and the late Harry Watts for information on cattle. To those who read and commented on my manuscript, Kathe Traynham, Marsha Mathews, Chris Jennison, Anne Turley, Carol White, Susan Richards, Amber Lanier Nagle, Ruth Parrish Watson, Carmen Tanner Slaughter, Frances Haman Prewitt, Cassie Dandridge Selleck, Marsha Atkins, and Ray Atkins, your comments were invaluable. And thanks to Addison Allen, Sherry Dee Allen, and Freida Dubin for their help formatting and proofing. And for their support, I am grateful to Ellen Young McCashin, Susannah Colby, Ned Colby, Dean Watts, Gail Watts, Judy Watts, and Emily Card. For my horse helpers Rachel and Cody Kelly, thank you. Thanks to Pat Shadden for her handwritten note of encouragement at the exact moment I needed it. I am grateful also to all the readers of my first novel who asked for another book. A special thanks to my dear friend Amber Lanier Nagle for designing my cover and for spending countless hours helping me see this book to print. To my husband Stephen and our sons, Anthony and Jack, and their families, thank you for having faith in me and seeing me through the journey.

To each and every one who has cheered me along the way, I appreciate your support. Thank you one and all!

ABOUT THE AUTHOR

A Chattanooga native with strong roots in Georgia, Janie Dempsey Watts lives not far from Taylor's Ridge in North Georgia. Her curiosity about most everything led to a writing career. Her first novel, *Moon Over Taylor's Ridge*, is also set in Taylor's Crossing, a fictional community. To learn more about her stories, please visit her at www.janiewatts.com, or see her Facebook page at Janie Dempsey Watts.